Andy threw the door wide open to see both Ford and Gizzard writhing on the floor. There wasn't time to see anything else because the bartender shouted a warning and men started reaching for their guns.

Andy opened fire with both pistols. He kept squeezing the triggers of both guns as fast as he could, not bothering to aim, not even aware of any conscious thought as men howled and died.

He kept firing until they were all knocked down, then he shoved his pistols into his coat pockets, choking on gun smoke as he dragged Hoyt Ford erect and stooped to cut free the ropes that bound Gizzard.

Moments later, they staggered out of the room in a cloud of blue gun smoke.

RIVERS
WEST

THE
CIMARRON RIVER

Gary McCarthy

BANTAM BOOKS

NEW YORK • TORONTO • LONDON • SYDNEY • AUCKLAND

For Frank Roderus
Great writer—great friend

THE
CIMARRON RIVER

One

Andy was almost sixteen, big and well coordinated for his age, when Avery Parmentier returned to their 120-acre Indiana farm one afternoon and announced to his family that he had joined the Union Army's newly formed Brighton Township Volunteers.

"It's the right thing to do," Avery proclaimed to his stunned wife and three children, the youngest still breast-feeding. "The War Between the States won't last long. As soon as it's over, I'll be given a eight-dollars-a-month Civil War pension, a free Missouri mule, new Springfield rifle, and a Colt Army pistol. When you add up the value of the whole outfit, it's worth over a hundred dollars!"

"No, please," Mildred Parmentier whispered, face turning the color of lye soap. "Avery, we've a family to raise."

"And I've a patriotic duty to help preserve the Union," Avery replied firmly. "Besides, we could use that pension. We've had some real bad farming years and they'll come around again all too soon. With that pension and a good mule, we can all eat a lot more and worry a lot less."

Mildred stood, gripping the table's edge and almost spilling little Gilbert to the dirt floor. "You could be killed."

"Naw! I'm going with my friends and we'll take care of each other. Don't you worry. We'll kick the . . . the tar outta Johnny Reb and be back before Christmas! I'll bring you a fine cotton dress from Dixie and a souvenir minie ball for each of the boys."

"Don't . . . go," Mildred begged in a small, strained voice that Andy had never heard before.

Up until that very moment, Andy had thought that his father was doing the right thing. He'd heard that Billy Wilson's pa had already joined and so had Chad Pickery's father and a whole lot more from the Brighton Township in the last few weeks. In truth, Andy had been a little disappointed that his own father wasn't going to go off to war against the dirty graycoats. But now, seeing his nearly hysterical mother, Andy had second thoughts. Maybe it wasn't such a good idea—even if his family would be recipients of an eight-dollar-a-month pension and an honest-to-gawd Missouri mule and two fine percussion weapons.

Maybe not.

For a moment his parents stood toe-to-toe, staring at each other with such defeat that Andy felt sick to his stomach. Finally, his mother asked, "Mr. Parmentier, have you signed the government papers?"

"Yes." Avery reached into his pocket and slapped not only his signing papers but also eight dollars on the table. "And that is good government money *paid in advance* so that you and the kids don't have to worry about cash money . . . for a time."

"Eight dollars?" Mildred questioned, unable to hide her scorn as she looked at the bills and the simple document that said Avery Parmentier was already a soldier in the Union Army. "Eight dollars!"

Avery looked uneasy. "Now, Mildred, I got more comin' soon from the government. Enough money every month so that you and the kids don't have to worry."

"Who says there is more coming!"

"Sergeant Billford."

Avery scooped up the paper and unfolded it in such haste that he tore it almost in half. "Look! Right here on the bottom line. It says that Avery B. Parmentier, having joined the Brighton Township Volunteers, who will soldier together for the duration of the conflict, is to receive eight dollars a month while on active duty and *forever* after as long as he shall live."

"That may not be very long!"

For the first time Andy saw that his mother's clenched fists were as white and bloodless as snowballs. "Don't you understand that you could get killed?"

"I won't!" Avery insisted.

"Then what if you are just maimed and return to us missing an arm or a leg? Or . . . or some other part of your body, or even your mind!"

"Mildred," Avery said, struggling to sound reasonable, "I got my friends all around me for protection. Sharpshooting fellas like Will Slatter, Ben Otto, and George and John Milford. I got good men to watch my backside and my frontside just as I'll be doing every minute for them."

"People are already dying in this war," Mildred insisted. "Or haven't you heard the reports that the war isn't going very well for the Union Army?"

"Well, that's why I'm joinin'!" Avery cried, glancing at Andy. "Son, how would you feel if I stayed here and every other boy's daddy went off to war? How would it make you feel when the other boys called your daddy a coward?"

"Leave Andy be! He wants to grow up to *have* a father," Mildred cried. "Don't you dare start shouting and carrying on toward your family. Not after what you've just done to ruin us!"

"Ruin!" Avery exploded. His hand streaked out and

Andy heard the sharp pop of hard flesh on soft. A cry and then his mother stumbled into the china cabinet, sending most of Grandma's china dishes shattering against the floor.

"Get out!" Mildred Parmentier shouted, blood trickling from her mashed lip as she struggled to her feet. "Take your government death warrant and leave this house!"

Avery balled his fists and that was when Andy stepped between his parents, saying, "Pa, you'd better go off to war. You'd just better not hit Ma again, so . . . so just pack your things and leave!"

"All right," Avery said, the anger washing out of his body, so that he seemed smaller. "All right. I signed up and I can't go back on that, so I'll gather my things. I got friends that still care for me even if my own family don't."

His mother broke forward at the hips and covered her face with her hands to smother a sob. And then, while Andy and the rest of them stood like dumb animals, Avery gathered his clothes, stuffing them in a bag and grabbing up his coat, gloves, and extra boots.

"Take the money," Mildred said woodenly. "You're going to need it worse than us."

"No," Avery said tiredly. "I signed up to help this family and you can by-gawd burn the damned money before I'll lay a hand on it."

His mother collapsed and Andy watched helpless as her shoulders worked up and down while she sobbed. Only she didn't make any noise, which would somehow have been easier.

"Son, you're the man of the family until I get back," Avery said as he stood at the open door with shadows stretching long across their corn-stubbled fields. "I left the old Navy Colt and ammunition aplenty. The rifle is broke, but you're a good shot and you can still kill a rabbit or a bird for the pot now with that pistol."

"But what are we going to eat?" Andy asked, knowing that there wasn't much food around the house or grain in the barn for the animals.

"You can sell the cow," Avery decided. "She'll bring eight or ten dollars and then you won't have to feed her through the winter. And we still got chickens, don't we?"

"Sure, but—"

"Eat them! And try not to butcher the hogs before I return. There's beans and corn in the cellar. Some of your mother's squash, too. There's plenty enough to tide you over until I return in a few months."

"But what if you don't?"

"Then spend the eight dollars that the government will send every month," Avery said, coming over and tussling Andy's long brown hair. "You're the man now. You got to use your head and take care of the family. And there's Mr. Loomis just down the road. I know he has a hard reputation, but Eldridge is a good man and he'll help out in any emergency."

"I liked Mrs. Loomis a whole lot better," Andy said. "Mr. Loomis is mean."

"No, he's not. He's just . . . well, he is still grieving and he's got a bad back and is in considerable pain, which can make any man testy at times."

To Andy's way of thinking, Eldridge Loomis was meaner than a teased snake and he'd be the *last* person to call in a bad fix. But he just said, "Yes, sir."

"And there's one more thing you need to know."

Andy waited, seeing his father struggle to find the right words.

"Son," he whispered low so that only Andy could hear. "I shouldn't have hit your mother. I never hit her before."

"I know that."

"Well, I am ashamed of myself. Tell her that when the time seems right. And you made me proud the way you stood up for her. Mildred worries way too much, but she's the best and you never forget that. Never let anyone hurt her while I'm gone."

"No, sir!"

Avery looked across the room and took a hesitant step toward his daughter, but Wilma shrank away, so he dipped his prominent chin to them both and he was gone, striding across the yard, melting into the sunset.

Andy rushed to his mother, trying to think of something that would stop her from crying, but he couldn't dredge up a single word. Gilbert was wailing, too, and having no stomach for the baby, Andy chased after his father. He overtook him at the edge of their cornfield as the sun was burrowing into the earth.

"Pa, I wish you wouldn't go," he said, falling in step with Avery. "Ma is real upset, and so is Wilma and Gilbert."

"They'll be better in the morning," Avery said, not breaking stride. "Go look out for 'em now. You're a strong boy."

"Ma is strong, too."

"I used to think so, but I guess having babies sucks the courage from a woman. I don't know. She's changed. Used to be, she'd have been proud. Now . . . well, she's just afraid."

"Pa, be sure and duck your head when the bullets come too close," Andy blurted. "I want you to be brave, but it's more important to come back home alive."

"No, it isn't," Avery said. "Not if you have to be craven. A real man either stands and does his duty, or he runs and hates himself for the rest of his miserable days. I won't run, Andy. No matter what happens, you remember that I *didn't* run . . . because I won't in a hard fight. And don't you ever run either."

He stopped and turned. It was getting very dark, so Andy could hardly make out his father's expression, but he knew it would be sad and maybe a lot worse than sad. "Son, promise me you won't turn tail every time there is trouble."

"Yes, sir! But . . ."

"What is it?" his father asked, sounding as if his mind had already left for the war. "Andy, I'm in a hurry."

"Nothing. I was just going to say good-bye and don't forget to come back from the war with the mule and Springfield rifle and the Army Colt."

"And the eight-dollars-a-month pension for life," Avery added. "That's the most important of all."

"Yes, sir, but you can remind me then, can't you?"

"I will," Avery promised. "I swear that I'll come back and we'll talk more about this. It's real important."

"I can see now that it is," Andy said.

And then his father was moving on. Heading down the road. Going south. Going to war.

Thanksgiving came with a letter from Avery Parmentier, but it was poorly written and didn't say much except that the Milford brothers had both gotten themselves killed while on patrol and that the weather was rainy but not too cold yet. Avery ended by saying that he hoped that they were all doing well and that they were living fine on the government's monthly check and not selling off any of the hogs because he was hoping to get better prices after the war.

"What government checks?" Mildred muttered while stirring yet another pot of corn-and-potato porridge. "We haven't gotten a single check and neither have any of the other families in Brighton. Do they want us to starve?"

"I heard that the mail has been having trouble. The trains are all off schedule and the war is making things a mess."

"*That* isn't the problem," Mildred said, voice shaking

with anger. "It's the whole government of these United States that is falling on hard times! President Lincoln doesn't know what he's doing and neither do his generals. The whole bunch of them are worthless and dragging this country into ruin."

"We gotta free the slaves," Andy said. "There is an underground railroad that I read about and they—"

"I don't want to hear another word. As far as I'm concerned, the slaves ought to fight for their own freedom and leave our Northern men out of it!"

Andy could see that there was no sense in talking about the war.

Christmas came cold, with leaden skies and hard winter winds that sometimes blew for days without stopping. When Avery failed to appear as promised, they ignored Christmas, but Mother went out into the barn and shot Avery's best sow. They boiled and scraped the hair off of her and feasted all the way into the new year, braving the wind every time that they wanted to cut off some more meat and fat.

"He's dead," Mildred said one night, with the wind shrieking like a banshee and the house shaking like it was ready to fly apart. "Children, your father is dead."

"No, he isn't!" Andy shouted. "He's alive and hunkered down in the South, where it's warm. Pa said it's always warm in the South."

Ma didn't raise her voice or even look at him as she rocked back and forth in front of the fire. Her face looked tired and old and he saw her lips move as she whispered softly to herself—something she was starting to do more and more often. Andy wondered if she was praying to the Almighty, or cursing his father and President Lincoln.

February brought a chinook and a letter from the War Department. It stated that First Sergeant Avery Parmentier and the entire company of Brighton Volunteers had been wiped out trying to defend a battle line under General George H. Thomas at a place called Chickamauga Station. Andy stared through tears at the last sentence, which read, *Although greatly outnumbered by the enemy forces under Confederate General Bragg, your husband and his regiment refused to retreat and fought to the very last man. Such courage has no equal and the name of your husband and his Indiana Volunteers will forever sound the cry of patriotism and honor.*

Andy looked up at his mother. She was frozen until her lips began work silently and he then heard a tortured cry well up from the darkest depths of her soul. It came out like a scream, a curse, and a wail that shook him to his boots.

"Gawdammit, Avery, you proud, stupid son of a bitch!"

Chapter
Two

Eldridge Loomis was a taciturn man with black hair turning white and a long, hooked nose tacked on a hatchet-shaped face. His shoulders and back were bent and his thin lips turned down at the corners as if he'd just been forced to drink a glass of sour milk. Some said Loomis had once been the best farmer in the county before he'd hurt his back falling out of his hayloft. Andy didn't know about any of that, but he did know that Loomis starved his livestock and pinched every penny. The man's stinginess was legendary; he was so cheap that it was said Loomis could feast on a skinny rooster for an entire month.

The Loomis farm was right next to the Parmentiers' and Andy often heard the crotchety widower screaming at his hired hands. It had gotten so bad that no one would work for Loomis anymore and now his crops grew weedy, his fences sagged, and his house and outbuildings were as bent as their skinflint owner. Loomis had fathered three sons, but they'd all lit out and not one of them had ever been seen since. The women of the town said that they were the smart ones, and that Ruth Loomis should have run off with her boys before she'd died of overwork and sadness.

"Here comes Mr. Loomis again," Andy complained to his mother. "What does that old goat want *this* time?"

"Don't you be so hard on Mr. Loomis," Mildred scolded. "You've never dealt with pain, so you don't understand how it can wear a person down."

"But this is the third time he's been here since we got the letter about Pa," Andy pointed out. "I know he wants something from us."

"Oh, bosh! Mr. Loomis is just concerned about his neighbors. I appreciate that," Mildred said, smoothing her apron and then her hair. "Have you forgotten the two chickens he brought over last time he came to visit?"

"Both of 'em roosters hardly bigger than crows," Andy groused. "And he isn't bringing any food for our table today."

"That's because I asked him not to," Mildred said. "I . . . I asked Mr. Loomis to come on by and promised I'd fix him a good meal in return."

"Ma! Why'd you do that?" Andy could hardly believe this and reckoned that if Pa were here, he'd run Loomis off quick, having no more use for the crotchety old bastard than anyone else in these parts.

"Shhh! Andy, don't you dare be rude. Mr. Loomis is a fine, God-fearing man and I'll not have him insulted in my house! Now, be a good boy and go kill and pluck us a good chicken for supper."

"I'll wring the neck of a thin rooster, the kind he brought us," Andy vowed.

"No, get that speckled hen. She's fat and is always pecking Gilbert when my back is turned."

"Ma, that's our best layer!"

Mildred took a deep breath. "All right, then. But I want you to kill one of them young roosters. I'll stew him with potatoes and greens. And pluck him clean. No pin feathers."

Andy was furious as he headed out to their barn. Since his father had died, he'd had to drop out of school in order to do a man's work. Now he was always tired and missing the sight of one Ginny Olsterdorf, the cutest girl in Brighton. Last summer, he'd thought that Ginny had admired him, too, but now Andy was sure some other kid who had time to joke around and put on a show had won Ginny's eye. Life was damned unfair.

To make matters worse, none of Brighton Township's Union Army widows had received so much as one thin dime from Lincoln's damned federal government, let alone the promised eight dollars a month.

"Andrew," Loomis called before he could duck into the barn. "I want a word with you, boy."

Andy slowly turned around to watch Loomis gimp and jerk his way across the yard like a crippled crawdad, face all pinched up with pain and bushy eyebrows knitted down, so they formed a big Y with his hooked beak. Eldridge Loomis wore shoes, but they were worn-out about as bad as the man himself. His poorly patched and baggy pants were hitched up with leather reins made into suspenders and his shirt was dark with dirt and fouled with dried food. Andy had an overwhelming urge to ask Loomis if he had taken even one bath since last summer, but he didn't.

While waiting for the man to gimp across the farmyard, Andy took a deep breath and shoved both hands into his pockets just so that Loomis couldn't see that they were shaking. He didn't know why his hands were shaking, but they were and Andy told himself that it was because of hatred rather than fear. In a few years he'd be bigger and far stronger than Loomis—hell, he almost was already.

"Boy, you had best be preparing your soil and getting to the planting," Loomis said, disapproval stamped all over his uglier-than-a-coon-dog face.

"I was just fixin' to, Loomis."

"Sir," the farmer snapped.

"Huh?"

"You should address your elders as 'sir.' Weren't you taught any manners?"

"I got manners," Andy said, teeth clenched and the hair on the back of his neck bristling. "But I never heard your boys call any man 'sir.' Mostly, they just cussed."

Loomis's lips drew tight across his crooked teeth and he said, "You've gotten cocky since your pa went off to war and got hisself killed. You've got to thinkin' that you're a man now, but you're a long, long way from it."

"I got to kill a rooster if you're staying for supper. Are you?"

"Haven't put any thought to the matter."

Andy knew that was a lie. Loomis probably hadn't eaten all day so he'd be able to wolf down most everything put on his mother's table.

"I got chores to do."

"You know how to do the planting?"

"Yep."

"Got good seed?"

"Yep."

"Maybe I should look at it."

"Don't need your watching over," Andy heard himself reply as he toed the earth with his bare feet.

"That's for a man to judge, I reckon."

Andy didn't trust himself to speak.

"Yeah, maybe I ought to look at that seed," Loomis said, squeezing on his pointy jaw. "If you plant bad seed, you're going to starve your family off this farm for certain, although I suspect it will happen anyway."

"The seed is good! Me and my pa saved the best from last year's harvest."

"No disrespect to your pa, but he wasn't any better at farmin' than he was at soldierin'."

Andy exploded. "You ornery son of a bitch! My father was ten times the man you are! He died a war hero!"

Loomis took a jolting step forward and swung at Andy, but he was much too slow. Andy ducked and ran under his arm, then shot across the yard, scattering chickens. He jumped an irrigation ditch clotted with cattails and didn't stop running until he was into the far woods. Andy thought he heard Loomis shouting, but it might as easily have been Ma, because when he hooked his arm around a tree and gazed back, with his chest heaving and his brain on fire, he could see both Loomis and his mother standing in the yard.

"To hell with them!" Andy swore, hitching up his pants and moving deeper into the trees, allowing the shadows and the coolness to settle his mind.

Whenever things got bad, Andy dreamed of faraway places. Places most always on the Western frontier. Andy liked to pretend that he was Daniel Boone or Davy Crockett, conveniently forgetting that the latter had already died at the Alamo. Or perhaps he was a California forty-niner, tall and striding across the Sierra Nevada Mountains discovering pockets of pure placer gold that no one else had a chance of finding because he had an amazing sense for prospecting wealth.

Another one of his favorite daydreams was that he was a Pony Express rider thundering across the plains or conquering the searing Nevada desert, outrunning Paiute Indians trying to lift his scalp. Andy wished so bad that he were just about anyone other than a poor Indiana farm boy with a couple of broken-down plow horses and no grain in the barn or corn in the bin. The milk cow was sold in January, so now both Wilma and Gilbert had become almost as skinny and ill-tempered as Loomis. There was no Ginny to bat her pretty eyelashes and say something fine like, "Why, Andy, I do so admire how you act now that you are the man of your family."

No, sir! None of it. Just their farm, the constant, gnawing hunger, and work that never ended even after sundown. It was wrong, just plain wrong, and no way to live at all.

"Gawdamn you Pa," Andy choked, hugging the trunk of an old cottonwood tree, "you put me in a bad fix and now here comes that horrible old man, scheming, I'll bet, to make things even worse, though I don't hardly know how that would be possible."

The next day, Andy hitched up the plow horses and set to work preparing for the planting. He worked the day after that, too. And the next and the next, until the fields were ready and then he and Ma went out and stomped in the corn seeds, one by one, and covered and watered them all like they were roses.

It was backbreaking work, but Andy took some pleasure in knowing he had his field planted a week before Loomis and his hired help.

"You've done good, and your father would be most proud of you, Andrew," his mother said early one evening when Andy had fallen asleep at the table. "Now go to bed. The weeds are starting to come up and the ditches need work."

"Yes, ma'am," Andy said.

"Tomorrow is the Sabbath. I think we'll hitch up the wagon and go to church and offer our thanks to God for getting the corn planted on time. Would you like that, Andrew?"

Would he ever! Ginny would be there and it seemed like forever since he'd had the pleasure of her smile. Never mind that she'd most likely have a new beau. It didn't matter. Just looking at her instead of the south end of a plow horse was going to be fine.

So the next morning, they hitched up their rickety buckboard and went into town. Wasn't much of a town, but it did have a few stores, a schoolhouse, silo and blacksmith shop, and the Holy Jesus Church of God. That was where everyone in town would go at eleven o'clock Sunday morning.

The arrival of the Parmentier family, so long absent from any social event, caused a stir. Andy didn't appreciate being gawked at and Gilbert wouldn't stop crying, so things were tense. Maybe, Andy thought, these townspeople had figured the Parmentiers had starved out. Well, come harvesttime, when he had the corn buyer out to put a value on his crop, standing proud and tall in their fields, these people would know that Andy Parmentier was a man. And never mind that he was missing school. Andy could read and he could write better than a lot of folks. He had his mother to thank for that, because she read stories rented from the traveling drummer that passed by their homestead every month. It only cost a nickel a book, and Ma had never been one to scrimp on learning.

"Andy!"

He turned toward the church and there Ginny was, prettier than a peach. She was dressed in white trimmed with yellow lace the color of sun-kissed corn tassels. Andy thought he was going to choke he was so happy to see Ginny again.

But then Jim Pullman rushed over and handed Ginny a damned flower and she giggled. They talked for a moment, giggled some more, and hurried off toward the church.

"Well, I'll be gawdamned if that don't fry me!" Andy swore, removing one of his father's old hats that had put a bend to the tops of his ears and slamming it to the ground.

"Andrew! This is the Sabbath and you are standing outside the temple of the Lord!" Mildred Parmentier scolded, trying to clean Gilbert's dirty little face. "I will not tolerate such behavior and profanity!"

Andy could see that it was going to be close as to whether Gilbert or his ma started the tears first. Feeling bitter and betrayed, he turned on his heel and went stomping off toward town.

"Andy! Andy come back!"

But he wasn't going to. No, sir! Neither the Lord nor the pastor of the Holy Jesus Church of God had done a single thing to help out the Parmentiers since Pa had died, and that was why Andy figured he wasn't about to go in and offer prayers.

Sure, they'd had a good spring, with plenty of rain followed by sunshine, so that they might even hope for a banner-year crop—if the locusts didn't eat it first or the wind and hail beat it flat, or there was no more rain. This crop was Andy's and by jingo he'd done it pretty near all by himself, except for the planting. His back was strong, his hands were callused, and he had grown an inch this year. And somehow, despite the backbreaking work, he'd gained maybe twenty pounds of pure muscle.

Having no particular place to go, Andy plodded around the town, but there wasn't anything much to see. The stores were all closed up tighter than Loomis's wallet and even the combination blacksmith, saddle, and harness shop was shut down. Andy removed his shoes and tied the laces together before slinging them over his shoulder. No sense in using up good shoe leather for nothing, and besides, the shoes were too small and pinched his toes.

Maybe he'd see what kind of horses, mules, or oxen Mr. Gaines had in the back corral. He might even feed them a little hay, if there was some dropped outside the corral. At least livestock wouldn't betray a man, if he treated them fair.

Andy was disappointed to see that there were only two cows and a donkey in the corral. But then he heard loud snoring and turned to see dirty bare feet sticking out of the straw pile, and that seemed pretty interesting. So interesting that Andy sat down cross-legged and waited for a while to see who it might be inside that straw pile. But when the man showed no sign of coming to life after a long while, Andy got a piece of straw and crept up to tickle the bottom of his feet.

"Ahem! Eh . . . ahem!" was followed by a series of grunts, mumbles and then moans. But when the snoring continued, Andy tickled some more, until finally, the sleeping man sat bolt upright, straw spilling from his face.

The stranger was maybe twenty, thin but taller than Andy, and wearing a stringy goatee such as Andy had been told was worn by Southern gentlemen and old Chinamen. He was dirty and unshaven, with bloodshot eyes and a mop of shaggy black hair.

"Shit!" he swore, glaring through unfocused eyes at his tormentor. "Did you tickle my feet?"

"Uh-uh," Andy lied. "I wouldn't do that. But I did see flies crawlin' all over 'em."

The man clamped both hands against the side of his head and moaned, hands fumbling around in the hay, probably for a lost gun or some food.

"Thanks be to God!" he said, producing an earthen crock and popping the cork an instant before his Adam's apple bobbed up and down four times. Andy counted each long, shuddering gulp and then watched as the stranger closed his eyes and sighed like a fat sow in mud.

"Damn but I needed that!"

"What is it?"

"Corn liquor. You a farm boy?"

The way he said "farm boy" made Andy want to deny the fact, but he thought of his father and nodded. "Yep."

"Yeah, that's what I figured. You got any money, kid?"

"Nope."

The stranger clucked his tongue with a rueful sound. "Nobody has any money anymore in Indiana. Or Illinois or

Iowa, either. Only people left with money are the preachers and the drummers and the whores in all the cities. That's all, and I can't do any of them things, especially the last one."

He chuckled.

Andy chuckled, too—though he had no reason.

"Say, my name is Gizzard O'Reilly."

" 'Gizzard'?"

"Yeah," Gizzard said. "I know it's unusual. My ma named me that 'cause I showed a love of fried chicken gizzards at a very young age. They're still my favorite food. I could probably eat twenty or thirty pounds of 'em at a single sitting, but that would take a lot of chickens."

"I expect so," said Andy. "What are you doing here?"

"I come up this summer to help my uncle Ben Morgan. He lives about fifty miles north of Brighton. But I didn't come just for the money he'll pay me. No, sir! I came because he once pulled me out of a creek so I didn't drown. After I help him out this summer, I'm heading back down to Old Santa Fe in the New Mexico Territory."

"I heard of it and always wanted to go out west. Maybe hire on as a cowboy or a soldier."

"Soldiering is hell. Cowboyin' isn't much easier. Say, do you want a little hair of the dog?"

"Why'd I want to drink anything with dog's hair floating around in it?"

Gizzard shook his head. "You are nothing but a hayseed farm boy and that's for double-damned certain."

Andy didn't like the sound of that so he said, "I am the man of a good section of land owned free and clear. My father was a farmer, but he was also a war hero. I reckon that I don't want your dog-hair drink, nor do I want to share your sorry company."

Looking offended, Gizzard tried to jump to his feet,

but lost his balance and toppled back over, then began to laugh hysterically.

"What's so damned funny!"

"You," Gizzard said. "You're all worked up over something that didn't mean nothing and you won't take a drink of corn liquor 'cause you're just a kid. The only thing good to drink in Old Santa Fe is whiskey or tequila. Nobody down there drinks milk or even water."

"My name is Andrew Parmentier and I *am* young," Andy admitted, "but I got a grown man's responsibilities and I do a grown man's work. What do you do besides get drunk and sleep in a pile of straw?"

Gizzard sat up. "I can fix about anything made of wood, steel, or leather. I can tame bad horses or beat 'em to death so they won't kill you first."

"Got no bad horses, only slow ones, and I do my own mending."

"You got any food at your house?"

"Maybe some." They had just butchered the last of their pigs, but it would have to last the summer. Nothing to spare.

"What you got? Beef?"

"Nope."

"Corn and potatoes?"

"Some."

"That's good, but I need meat. I sure would love some chicken gizzards right now. The rest of a chicken wouldn't be bad, either."

"You need a bath even worse."

Gizzard scowled. "I could whip your ass, Andrew Parmentier."

"I don't believe you could," Andy said, feeling a surge of expectancy. His father had taught him a few things about fighting. More than a few things, in fact. "I don't believe that you could at all."

"All right, I'll show you," Gizzard said, coming to his feet with clenched fists and staggering forward.

Andy waited until Gizzard took a big looping swing and then he stepped in close and nailed him in the stomach with a wicked left uppercut right where the ribs come together. He hit him so hard that Gizzard's mouth flew open like a hooked fish. Then Andy sledged him with an overhand right to the jaw and he heard the sickening pop of bone.

Gizzard howled and collapsed, both hands cradling his jaw as he struggled to speak.

"Oh, Jesus," Andy swore, appalled at the untapped power in his fists, "I ruined him!"

But it turned out his jaw wasn't broken after all. When Gizzard finally got it back into its socket, he explained how it had once been broken and sometimes could be knocked out of joint with a perfect punch.

"I apologize, Andrew."

"Andy."

"Whatever. I judged you wrong. You *are* a man."

Andy couldn't help it. He swelled up like a toad in a milk bucket and grinned. "We got some pork," he said, helping Gizzard to his feet. "Not much. We're poor."

"I'm poorer. Have a drink."

Andy drank. It was terrible!

"Gets better with the effort," Gizzard promised. "Have another. Got a second jug hidden in this straw pile and I may need your help finding it."

Andy fought down the fiery liquor.

"One more," Gizzard urged, massaging his whiskery jaw with a pained expression. "Third one is always sweetest, or so they say in Old Santa Fe."

Andy drank more whiskey, wanting to forget about Ginny, the farm, and especially about Eldridge Loomis coming around more and more often.

"I can go find my uncle Ben tomorrow. Today we'll

steal a chicken while everyone is at church," Gizzard said, eyes sparkling. "Then we'll roast her good in the blacksmith's forge barn, 'cause I already pried a barn board loose and we'll get drunker'n pigs in a whiskey barrel!"

"Why would pigs—"

"Aw," Gizzard moaned. "Don't ask me that. Please! Just help me up and let's catch a chicken or two."

"All right," Andy said, grinning like a fool and deciding that was just about the funniest idea he'd ever heard in his whole short life. "We'll do 'er, by crackie!"

They'd gotten caught, but not until after they'd torched two chickens and finished the second jug. Gizzard had gone straight to jail, but Andy had been set free by the town magistrate after a hard sermon.

"We're ruined!" Mildred wailed. "All that your father did to make the Parmentier name respectable has been soiled by your drunkenness and thievery! Mr. Loomis was right. You do have a bad streak!"

"Don't tell me about Loomis!" Andy struggled to lower his voice, shocked that he'd raised it to his own mother. "Ma, please. I just got a little drunk and then hungry."

"Oh," she cried, "and on the Sabbath, too! Can you imagine how mortified we were?"

" 'We,' Ma? Gilbert sure don't understand."

"And it's a good thing!" She came over and threw her arms around his shoulders. "Andrew, promise me you'll never act that way again!"

"I won't," he promised, head feeling like one big stinging nettle. "I surely won't."

"Who was that awful stranger?"

"Gizzard O'Reilly. He's from the New Mexico Territory and has lots of stories that—"

"Figures," she snapped. "He's an outlaw and he'll stay in jail a good long while, unless I miss my bet."

"For stealing a couple of chickens?"

"A chicken, a horse! What's the difference? Stealing is stealing!"

Andy thought to himself that there was a huge difference, but he supposed this was not the time or the place to argue his point.

"Tomorrow you get out in the fields, weed and irrigate and work like you never worked before. And you don't stop working until the harvest is done. Hear me?"

"Yes, ma'am."

"And you don't ever drink demon rum again or—"

"It was just corn liquor. After the third gulp, it tasted all right. We could make better right out in the barn. Gizzard told me how and . . ."

Mildred Parmentier couldn't stand to hear another word. Mortified, she crushed her two innocents to her breast turning her back on Andy.

That was fine. He would bring in the corn this fall and then he was heading for Santa Fe. Or maybe California. He and Gizzard had it all figured out—except for the small details.

Yep, harvest the corn and go west to make his fortune one way or another. Then return someday to buy his ma a fine little business in town. He would come back to redeem himself and restore his reputation.

He was, after all, a Parmentier right to the bone.

Chapter Three

Andy was out hoeing weeds one muggy August afternoon under a hot, sullen sky when he saw Eldridge Loomis come gimping through his cornfields looking for him. Tired, depressed, and definitely not up to facing his cantankerous neighbor, Andy ducked down in his corn and ignored Loomis's calls. After a few minutes the old man headed for Andy's farmhouse—something he had begun to do more and more frequently.

Watching Loomis greet his mother and then go inside, probably for a cool glass of water, made Andy even more depressed. What was that crotchety son of a bitch *really* up to, anyway? Andy figured Loomis was trying to get into his mother's good graces so that he could buy the farm if their corn crop failed. Either that, or maybe to purchase equipment or harness at less than a fair price. That was the way of a man like Loomis. He was always conniving to get a deal or chisel someone out of something. Well, Andy wouldn't let the man buy a single thing, unless it was for twice its true value.

Andy continued weeding, giving his anger a constructive outlet. Try as hard as he might this summer, one man couldn't keep up weeding over a hundred-acre corn patch. Andy's only consolation was that Loomis had two hired hands working in his adjoining fields practically from sunup to sundown. And Loomis's fields didn't look all that much better. Yeah, Andy thought, I have to remember to think of the good things I'm doing and how much this crop will bring in just another month or six weeks. He'd heard that corn prices were down somewhat because everyone in the county had a bumper crop this year. No matter. Even if the prices were only half of what they had been last year, he'd still make more money than he and Pa had a year ago.

No more potatoes for nearly every meal. No more gnawing, ever-present hunger in the belly after leaving their supper table or hearing little Gilbert beg for milk. It had been hard, but now Andy could see the fruits of his labor. He kept reminding himself of how happy and proud he'd be come harvesttime and the sale. After that, everyone in Brighton would say what a fine man Andy had become and never mind that he'd gotten drunk on the Sabbath with a wild young drifter from the New Mexico Territory. Eldridge Loomis had crowed about how Gizzard had been locked up for ten days then run out of town.

"We don't tolerate that kind of drunken trash in Brighton," Loomis had declared, speaking directly to Andy. "A thief like that won't last long in any God-fearing community. The good folks will take care of his kind in a hurry."

Andy hadn't missed the thinly veiled implication that he also would be run out of this community . . . if he ever got drunk and stole a few chickens again. Even his mother had seemed uncomfortable as Loomis continued his vitriolic tirade over the chicken thievery, which Loomis managed to place on the same level as murder. But then, come to think of it, his mother had said that stealing a chicken wasn't any different from stealing a horse.

It was growing late in the afternoon when Loomis finally left their farmhouse and headed on back to his own ramshackle house. Andy had worked almost to sundown, not wanting to see Loomis in their house, and now he was relieved to see the man heading home. Maybe Loomis and his mother had gotten into an argument and she'd thrown him out for keeps. That sure would be a welcome bit of news! But Loomis didn't appear to be upset and Andy had grown accustomed to how he walked a little more bent and crabbed along a little faster when he was angry, which was most of the time. In fact, this evening Loomis was actually . . . smiling.

That scared Andy. Scared him near to death.

I'll bet that old bastard cheated Ma out of something and that's why he's so happy, Andy thought, vowing in the next moment to get his gun and make things right again.

Loomis coughed, then spat on the corn. Andy swore to himself and ducked to let the old geezer pass by, and damned if Loomis wasn't humming a tune as well as smiling.

Yep, Andy thought, he made himself some damned fine deal swindling his mother out of something pretty good, although there wasn't much of anything that the Parmentiers owned that was worth much, other than their . . . farm.

The farm!

Andy started running toward the house with the hoe still clenched in his fist. He didn't know if Loomis glanced back and saw him, nor did Andy care as he shot across the farmyard and landed on the porch to tear open the door. "Ma, what happened!"

She was at her iron stove, cooking supper, and damned if he didn't catch *her* smiling, too!

"Ma, what's wrong?"

She turned, and at the sight of Andy, her smile died. Andy looked to Wilma and her face was blank as a board, which was pretty typical. Little Gilbert was playing on the floor.

"Ma, what'd you sell to old Loomis!"

She frowned. "Sell?"

"Yeah! What did he cheat you out of?"

"Andy," she replied, "I think you'd better go out and feed the livestock before it gets dark and you have to use a lantern in the barn. I didn't have time to collect the eggs. See if you can find at least two."

Andy was in the habit of doing his mother's bidding, but not now. Instead, he marched over to the table and dropped into a chair. "Ma, I need an answer. What kind of a deal did you make with Eldridge Loomis? I'm the man of the house now and I got every right to know."

Mildred Parmentier set her ladle down and sniffed at the pot of potato stew that she had cooking. Then she made a big deal out of washing her hands in the bucket and drying them on her apron before she turned completely around and came slowly across the room.

"Andy," she said, not quite able or willing to meet his questioning glare, "you've done a man's work and then some and I'm proud of you. Your father would be—"

"Ma, what happened in here this afternoon!"

"I wish we could talk about this after dinner. Maybe outside, where we can discuss this in moonlight."

"Moonlight?" Andy was getting more upset by the second. "Ma, did you sell him the horses? Or . . . or our plow? What did you let him swindle out of us!"

"Nothing. Nothing at all."

Andy blinked. Could he have been so wrong? "Ma, I saw that man and he was smiling. Something happened in here."

"Yes," she admitted. "A lot happened, but I'm not sure that you will be able to understand. This is going to be very difficult for you, Andrew. I think . . ."

"Tell me!"

She took a deep breath. "All right, I guess there is no

way around this. The truth is that I just agreed to marry Mr. Loomis as soon as we bring in the harvest."

Andy's mind locked up and burned like brakes on a runaway wagon. His jaw sagged and he stared at his mother in disbelief.

"Andrew," she said, hurrying over to kneel before him and gather his big, callused hands in her own. "You've been working yourself to death. We all have. And the corn prices have gotten real, real low, so we aren't going to do too well after all."

"How low?"

"A bushel isn't going to be worth much more than a pound of flour or potatoes. Eldridge says that it's so bad that some farmers have even stopped working their fields. They're . . . they're talking about burning crops and trying to organize something called a cooperative."

Andy scrubbed his face, but it was numb. He shook his head as if he could throw off a bad dream . . . or, rather, a full-blown nightmare, and his mother's words seemed to come at him from a great distance.

"Mr. Loomis said that if we combine our farms, we'd have a lot more bargaining power. He said that we could command a better price because we'd have more—"

"No," Andy muttered, his head shaking faster now. "No, Ma, we're not going to team up with Loomis. You can't marry him!"

She recoiled. "You've no right to tell me what I can or cannot do! This is my farm and I will do whatever is best to make sure that it is not lost to the bankers."

"It won't be 'lost'!" Andy jumped up and shouted, "We're going to be all right. I swear I'll always take care of you and Wilma and Gilbert."

"Will you? Once, I thought you would. But that was before . . ." Her voice trailed off like smoke in a stiff wind and she wrung her hands in futility.

"Before what?" he managed to ask.

"Let's just not talk about things for a while, all right?"

"I want to know right now!"

"All right," she said, taking a deep, ragged breath. "Before you got drunk and showed yourself to be a thief."

"Two chickens, Ma! Two lousy, skinny chickens that we paid back!"

"Andrew, a responsible man would never do such a shameful thing to his family. Never. Eldridge says that it'll likely happen again. That you can't be trusted and that you've shown your true colors."

"And you believed him!"

Andy couldn't believe this was happening. It was worse than being thrown in jail, even worse than losing face in town and imagining what Ginny and all the other kids were saying about him since he and Gizzard O'Reilly had themselves a little fun.

"Ma, I just got drunk for the first time in my life. I'm no thief. I'm your son! You raised me. You know me."

"I thought so," she replied, chin quivering. "But the son I thought I knew would never have gotten drunk on the Sabbath and stolen chickens."

This couldn't really be happening! In desperation, Andy rushed over to Wilma and scooped his sister up in his arms. "Tell your mother that Eldridge Loomis is an evil man! Tell her that we can see his true nature and that it is bad. You don't want him to become your new father."

Wilma began to cry. She always cried when anyone raised their voice in the house. Wilma had never been much use for anything and Andy knew that she never would be. The girl was the only daughter, spoiled and doted upon by both her parents. He set her down roughly and she ran to her mother, crying. It filled Andy with such a rage that he could not help but ball his fists.

"I have worked like a mule all summer and this is what

I get in return! You're going to marry that skinny, ornery old son of a bitch and give him our farm!"

"I'll get half of his and . . ."

"And what!"

"I'll outlive him and then I'll have both," Mildred Parmentier said with uncharacteristic hardness in her voice. "I'll either give the land to you to farm, or sell it. Either way, I'll have food and a place to live in my old age. Something I won't have if I don't marry Eldridge."

"That's crazy talk!" Andy shouted. "All you'll get is a man who is mean and crotchety and who will treat you like a farmhand or animal. That old bastard will work you into an early grave just like he did his first wife!"

"She was always sickly and . . . and a slacker."

"Mrs. Loomis worked like a slave! Remember? We used to see her out in the fields even when she was heavy with child. Ma, that man killed her as sure as if he'd put a gun to her head or poison in her porridge!"

"That's not true! You just don't know him," Mildred cried, on the verge of angry tears. "Andrew, you don't know Eldridge at all. He's hard on the outside, but he's got a good heart and he's real smart. The reason he seems so mean is that he's hurting with back pain and he's terribly lonesome."

"I remember him when he had a good wife and a good back," Andy hissed. "He was mean then, too. That's the way Loomis is and he'll never change."

She raised her chin and squinted, face turning hard. "Andrew, after we're married, you can stay and help out, or you can run off to California or someplace out west like you've always dreamed about. I've got a little money tucked away that I never told anyone about and you can have that with my blessings as your stake."

"Uh-uh," he told her in a low, hoarse voice. "I'm staying until the harvesting is done. After that, I'll leave. But I won't take anything except Pa's watch, rifle, and pistol. That's all. Nothing more."

"That's fair," she said, turning back to her stove. "Now go out and wash up for supper and let's never talk about this again."

Andy didn't remember anything for the next couple of days. He worked with such savage intensity that his mind shut down, so that his energy focused on his body. Wilma came out to bring him food and water, and to lead him back to the house, where he would stagger to the table, gulp a few bites down, and then collapse on his bed in complete exhaustion. Andy didn't want to think, and he realized that he was even afraid about leaving Indiana.

He was afraid of Indians and was a long ways shy of being a Davy Crockett, Daniel Boone, or Jim Bridger. He was just an Indiana farm boy. But that was going to change, because if he lost his nerve about going west, Eldridge Loomis would make his life even more of a living hell than it already had been since Pa had gotten himself killed in the War Between the States.

And now Andy realized that Loomis's plan all along had been to marry his mother and increase his holdings. Andy knew that he should have killed the man when Loomis took a swing at him in front of the barn. He could have beaten Loomis to death with his fists and claimed he'd done so in self-defense. The people in Brighton would have believed him, because Loomis was mean and had a terrible temper.

"I could have killed him that day," Andy muttered to himself, "and nobody would have thought much about it one way or the other."

But now it was too late. Or was it?

The idea put its teeth into his mind and shook it back

and forth like a dog playing with a rope. It was a terrible thing to think about, and yet it was all that he could think about as he worked through the harvest, seeing Loomis coming over more and more until it was every day. Of course, he'd never kill a man except in self-defense but . . . what if it *was* self-defense?

That was an interesting idea. Loomis was notorious for losing his temper. Many was the time that Andy had seen him beat his wife and whip his kids or a farmhand. Not so much anymore, but he'd sure been quick to do it in the past. Loomis was older now and maybe not so ready to deal out punishment. But Andy was ready to bet that the man could be goaded into a killing rage.

But how? And when?

As the long days passed and he labored to harvest the fields, the idea of killing Eldridge Loomis wouldn't go away. At first, he tried to smother it like a live thing, but after a time Andy let the idea take shape and form both in his waking hours and even while he was sleeping.

Jim Pullman arrived one day from town and found Andy in the fields, face burned but wearing a big grin. "Hello, Andy!"

"Hello," Andy said without much enthusiasm.

"Andy," Jim said, "I can understand why you'd be mad at me for taking Ginny. I can also see that you're working like a dog. But when I watched you a minute ago, you were smiling!"

Afraid that Jim might read murder on his mind, Andy forced a scowl. "I was remembering my pa."

"I guess you're going to have a new man in the house," Jim said cautiously. "Old Loomis was in town bragging about the upcoming wedding."

Andy felt his heart begin to hammer and he concentrated hard to keep his voice under control. "Oh yeah?"

"That's right. When the news got out, everyone in town was shocked half to death. Why'd your mother ever agree to marry him?"

"I've been asking myself that very same question since she told me about it. The truth is, she don't trust me anymore since that time with Gizzard O'Reilly."

"Loomis is bad. He'll work your mother into an early grave. And then he'll mess with your little sister, Wilma."

"What do you mean?" Andy asked, his heart hammering even faster.

"It's pretty common knowledge that he once had a daughter but drove her crazy. Did it a few years before he brought his wife and boys to Brighton."

"How do you know this?"

"I'm living in town and you're not, so you don't hear everything. But some men were talking about it a few days ago. They didn't know I was listening, but I was. Seems they almost lynched Loomis over near Bookerville."

"Where's that?"

"I don't know, but it wasn't far enough away for old man Loomis to hide his past. You're gonna have to protect both your mother and Wilma, though everyone figures he'll be on his best behavior for at least a few months."

"Yeah," Andy said in a daze. "Thanks for the warning."

Jim dug his hands into his pants. He was smaller than Andy, but his pa had money and he looked a whole lot cleaner and smarter. "I come to tell you that Ginny is fickle."

"What do you mean?"

"I stole her from you and kissed and hugged her plenty. But then a new kid named Emory Bayer moved into town and she threw herself all over him. Now they're smitten and he's kissin' her and doin' other things that a gentlemen shouldn't even talk about."

"Ginny?"

"She looks innocent, but she's got a curious mind and a hungry body." Jim shrugged. "I'll say no more other than that we are both better off without her."

"That's good to hear," Andy said, not sure if it was or not. "I never even kissed Ginny."

"You should have. She's a good kisser and hugger. She liked you a lot, too."

"She did?"

"Sure! Ginny said more than once that if you weren't so poor and dirty, she'd have catched you good."

"She said that?"

"You bet! Made me real jealous. Don't anymore, though."

"Yeah," Andy said. "How old is this Emory fella?"

"About twenty. He's a man and I'll bet he'll turn Ginny into a woman soon . . . if he hasn't already."

Andy turned and gazed toward town. It was too far to see, except for the distant line of trees that would be near the Holy Jesus Church and the schoolhouse, where he used to go most every day when it was in session. Just thinking of Ginny, Emory Bayer, and Eldridge Loomis filled him with a sadness so profound that he could hardly swallow.

"What's the matter with your eyes?" Jim asked. "You're not . . . crying, are you!"

"Naw!" Andy roughly dragged a sleeve across his eyes, damning them for their betrayal. "It's the ripening corn. It lets off something when you pull the ears off the stalks and it burns my eyes."

"Huh." Jim also turned back toward town. "Well, I best go home for supper. I just had to let you know what I heard about Loomis so you'd be warned. And I've been feeling guilty about Ginny for a while, too. Wasn't fair for me to take her while you had so much work and troubles."

"Forget it. I have."

"Thanks. Ginny wouldn't have stayed with either of us after Emory came to town."

"Is he a big fella?" Andy asked, suddenly wanting to know.

"Yeah. Emory's father intends to open up a new livery and auction barn, but Emory is telling everyone that he'll be the proprietor and will be hiring a few stablehands. You can tell the Bayers have money behind them."

"Even more than your own pa, huh?"

Jim sighed. "I'd guess so."

"I got to get back to work," Andy said. "Thanks for the warning."

"Sure don't envy you," Jim said, looking out at the sea of gently waving corn. "Are you really gonna try and pick all of this?"

"Yep."

"Prices aren't good. In fact, they're real bad."

Andy had heard enough bad news for one day. "Sure," he said, moving deeper into the cornfield.

Chapter Four

The Parmentier corn harvest sold, but not for much. To make matters worse, the following week Mildred Parmentier became Mrs. Mildred Loomis. It would have made Andy sick had he not decided that the marriage was very much in his family's best interest. That's why he had attended the wedding, surprising both his mother and Eldridge Loomis.

"Boy, now that we're joined," Loomis told Andy the next afternoon, "I'll be expecting you to follow my orders. You've got a man at the helm of this household now. And by gawd, I'll make these farms pay handsomely! We'll plant wheat and barley next year and capture the market."

"Yes, sir," Andy said, as meek as a mouse.

Loomis studied him suspiciously. "You finally gettin' some manners, boy?"

"Yes, sir."

"Manners are important," Loomis said, relaxing a bit. "But hard work and taking orders are just as important and I'll brook no argument. You'll be working on my farm same as this one."

"I thought that the two farms had become one farm," Andy offered, forcing a thin smile. "Isn't that what happens when you get married?"

"Well, sure! But I don't want you messin' around in my house or my barn. Once a thief always a thief. No sense in putting temptation before a sinner."

It was all that Andy could do not to grab the old man by the neck and throttle him on the spot.

"Can you shoe livestock?" Loomis asked.

"No, sir."

"Damn! I should have guessed as much. Your pa couldn't shoe either. I tried to show him once, but my back wouldn't allow it. A man can save a pile of money if he can shoe his own stock. I'll teach you how to shoe them skinny plow horses. But first, I reckon we can start cutting some of that timber at the back of my new farm. Had my eye on that stand of timber for a good long while."

"Doesn't surprise me."

"What?"

"Nothing, sir."

Loomis glared at him for a moment, then said, "We'll clear out the pines first and sell 'em in town by the cord. We can use your old buckboard."

"It won't stand up to heavy hauling," Andy said, feeling the first faint hammering of his heart. "Not unless the spokes are—"

"Don't you go tellin' me what it will or won't stand up to, boy! We'll start chopping and hauling firewood at the crack of dawn!"

Andy saw blood rise up in Loomis's shrunken cheeks and he heard the shrill anger in his voice. It would be very easy to goad Loomis into violence. The only questions were how, when, and where to make his move. Certainly not in town, where people could interfere and save Loomis, and certainly not in front of his family.

They were up long before daylight. Andy hadn't slept at all, but he wasn't afraid. He had it all figured and it was going to work out even better than he'd hoped. It was going to end . . . perfectly.

Andy hitched the plow horses to the buckboard, then he and Loomis drove in silence out to the stand of trees down near the creek, where Andy had played beside a shallow frog pond since he was old enough to walk. He knew every tree and every square foot of this forested area. Today, they would be alone and he'd goad the old man into a fighting rage. Afterward they'd see who was a man and who was not, and his mother would own both farms. Yeah, he was ready for a showdown with Loomis, who had been gloating about the marriage and riding him far too long. If he, Andy, won, as expected, Wilma would never have to worry about her lecherous father-in-law or going hungry.

"Boy," Loomis shouted, stomping around in front of a tall perimeter pine, "you might as well start with this one. Cut her so she falls away from the others and out in the open."

When Andy pretended not to understand, Loomis grabbed the ax and rushed over to the pine. He measured it with one eye closed and then planted his sorry boots and sent the blade biting into bark.

"There," he hollered, stepping back from the tree and eyeballing it again. "You just chop into her right where I did and she'll fall where she ought."

"How can you be sure?" Andy asked with a bland expression that hid the seething hatred he felt inside.

Loomis gaped at him. "What do you mean, boy?"

"I mean that maybe you're wrong and it'll fall into the forest."

"Are you crazy or just stupid! Of course it won't fall toward the other trees!"

Andy shook his head as if he were doubtful . . . or a bit confused. "I don't know," he said. "My pa told me a thing or two about chopping down trees, and he'd say that if you cut it there, it will fall the wrong way."

Loomis's face drained and his eyes bulged. He choked the ax in his hands and hissed, "You better shut up and start working like I tell you."

"Well," Andy said, toeing the thick layer of dead forest leaves. "I just think that the tree is going to fall the wrong way. I got a right to my own opinion, don't I, Eldridge?"

Loomis began to shake. "You address me as 'sir'! And you got a right to nothing! You either do what I say or get off my gawdamn farms, you stupid bastard!"

"*Your* farms?" Andy advanced a pace. "I thought they were now *our* farms. That's what the law says when two people get hitched, doesn't it?"

Loomis raised the ax to the level of his narrow, heaving chest. "What are you doin', boy? Are you looking to get hurt? Is that what you want?"

Andy played dumb. "Hurt? What do you mean?"

"You know what I mean! You're testin' me and you won't find me wanting! Mess anymore with me and I'll chop you down deader than a sapling."

"How you gonna do that, Eldridge?" Andy asked, managing to sound naive and curious even as something inside of him coiled with the deadly purpose of a rattlesnake.

Loomis's eyes dropped to the ax, then moved back up to Andy. "You really must be stupid," he said in a pitying voice.

"Why, Eldridge, you wouldn't really take that ax to me, would you?"

"You're no damned good." Loomis raised the ax. "I should have figured it would come down to this, but I thought I could work you awhile first. Now I realize that isn't the case, so you're about to have a terrible accident."

"Accident?"

"That's right. You don't know how to cut a tree down and so you'll have an accident."

"One that will get me killed?" Andy asked, playing him like a fish while reading his murderous intentions.

"That's right, boy."

Andy was suddenly struck with the realization that they both had the capacity for killing. The big difference, though, was that Loomis preyed on weaker things like women and children and when he killed, he probably had to first work himself into a rage.

"Say your prayers," Loomis wheezed as he stumped doggedly forward, ax coming up in his bony fists.

Andy retreated deeper into the shadowy woods. Loomis charged, ax whistling far short of its target.

Feigning terror to make the man ever bolder, Andy cried, "Please don't kill me."

"Too late," Loomis gasped, already winded. "Way too late. I hated you from the minute I first set eyes on you. Hated your pa, too."

Twice more the man charged, swinging his ax. Each time Andy jumped farther into the woods. Loomis was in poor physical shape and Andy saw pain seeping into the deep creases of his face. "Is your back hurting you?" he asked.

Loomis sucked hard for air and finally managed to hiss, "Yeah, but not nearly as much as you're going to hurt!"

"Broken-down old son of a bitch," Andy taunted. "I heard that you drove your daughter crazy in a place called Bookerville. They say you did dirty things to her. How old was she when you started messing around?"

Loomis lunged with a sputtering curse and Andy retreated just out of his reach, shouting, "What happened to your little girl, Eldridge? Because of you, she's locked up in some crazy house!"

This time Loomis charged with demented fury even before he could raise the ax. Andy leaped forward and his powerful hands clamped onto the handle. For a moment they strained against one another, eyes locked and hate-filled. Andy threw Loomis across his hip then jumped on him and forced the ax handle under his stubbled chin.

"If there is a God, I'll wager that He'll forgive me," Andy said, bearing down with relentless pressure on Loomis's throat until the man began to gag.

Desperate, Loomis released the handle and tried to claw Andy's eyes out, but his arms weren't long enough. His heels began to drum against the dead layer of leaves and his hands flapped wildly. He stared upward, tongue protruding, lips turning white, eyes bulging in horror.

"I guess you're the one that had the terrible accident," Andy said, choking the last miserable thread of life out of his hated stepfather. "This is for the wife you worked to death and who was way too good for you, and it's also for your daughter, who never had a fair chance in life!"

After a final and convulsive effort, the man's body went limp. Andy checked his pulse, knowing Loomis was dead. He pushed to his feet and stared down at the man, try-ing to decide what he felt after just killing another human being. In truth, he felt no remorse whatsoever. Eldridge Loomis had been as sick a creature as ever walked the good soil of Indiana. Andy felt vindication and no more guilt than if he had slaughtered an animal to put food on the family table. Actually, he felt less guilt, because animals were innocent, while old man Loomis had been cruel and savage.

Andy picked up the ax and went over to the big pine tree that Loomis had chosen to be felled. Taking a wide, well-balanced stance, he reared back with all his might and sent his blade biting deep into the tree, making it shiver all the way to its top. He attacked the tree with the same measured purpose that he had attacked the weeds in his cornfield. The pine crashed down right on Loomis's body just as he'd expected. Andy went over and spread the branches. Yep, one of them was pressed down hard across the man's face and throat—a choker for certain.

Andy pitched his ax in the waiting buckboard, deciding that he would claim there had been an awful accident. Loomis had been trying to teach him how to drop a tree in the desired direction. But he'd lost his temper and rushed forward to demonstrate at the wrong time and place. And damned if the tree hadn't twisted just a little and landed right on him! Poor Eldridge had choked to death with the weight of a thick branch crunching down on his throat while Andy had struggled to lift the tree.

What a shame. Would everyone believe it? Probably not. Did it matter to Andy? Not a whit. The important thing was that it looked like a real accident. Loomis had been so despised in these parts that everyone would give Andy's unlikely story the benefit of the doubt.

No one had bothered to come to Eldridge Loomis's simple church wedding, but everyone attended his funeral out of morbid curiosity. Andy didn't act sad, but neither did he look happy, because that wouldn't do. So he just stood there beside his now twice-widowed mother, who was going to be quite a marriageable catch because she owned two good farms. Even better, the town banker had informed his mother that she'd inherited a considerable amount of cash. In this day and age, twenty-seven hundred dollars was considered a small fortune.

"You'll be all right now, Ma," Andy said after they returned to their farms and changed out of their funeral clothes. "So will Wilma and Gilbert. You'll be well-fixed for life."

She looked right through him and said, "Andy, you

know how to fell a tree. Can you live with what you done to him?"

Denial sprang to his lips, but Andy squeezed them tight and simply nodded his head.

"I hope so," the widow Loomis said with sadness. "Will you stay here and hold this family together now that Eldridge is gone?"

"I can't."

"Why not?"

"There's too much death all around. Too many bad memories I can't throw off. And there's liable to be a lot of talk about what happened in the woods. Already I could see the questions in their faces."

"Whose faces, son?"

"The ones that guessed the truth like you have. If I lived here another fifty years and went to church every Sunday, they'd still never trust me. In time I'd become as much of a loner as Loomis. Like him, I'd probably go bad, if I haven't already."

"You haven't, Andy. And as for Eldridge, I had hoped to change him for the better."

"You'd have failed, Ma. Loomis would have changed you instead, and much for the worse. Everything that Pa loved in you would have been destroyed by that man."

"How can you be so sure?" she asked. "Sure enough to appoint yourself judge and executioner?"

Andy shrugged. "If it helps, I can tell you that Loomis came at me first with the ax. He was trying to kill me just like I meant to kill him. The difference was that he lost his head. He went crazy and so I was able to kill him in self-defense."

"No, you didn't. But it don't matter now. You're the only one that will have to live with what happened out there in the woods."

"I can live with it just fine," Andy said truthfully.

"But how!" She was pleading for understanding more than an answer.

Andy thought about it for a moment, then said, "Didn't you ever hear about what Eldridge done to his own daughter in a place called Bookerville?"

"No."

"I suspect you don't even want to know," Andy said, laying his hand on his mother's shoulder. "But sooner or later you would have."

Leaving it at that, Andy packed up his father's rifle, pistol, and a few other things. When he was finished, he felt her gentle touch on his arm and heard her whisper fervently, "Thank you, Andrew, and God be with you always."

He went outside and had a long last look around the farm, trying to lock it into his memory. This was a good farm and it would improve with time and a little money. Andy wandered out to the barn and briefly considered saddling one of the family's plow horses, but they were a team and had been together almost since they were colts. He killed a chicken instead, then plucked and gutted it and stuffed it raw into his knapsack. It would last him a few days and then he would have to steal another. Once a chicken thief, he thought with a self-deprecating grin, always a chicken thief.

"Andy!"

He turned to see his mother rushing across the farmyard. "Here," she said, offering a handful of cash. "You earned it."

"Loomis's money?"

"Most of it."

"Then you keep it," he told her. "I want nothing of his to cause me bad luck."

"I understand." She stuffed the bills into her dress pockets, eyes pulling toward Brighton.

"Ma, what are you going to do now?"

"I'm going to rent out these farms and buy me a nice little house in town with a front porch and a swing to rock on come warm summer evenings. I'll do some sewing and laundry and a lot of reading and visiting. With the rent money and what I can make at easy odd jobs, I'll do just fine. It'll also be a much better life for Wilma and Gilbert. So we're all grateful to you."

"Maybe someday you'll marry another good man like Pa."

"Avery was a good man. And . . . and so are you."

Andy needed to leave before he started to cry. He hurried back into the house to say good-bye to Wilma and Gilbert. Seeing the devastation on his face, they both began to wail, so Andy retreated outside. He kissed his mother on the cheek, then scooped up his things and rushed on down the road.

School was just getting out when he saw Ginny for the last time. Emory Bayer was waiting to greet her. Brazenly, the prosperous young liveryman took Ginny in his arms and gave her a kiss. Andy heard Ginny giggle and he averted his eyes. Head down, he kept marching.

"Andy!"

Ignore her, he told himself.

"Andy, wait! I need to talk to you! Are you leaving!"

He kept walking but heard Bayer's protests. Andy wasn't happy about this, but he had nothing to be jealous about because he was going away forever.

Ginny overtook him and cried, "What is the matter with you! Can't you even say good-bye!"

"Get out of my way. Go back to kissing Emory."

She grabbed him and pulled him to a reluctant halt. "You shouldn't go away. You've got two farms now, and I heard the rumors that Mr. Loomis was worth a lot of money. Is that true?"

"Why do you want to know?"

"Because if it is, you can stay and become a . . . a respected leader in this town!"

"He's nothing but a drunk and a chicken thief!" Emory shouted. "And some are saying Andrew Parmentier is also a cold-blooded killer!"

Andy dropped his pack and took a deep breath. His heart began that hammering again and he brushed Ginny away like a pesky fly, walking slowly toward Emory Bayer. They were about the same height, but Andy was far broader in the shoulders and his muscles were as hard as the limbs of that killer pine tree.

"What did you say?" he asked in a soft voice that was somehow all the more frightening.

Emory's contemptuous smile dissolved. He retreated a step but Andy stayed close. "What did you say?" he repeated.

"Nothing!"

"Oh yes you did," Andy told him. "Among other things, you called me a drunken chicken thief."

"Yeah, but—"

"And you were right," Andy said, yanking his mother's plucked and gutted chicken from his pack. "Look! You caught me red-handed. So what are you going to do with the evidence?"

"I . . . I don't know what you mean!"

"Hmmm," Andy mused. "I think that you should take this poor chicken to the city constable and see if he wants to arrest me again."

"No!" Emory looked toward Ginny for help but received none.

"Well, Mr. Bayer," Andy said just as pleasant as anything, "if you don't want to give the evidence up to the law, I guess the next best thing you could do is . . . eat it!"

"Andy," Ginny cried in alarm. "Don't do this!"

He ignored her and shoved the pale, limp carcass in Emory's face. Emory attempted to run, but Andy grabbed him around the neck and mashed the dead chicken even harder into his face, hearing him bellow in protest.

"Andy, stop it!" Ginny screamed, grabbing him by the ear and twisting it hard enough to bring him to his senses. "Let Emory go! Leave now and don't you ever come back!"

Andy released Emory and, at the same time, released Ginny and every good thing he had ever felt about Brighton, Indiana. He took her roughly into his arms and kissed her, feeling nothing but pleasure and the satisfaction of putting this last question mark to rest.

She nearly swooned. "Andy," she panted. "I never expected it would be like that."

"Aw, it wasn't so much," he said with a grin. "No big deal at all, Ginny."

He left her in the street in front of the schoolhouse and sauntered out of Brighton as if he had not a single care in this world. He'd find Gizzard O'Reilly, then visit the great American West like he'd always dreamed. In a way, it would be like finally going home.

Chapter
Five

Andy remembered that Gizzard's uncle was named Ben Morgan and that the man lived on a farm about fifty miles to the north. That had seemed simple and easy enough to find when he set out from Brighton, but after walking for two days, Andy decided that fifty miles was a stretch farther than he'd expected. The chicken was all gone when he arrived in a little farming town called Sperryton and learned that Ben Morgan's farm was another five miles north.

"You look half-starved and pretty wore down," the old man that told him about Morgan opined. "If you chop us some firewood, my wife and I will put you up for the night and give you a good bait of feed."

Andy looked up at the pair who sat rocking on their front porch and thought about how nice it would be to see his own mother sitting and rocking. "All right," he told them, "where's your woodpile?"

"I'll show you," the old man told him as he struggled out of his chair. "My name is Willard Gibbons and this is my wife, Louise."

"Mine is Andy Parmentier. I'm from down around Brighton."

Mrs. Gibbons looked at him closely. "Did you walk all that way?"

"Sure did. Wasn't bad, though."

"That's a pretty long walk, but you look fit and strong."

"Yeah," Willard agreed, "I'll bet Andy could walk all the way to California without wearing out."

Andy was flattered. "As a matter of fact, I'm going to find my friend and we'll walk clear down to Santa Fe in the New Mexico Territory."

"You try that and you're liable to get scalped," Louise warned, wagging her finger at him as if he were a truant schoolboy. "You'll be taking that awful Santa Fe Trail."

Andy had heard of the Santa Fe Trail because it had long been famous. But he hadn't realized that it would be his road to the West. Now that he knew, however, he was even more excited about leaving.

"My friend knows the way right well, ma'am. I guess those Indians will think twice about giving us any grief when they see how well armed I am."

"Hmmph," Willard grumped, "you ain't so well armed. Might even be soldiers fighting out that way. Maybe they'll conscript you into the Union Army. That's happening now'-days, you know."

"Willard, he's still too young!"

"I don't think so," the old man said. "How old are you, Master Parmentier?"

"I just turned sixteen," Andy said proudly.

"Then you're plenty big and strong enough to put on a uniform and fight for the Union."

"No, sir," Andy told them. "The Civil War already killed my pa and a whole lot of other good Brighton men. Their families were all promised eight dollars a month for the rest of their lives, but we never saw a penny. I figure Lincoln is a liar."

"They're all liars!" the man swore. "Damn foolish war, if you ask me. What do we care about preservin' the Union? If them Rebs want to form their own government, then let 'em! Ain't worth all the dying."

"Amen," Andy said. "Now, where's your woodpile?"

"Forget the woodpile," Willard decided. "If your pa died fighting for the Union, that's payment enough. Just take your things inside. Empty bedroom is first door to the right."

"And I'll heat you some water for a bath, young Parmentier," the old lady said, easing out of her chair. "You do smell ripe."

Andy blushed with embarrassment. He hadn't really taken a bath since the day he'd strangled Eldridge Loomis, and then he'd only done it to wash the stench of Loomis away. Andy found the spare bedroom, thinking, If I'm not careful, I'll end up smelling as bad as Loomis.

The bath was hot and they gave him plenty of time to scrub himself with better soap than he'd ever had the pleasure of using. Andy gazed contentedly around and saw that these people were living a pretty good life. They had pictures on the walls and rugs on a real wooden floor. Yes, sir, he thought, town living is sweet.

"So," Willard said a while later, after watching Andy wolf down a third helping of beef, butter beans, and collard greens, "before we get around to the apple pie Louise baked, tell me about Brighton and your family farm."

Andy told them everything, leaving out only his mother's marriage to Eldridge Loomis and her final ownership of his farm. When Andy was finished, Willard said, "You're strong and seem bright enough, so why do you want to go traipsing off to Santa Fe? You'd be a whole lot better off staying at home and farming."

"It's a long story," Andy said, "but the short of it is that

I've always wanted to see the Western frontier. I've read about it since I was just a little shaver and I'm sick and tired of working a farm."

"Won't be any easier where you're going, and it'll be a whole lot more dangerous," Louise promised. "I think that you're making a big mistake, young man."

"That may well be true," Andy admitted, "but it won't be my first or my last. I might come back after I've had my fill of adventure. I don't know."

"You don't sound like it," Willard told him. "I can see your eyes light up when you talk about Old Santa Fe and all that wild Colorado and New Mexico country."

"I guess that's true."

Andy woke up early as usual, although he had no reason except for the habit. He dressed in darkness and tiptoed into the kitchen and consumed a slice of pie before he headed out the back door and found the woodpile. The sun was just coming over the eastern horizon when Andy finished sharpening the ax and set to work chopping a hefty supply of firewood. Working hard woke him up and he didn't mind it at all, for it was a normal part of his everyday life. By eight o'clock, he had a cord cut and neatly stacked alongside a little shed.

"Mighty nice of you to do that for us, young Parmentier," Willard Gibbons said, still wearing his pajamas and looking half-asleep. "Now, why don't you come inside? Louise has breakfast about ready and we could all use some coffee."

"I didn't expect any breakfast," Andy replied. "I just wanted to leave some firewood behind."

"Put the ax in the shed and come inside," Willard said with a big yawn.

"Well," Louise said as she pushed a heaping plate of

eggs, bacon, and pancakes in Andy's direction. "Sit down and fill up. What'd you say the name of that fella was that you were trying to find?"

"Gizzard O'Reilly."

"Never heard of him, and I'd sure remember a name like that. What was his uncle's name again?"

"Mr. Ben Morgan."

"Now, he is well-known in these parts. Yep! I heard that he killed more than one man in his younger days. He was a bounty hunter, you know."

"No," Andy said, "I did not know."

"Well," Louise said, "rumor is that he played both sides of the fence and made away with a tidy fortune. He never had a family and keeps pretty much to himself."

"That's right," Willard said. "We seen him only a time or two all year, when he comes to town for provisions. He don't do a whole lot of farming. Mostly he's a hunter."

"Manhunter?" Andy asked.

"No, a trapper. He runs a trap line up in the northern woods and sells furs and meat. Are you sure he's the one that you're looking for?"

"Pretty sure," Andy said, wolfing down his victuals. "Anyway, guess I'll find out soon enough. I heard his place isn't but five miles north."

"That'd be about right," Louise said. "But he isn't very neighborly."

Andy didn't care a whiff about that. All he wanted to do was find Gizzard and head for Santa Fe before the winter snows became regular. There'd already been frost on the fields and that meant that heavy snow was soon to follow. So he finished up his breakfast and collected his things.

"Much obliged for all the food and hospitality," he said as he prepared to take his leave.

"I see you got a rifle and pistol," Willard told him. "But do you have a hideout gun?"

"No, sir. What'd I want one of them for?"

"Because they can't be seen and give a man a big advantage in a fight," Willard explained. "A hideout can often save a man's life."

"I'll try to remember and buy one someday," Andy promised.

"You won't have to, because I'm giving you mine," Willard told him. "It's a six-shot pepperbox, loaded and ready for close action."

"Oh, no, sir!" Andy said when Willard handed him the evil-looking weapon. "I wouldn't even know how to use it."

"It's a double action," Willard explained. "It'll keep firing as long as you can pull the trigger. Sometimes, though, these mean little bastards will fire all six barrels at the same time. If that happens, it would probably blow your hand off at the wrist. So only use this when your back is against the wall and it's do or die."

"Are you sure?" Andy asked, taking the weapon, surprised at its heft. "I mean, it must cost plenty."

"Naw," Willard said. "It's old and I won it playing cards. Actually, I never had the nerve to fire it myself."

"Willard," his wife said, "I'm not sure I approve! If it blows up and hurts or kills young Andy, it'll forever be on our conscience."

"No, it won't," Willard answered, "because I just warned Andy never to use it except when he's got no other choice. Hopefully, he'll be like me and never shoot the damned thing, but instead just give it to some other fella when he gets old."

"Who makes these things?" Andy wanted to know.

"Allen. You'll notice there's only one hammer," Willard explained. "I was told that the cylinder revolves around that center pin each time you pull the trigger. I was also told that these pistols are worthless at any distance beyond twenty yards and highly inaccurate beyond ten yards. But they go off like a cannon, and at close range, they'll rip a man in half."

"I don't know how to thank you," Andy said.

"Can you write?" Louise asked.

"Yes, ma'am."

"Then send us a letter when you get to Santa Fe and tell us about your trip and what you think of the New Mexico Territory. We've both heard of it and we have talked about moving south to avoid these hard north-country winters."

"Santa Fe is an awful long way south," he told them.

"We know that, but our bones ache something fierce by December," Louise explained. "Anyway, it's nice to at least think about a warm climate. We have a son named Oscar, who rushed off to California to find gold, but he doesn't write and I expect he hasn't prospered. He lives in a little mining town called Placerville, but I've heard all the gold in California has been mined out."

"If I ever go to Placerville, I'll look Oscar up."

"You do that and give him hell for never writing us," Willard ordered in a voice that mirrored his considerable exasperation and disappointment.

Andy left the nice old couple and headed up the road at a brisk pace. He expected it would not take him more than an hour to reach Ben Morgan's homestead, and that meant that he and Gizzard might even head for Santa Fe that very same day.

The Morgan place was easy enough to find because it was set off all by itself. Andy turned left off the rutted dirt road he'd been following and headed across fields that looked as if they had not yielded a respectable harvest in a good many years. He could see a rickety cabin up in some trees, and as he approached, a couple of coon hounds came bounding out braying and raising a mighty ruckus. Andy stopped and waited for the two brown-and-white hounds to give him a good sniffing. Their long tails were whipping back and forth, so he figured he was in no danger of being bitten.

"Hello the house!" he called.

A moment later Gizzard O'Reilly appeared in the doorway with a rifle in his hands. When he recognized Andy, he set the weapon down and came out with a big, loose smile on his face.

"Well, if it isn't Andy Parmentier, the infamous Brighton chicken thief! I was beginning to think that you'd either gotten locked up or had forgotten about Santa Fe!"

They shook hands and took each other's measure. Gizzard was thinner and smelled faintly of liquor, but he was steady and reasonably clear-eyed. From the swelling of his jaw, he appeared to have been on the losing end of a bad fight.

Andy dropped his things down in front of the cabin and followed him inside. The place was a real pigpen, crammed with clothes, traps, dirty dishes, a pile of furs, and all manner of filth.

"Whew!" Andy exclaimed, retreating back outside. "Kinda rank in there, isn't it?"

"You get used to it after a while," Gizzard said, looking amused. "Uncle Morgan is off setting trap lines. He won't be back for a few days, so we can just sit around and sip some corn liquor."

"I thought we'd head for Santa Fe as soon as I arrived," Andy said. "The weather is going to get nasty. With luck, we can reach Missouri and head on down the Santa Fe Trail in a few more weeks."

"Too late in the season for that," Gizzard told him. "We need to wait until spring."

"Not me," Andy told him, the smile sliding off his

lean face. "I'm leaving Indiana, and heading for Missouri today."

"Today!" Gizzard laughed, but paid for it and grimaced because of his jaw.

"Someone really walloped you a good one, huh?"

"Yeah, Uncle Ben hits real hard but not as hard as you." He rubbed the jaw. "Andy, why are you in such a big hurry?"

"I been waiting many a year for this."

"Well, we can wait a few months longer."

"I don't think so, Gizzard."

"Listen, we'll winter here with Uncle Morgan. Do a little trapping."

"No thanks."

"Hey, there's even some French-and-Indian girls about two days' walk north up near Lake Michigan and in the wintertime they get real hungry for some loving!" Gizzard tried to grin. "We'll have us a real good time and head out for Santa Fe next spring with a few dollars in our pockets, if we get lucky and don't get caught."

"Caught doing what?"

Gizzard winked. "Never you mind about that! We can talk business later. Let's celebrate and get drunk."

But Andy shook his head and picked up his things. "I guess I'll be heading south right now. When you come around next spring, maybe I'll still be in Santa Fe. I don't know."

Gizzard looked pained. "You sure are pigheaded. I remember when we got drunk you told me that you'd been working from sunup to sundown since you were just a kid. So now you have a chance to drink, screw some horny half-breed girls up in the north country, and add to your wealth and knowledge of good living."

"Guess I'm not your kind," Andy said.

Gizzard heaved a big sigh of disappointment. "You say you're going to start for Missouri and walk yourself to death in weather that's already turning foul. I say you'll likely catch pneumonia and die. And even if you do reach Missouri, what then?"

"Who knows?" Andy said, getting tired of being berated. "That's part of life's adventure."

"Adventure! Ha! You'll starve along with a couple thousand other fellas, maybe catch river fever, and for damn sure be broke and even skinnier come next spring! Andy, you just aren't making any sense. I thought you were smart."

"I guess I am an impatient fool to get on with what I set my mind to," Andy agreed. "But I can't help that. So long, Gizzard. Maybe I'll see you in Santa Fe next year."

"You won't make it!" Gizzard shouted. "Not without me and some money, and damn sure not in the winter!"

Andy figured otherwise. He would keep moving and working for his keep at farms along the way. He'd do enough odd jobs to keep himself in food, shelter, and shoe leather. He had a dream that had been with him since boyhood, and so he was going after it come hell or high water.

"Hey!" Gizzard yelled. "Wait up! You win. I'll go with you, gawdammit!"

Andy turned around at the place where the big road joined the little one up to Ben Morgan's cabin. "What about those coon dogs!" he yelled. "Who's going to feed them if nobody is home!"

"We'll sell 'em along the way or eat 'em if we get to starving!" Gizzard hollered in reply. "Give me a minute or two to gather my things."

Andy laid his rifle and pack down, then spread out and pulled his father's old slouch hat over his eyes. He knew that it would take Gizzard a lot more than an hour to get himself ready. Might as well take a nap. He had a hunch that sleep was going to come dear before he reached Santa Fe.

_____ Chapter _____
Six

They were worn down, wrung out, and flat broke despite having sold the coon hounds for ten dollars each. It had taken Andy and Gizzard three cold, hungry months to reach Independence. They had walked mostly; mornings with the sun at their back, afternoons with it in their faces, whenever it managed to break through overcast gray skies. Sometimes a sympathetic traveler had seen their weariness and given them a ride in his wagon. But that had not happened often. In the late afternoons, they'd stopped at farms where they were allowed to sleep in the barn in exchange for a few hours of odd jobs. Being bigger and stronger, Andy often cut firewood or hauled things; Gizzard had more talents, so he repaired wheels, harnesses, or whatever a farmer needed fixing.

"You two boys could make a go of it here," a successful freighter outside Hannibal had told them one night in his livery when the angry sky opened up and the rain came down in icy torrents. "Gizzard, I could especially use a good wheelwright. You've a skill that's hard to find."

"I appreciate your saying so, but I don't think we'll be

staying, Mr. Howell," Gizzard had replied. "We're bound for Old Santa Fe in the New Mexico Territory."

"If the Injuns don't scalp you, a Mexican will put a knife in your bellies."

"No, sir. I'll avoid the Indians and I can speak a little Spanish, so we'll get along just fine with the Mexicans. As a matter of fact, some of 'em are my best friends."

"Well," the freighter had groused, "that's not something I'd brag about."

"They're a real easy people to get along with," Gizzard insisted. "And their señoritas are mighty pretty."

"What about you, Andy?" the man asked. "You're worn down to a nubbin. Maybe you should consider wintering here. I'd pay you fifteen dollars. Can you handle animals?"

"I'm the son of a farmer and have been around livestock all my life."

"Good enough. And Gizzard, if you change your mind, you could work right here in this livery fixin' my wagons and harnesses. What do you say?"

The offer had been tempting, but they'd turned it down and pushed on until they'd finally arrived in Independence. It was mid-January and they'd struggled through a snowstorm at Christmas, then gotten lucky and found work refurbishing the salon, gaming room, and suites aboard a once-elegant paddle-wheel steamer. Fortunately, it was mostly inside work, replacing flooring, sanding, and painting. They were allowed to live on board and eat in the galley on a regular basis with a few other permanent rivermen.

"If you boys stay on until spring," John Marsh, the crusty old riverboat captain, told them, "we'll float down to St. Louis, hook up with the Mississippi, and steam all the way down to New Orleans. We'll load up passengers and freight and return by July. It'll be the trip of your lifetimes."

He winked. "I'll promise you this, young fellers, once

you get Missouri and Mississippi river water in your blood, you'll damn sure forget about Santa Fe and them spicy Mexican señoritas!"

Gizzard was tempted enough to ask, "What kind of women are there to be found on the waterfront of New Orleans?"

"The prettiest, man-hungriest women in America!" Marsh exclaimed. "They're dark and dusky Creoles. Once a man lays eyes and hands on 'em, he's ruined for any other kind."

"Creoles," Gizzard said, a forgotten paintbrush poised in his hand. "I've heard of them. French-and-Indian, aren't they?"

"I expect so. But who cares what their blood be when the lovin' starts!"

"Andy, what do you say?"

He was tempted. Their long, numbing walk across most of Indiana and then all of Missouri had left him twenty pounds underweight and bone weary. Furthermore, Andy enjoyed working for Captain Marsh and knew that this was the chance of a lifetime. For two weeks the captain had been telling them about all the perils to be experienced on the big rivers as well as the excitement, color, and adventure.

"Boys," Captain Marsh added, "the men I hired in the past to go to New Orleans and back with me have returned with hundreds of dollars. You could get a start for Santa Fe well outfitted and riding fine horses instead of dead broke and walking on worn-out shoe leather."

"But what if the War Between the States isn't over by then?" Andy asked. "Wouldn't it be impossible to reach New Orleans because of federal gunboats?"

There was a long pause before Marsh forced a smile. "I got lots of friends along the lower Mississippi. We wouldn't have to worry about any bluecoats."

Andy was willing to accept the captain's pledge, but surprisingly, Gizzard was not. "Captain, I've heard that the North controls the Mississippi River and that New Orleans is practically a Union Army fort."

"Nonsense!" the captain cried. "New Orleans may be controlled by the Union Army, but its heart still beats true to the South. And besides, if there is trouble on the Mississippi, then we'll only go as far as St. Louis and see what kind of cargo and passenger list we can sign on for a return trip. Either way, you will both have money in your pockets and meat back on your bones. What do you say?"

Andy and Gizzard were sold and nodded eagerly. Andy declared, "Captain Marsh, consider us hired!"

"Glad to hear it." Marsh looked well pleased. "And after today's work, stop by my cabin and we'll have a couple of drinks to seal our agreement."

"That would be dandy," Gizzard said, licking his lips. "What do you say, Andy?"

"I guess so," Andy said doubtfully, remembering the last time he and Gizzard had drunk hard liquor—they'd made a complete mess of things and gotten arrested.

"What do you mean you 'guess so'?" the captain asked, eyeballing Andy suspiciously. "You ain't no religious fanatic, are you? One of them temperance-minded, holier-than-thou Bible-thumpers?"

"No, sir!"

"Good. My sister and my aunt Harriet give me a temperance lecture every time I visit Atlanta. And they're both sanctimonious old prunes!"

"We like to drink," Gizzard assured him.

"Damned relieved to hear it." Captain Marsh consulted his pocket watch. "Hell, there's no sense in us waiting until quittin' time. I make the rules. Besides, you boys have been working real hard and could use some rum!"

Andy and Gizzard followed the captain to his cabin, which was filled with maps and books, and had pictures of paddle-wheelers tacked over every inch of his walls.

"I been navigatin' the Missouri and the Mississippi for nearly thirty years," Marsh boasted. "I know both rivers like most men know their women's curves. Ain't no man better than me at readin' currents, tides, and the drift of the sandbars."

Marsh opened a well-stocked liquor cabinet and poured generously. "Rum is good for your blood, laddies!"

Gizzard raised his glass in a toast and shouted, "To Creole women!"

The rum put a fire in Andy's belly, but he decided right away that he liked it better than cheap corn liquor.

"Captain, where do you hail from?" Gizzard asked.

"The river is my home and I go where it and the money take me. Why do you boys want to go to Santa Fe? Far better and easier times can be had on the river."

"I enjoy the señoritas." Gizzard forced a laugh. "Captain, I might even marry one someday."

Marsh's smile soured. "If you do, you'll have to become a papist and swear allegiance to the pope! No woman is worth that, and why bother when you don't even have to promise to marry a Creole gal, but they'll love you all the same?"

He eyed Andy and refilled their glasses. "What about you?"

"No more farming for me," Andy vowed. "I'd like to be a mountain man."

"They're a dying breed since beaver hats went out of style. And long before, most of them either got scalped, froze in the mountains, went crazy, or died young."

"Then an explorer," Andy said.

I'm sorry to be the bearer of bad tidings, but you are

fifty years too late, because all of America has already been mapped, except maybe for some of the Apache country, which ain't worth mapping or settling anyhow."

"Sir," Andy replied, "I know that's true. But I heard that there are mountains so tall that they never melt all their snow. And deserts and canyons so deep they could swallow every city in this country."

"So what?"

"I was raised in flat country and I hunger to see those places," Andy replied. "And maybe to prospect and find a gold mine. I expect that there is plenty of gold left to dig, don't you?"

"They dug it all out of the California goldfields," Marsh said, "and now everyone talks about the Comstock lode and Virginia City in the Nevada Territory. They say that's deep, hard-rock mining, where they send a miner down a thousand feet in a damned wire cage. And when he gets to the bottom of that hole, the air is poison and hotter than Hades."

"A wire cage?" Gizzard asked, looking shocked.

"Yep," Marsh told him. "Like a rat. But I talked to a few men who were going to the Comstock lode anyway, because they can earn three dollars a day once they get into the miners' union."

"That is a lot of money," Andy said. "Nearly a hundred dollars a month!"

"Sure," Marsh said, sounding unimpressed, "but what does it matter when the price of an egg or a drink is a dollar? And I've heard that the cemetery there is fillin' up so fast they're starting to drop bodies down mine shafts to save the work and cost of a decent burial."

"Maybe I could find a new strike someplace else," Andy said, unwilling to give up another of his dreams.

"Maybe," the captain agreed. "But remember that gold

strikes come and go in a hurry, but the Muddy Mississippi and the grand old Missouri rivers keep rolling along, creating commerce and opportunity for a man with guts and vision. As for the West, why, I've known many a good man to return from there with a ruined mind and body."

"I'm sure that's true," Andy said, "but there are lots of ways to die in the East as well."

Marsh nodded and drank in silence for a good long time. Finally, he said, "Why didn't you boys get into the war?"

"I tried," Gizzard said after an awkward silence, "but I was rejected."

"I won't ask you why," the captain said. "What about you, Andy?"

He told the captain about his father dying on the battlefield and about how he had been bound to bring in the harvest and help keep his family out of the poorhouse.

"War is terrible but it creates profits for those that are smart and willing to take risks."

"Captain," Andy said, "any man who'd profit from war deserves to be shot!"

Marsh looked down at the drink in his hand, swilling it 'round and 'round for a moment before saying, "Let's talk about good times and pretty Creole women. Boys, let's drink up!"

Remembering the sickness caused by corn liquor, Andy quit drinking early. But Gizzard said, "I'll be along soon."

"Suit yourself," Andy replied. "I'm not your mother."

"Damn right he's not!" Marsh roared. "But while we're on the subject, let's toast to our dear mothers, God bless 'em one and all!"

That's when Andy left the party. He wobbled down to his bunk feeling excited about heading down to St. Louis and maybe seeing New Orleans, if the war didn't get in the way. Even if it did, maybe they could steam right on past the battles and cheer for the Union to the roar of their cannon! It all sounded perfectly reasonable to Andy as he fell asleep to the snores of his shipmates.

But later that night, he awoke feeling as if he were being smothered. He couldn't breathe and struggled until Gizzard whispered in his ear, "Grab your things and come topside! Don't wake anyone!"

Andy was confused. The rum roiled in his belly and fogged his brain. He had to concentrate in order to follow Gizzard up on the deck, where it was cold, with stars as clean and glittery as broken glass.

"What is it?" Andy demanded.

"I discovered that Captain Marsh is a gun-and-supply runner for the Confederacy." Gizzard took a couple of quick, deep breaths. "I got suspicious when he said that his sister and aunt were in Atlanta. After you left, I told him that I was a Confederate sympathizer."

"What!"

"I had to find out! As soon as I said that, the captain admitted that he was, too. The next thing I know, he's opening a wall safe hidden behind that picture of the three-masted schooner. Then he showed me a big wad of federal money he was given to buy rifles and supplies for the Confederacy. Said not to tell anyone under order of death."

"Then why are you tellin' me?"

"Because maybe one of the rifles he's smuggled for the Confederate army killed our friends . . . or even your pa."

Andy was waking up fast. "I hadn't thought of that."

"I did," Gizzard said, "and that's when I started planning how to stop the man. Andy, these people are our enemies!"

"Now, wait a minute," Andy said, needing time to think this out.

"We don't have any time to waste," Gizzard cried.

"When the captain turned his back, I broke a bottle across the back of his head."

"You what!"

"I knocked him out cold," Gizzard said, teeth starting to chatter.

"Why!"

"How else was I going to get his blood money?"

Andy's jaw dropped. "You . . . you *stole* his money!"

"Damn right! It was my duty as a Northerner. What else could I do? Let Captain Marsh buy weapons that would kill federal troops?"

This was happening too fast for Andy. When he'd fallen asleep below, he'd been thinking about Creole women, and now—now he was thinking about being hunted down and killed by the captain and his tough crew.

Gizzard yanked a big roll of hundred-dollar bills out of his pocket. "Andy, there's thousands of dollars here," he whispered. "Enough to get us to Old Santa Fe in grand style! Hell, enough to take us around the world, if that's where we wanted to go!"

Andy couldn't believe what he was hearing. "Gizzard," he stammered, "we'd better stop wasting time talking and get moving! The crew will be up at daybreak and they'll discover us gone and start adding things up fast. I'd say we have about a four-hour head start. Five hours at the most."

"Then let's go!" Andy exclaimed. "But first, I've got to run below."

"What for?"

"I've got to know if Captain Marsh is dead or alive!"

"We'd be a lot better off if he's dead. He's the only one that could pin this on us. Andy, I didn't try to kill him, but I hit him real hard. He could be dead."

Andy expelled a deep breath. "Gizzard," he said, "I

ought to let you take the money and run, then go back to bed."

"Some friend you are!"

"What is *that* supposed to mean?"

Gizzard glared at him with hard, bloodshot eyes and hissed, "Well, aren't you the one that told me anyone who'd profit from war ought to be shot?"

"Sure, but—"

"But nothing, Andy! I didn't shoot Captain Marsh! All I did was to relieve him of the moral burden of his blood money. That's right, I might have saved his soul!"

"Horseshit!" Andy cried, not believing it for a moment. "You saw a chance to steal his money and you took it."

"Better we have it than if the money goes to buy Confederate rifles. Or have you changed your mind about that, too?"

Andy knew that Gizzard had him cold. "All right," he said, "but I still have to know if he's dead, dying, or just knocked out cold."

"If he's dying, we ain't got the time to play doctor."

But Andy wasn't listening. He dashed downstairs and found the captain lying on the floor, alive. "Thank God," he whispered with relief a moment before running back up topside to join Gizzard.

"Well?"

"He's alive. Let's get out of here!"

They ran down the long pier and plunged into the seedy waterfront, where drunks and all manner of riffraff were ready to grab a man and kill him for small change. But no drunk or degenerate could have caught them this night, because fear gave wings to their feet and steel to their legs.

"I remember that there's a big livery just down the street," Andy wheezed. "We need horses!"

"Yeah, but that's the first place the captain and his men will look. We'd better try to steal a couple from someone's backyard and hope that they're not missed for a while."

"Gizzard, horse stealing is a hanging offense!"

"And getting caught by Captain Marsh and his crew wouldn't be fatal?"

"You're right," Andy said, sweating profusely despite the cool air. "Let's find an alley and a barn."

They found an alley but were almost immediately challenged by a pack of stray dogs, and had to hurl rocks at them and make a hasty retreat.

"We're losing time," Gizzard wheezed. "In a few more hours it will be daylight."

"What else can we do?" Andy asked, feeling his own rising panic.

"I got an idea!" Gizzard cried. "Follow me!"

Andy was seized by a nearly overpowering urge to ditch his friend and strike off on his own, because much as he hated to admit the fact, Gizzard O'Reilly was trouble.

Seven

A ndy and Gizzard ran until they'd left Independence
far behind. Now, with a cold moon shining on a
countryside dotted with farms and trees, Andy wondered just what was going to happen next.

"We wait for a freight wagon to come along and we
jump on behind," Gizzard explained between deep gulps as
he tried to catch his breath. "This is the road to State Line."

"Where is that?"

"In Kansas," Gizzard told him. "Before we get to
New Mexico, we have to cross Kansas. After that, we'll
follow the Cimarron River and either take the mountain
route or the Cimarron route but—"

"Shhh!" Andy hissed, not caring a damn about anything except getting as far away from Captain Marsh and
his crew as possible. "I hear a wagon coming!"

Out of the gloom, a high-sided freight wagon, pulled
by six yoke of oxen, did appear. Andy saw the thick silhou-
ette of a bullwhacker plodding beside the leaders. His hat
was pulled down and his face was shielded from the moonlight. A large dog trotted along, his head low to the ground
except when the man snapped his whip so that its buckskin
popper cracked like the shot of a rifle. The oxen bearing

their cumbersome wooden yokes did not seem to pay the man any attention as they slowly plodded forward, great heads swinging back and forth like pendulums.

"We're in luck!" Gizzard whispered. "If it was a supply train, we'd have to wait until the last wagon and hope that there were no livestock tenders following along with extra animals who might catch us hopping aboard."

Andy could see the first faint glow of morning light seeping out of the east and was anxious to be on the move. He could imagine the rage of Captain Marsh when he was finally awakened by his crew. The man's head would ache and he'd be looking not only to get his money back but for the worst kind of revenge. Andy had a feeling that they had not seen the last of Captain Marsh.

"All right," Gizzard whispered as the freight wagon drew near, "this is going to be simple. When the wagon rolls past, we jump in the back, cover ourselves with the tarp, and enjoy a nice, long snooze."

"What if that bullwhacker takes a rest stop when we're asleep? He might decide to shoot us!"

"Why on earth would he want to do that?" Gizzard asked. "It's not like we stole anything from him. And besides, my head is pounding something fierce. I shouldn't have drank so much rum."

"You shouldn't have knocked out and robbed Captain Marsh is what you shouldn't have done," Andy replied, accusation thick in his voice.

"If you don't want half the money, then just say so right now and find your own way to New Mexico!"

"Nope," Andy said as they came to their feet and began trotting after the freight wagon. "If I'm going to be blamed by the captain for having a hand in stealing his money, then I might as well enjoy the rewards."

"I figured you'd say that," Gizzard wheezed. They caught hold of the lowered tailgate and swung onto the wagon, then burrowed under the heavy canvas tarp under cover of the loud creaking of the heavily laden wagon. "See, I told you this was going to be perfect."

"He's hauling oats, barley, and sacks of corn," Andy whispered. "Beans and sowbelly, too."

"You're a farmer, all right," Gizzard said, curling up in a ball. "Go to sleep and let's hope this fella don't stop until he gets to Kansas."

"*Then* what are we going to do?"

"We'll pop up like a couple of ground squirrels and pay him a dollar to take us on to Round Grove, where we can buy horses and make fast tracks for Santa Fe."

"That sounds simple enough."

"It *is* simple."

Andy hoped that his friend knew what he was talking about. He didn't even want to think of what lay behind them, so he forced himself to imagine his mother rocking away on the front porch of a fine cottage in Brighton surrounded by roses and a white picket fence just as pretty as anything. Never mind that it was much too cold and the wrong time of year. The main thing was that the Parmentier family now owned two farms and had money in the bank.

"I sure am thirsty," Andy complained later that morning, after the wagon hit a rock and jolted him into wakefulness.

"Go back to sleep!"

"I am," Andy said, giving in to the sway of the freight wagon and soon to blessed sleep.

The sun was high when Andy awoke again. The wagon was still bumping along. He raised the tarp and peered out at a vast, mostly empty expanse of trees and grass, wondering if they had crossed State Line and if this was really Kansas. If so, it looked pretty much like Missouri and that was disappointing, because Andy had been hoping for a change in scenery. Not that Missouri wasn't a handsome country, but he was hoping he would get some idea of the West that he'd read and heard so much about. After all, Kansas was still home for the fierce Kiowa and Comanche, who had killed the famous mountain man Jeb Smith and a whole lot of other pioneers over the past thirty or forty years.

Could there possibly be Indians watching them from the surrounding countryside? Andy wished he still had his father's weapons, but at least he still had the pepper-box. Gizzard had a pistol that he must have stolen from Captain Marsh along with the money. By comparison, last night made their Brighton chicken-stealing days seem small time.

Later that morning Andy had to take a leak but was afraid to risk jumping off the wagon. If he were caught, the bullwhacker might decide to leave them stranded in the middle of nowhere. Then what would become of them? They could get scalped, for one thing, or just starve, for another. Then again, Andy thought, we've got God only knows how much of Captain Marsh's money and we probably could buy this whole freight wagon lock, stock, and barrel and still have plenty of dollars.

Andy stewed, squirmed, and . . . finally, he rolled back the tarp and jumped down on the road, where he hurriedly dropped his pants and relieved himself. Then he sprinted after the wagon, and everything would have been fine except for the bullwhacker's large spotted dog, which came rushing at him with bared teeth.

It was a close race, but Andy managed to beat the dog into the wagon. Trouble was, the animal came flying in, too! Andy squealed and ducked under the tarp, feeling the dog snap and bite.

"What's going on back there!" the bullwhacker shouted, stopping his team of oxen and hurrying around to investigate. "Julius, you better shut up!"

"What'd you do now?" Gizzard whispered as they huddled under the tarp.

"I had to piss."

"Dammit, Andy!"

"I couldn't help it!"

"So," the driver bellowed, whipping the tarp to one side and exposing them, "I've got stowaways! Good work, Julius!"

The dog wagged its tail but kept on growling.

"All right, boys, get out!"

Andy and Gizzard bailed out of the wagon. In the gathering light, they saw a stout man with wild red hair, a matching beard, and pale blue eyes. His boots laced up almost to his knees and his hand rested on the wooden handle of a knife that must have been two feet long.

"Well," he shouted, brandishing the knife and spitting a stream of tobacco between their feet, "what do we have here—stowaways!"

"Hold on!" Andy cried, throwing up his hands. "No need to shed blood!"

"Why not?" the bullwhacker demanded. "You are thieves!"

Oh, God, Andy thought as his blood ran cold, how did he learn about us stealing Captain Marsh's money!

If Andy had been in possession of the thick money roll, he'd have dragged it out, handed it over, and begged for his life. Fortunately, Gizzard had the presence of mind to say, "You mean we stole a *ride*."

"That's right! I own and feed these oxen. I bought this wagon and you're enjoyin' both for free."

"You're right," Gizzard said, looking as if he suddenly saw the truth of the matter. "We're ashamed and we owe you money."

The driver eyed them suspiciously. "You boys look awful poor. How you gonna pay?"

Gizzard proved to be much too smart simply to drag out Captain Marsh's bankroll. Instead, he reached into the other pocket and produced a bone-handled pocketknife. It was a good knife, one that Andy had often admired. "This ought to be worth a dollar and a lift to the Kansas border."

The bullwhacker inspected the pocketknife with care, snapping out both blades and holding them up to the light, then testing their sharpness. "All right," he finally agreed, "the knife for a ride to Kansas."

Andy couldn't help but heave a deep sigh of relief. "Thank you, sir!"

"You boys could have just asked for a ride in trade for the knife." The way he said this almost made Andy think he was insulted. "I mean, you're too old to be sneakin' around in the night like thieves."

"Sorry," Gizzard said, managing to sound contrite.

"Well, I accept your apology. Get back in the wagon, but I'm going to search you when you leave to make sure you didn't steal nothing."

"We wouldn't do that!"

"Hoyt Ford trusts no one—not even his own mother. I'll search your packs and your pockets or I'll keep the knife for the ride you've already taken, and you'll walk the rest of the way to Kansas. What's it going to be, boys?"

This time Gizzard didn't sound so apologetic or contrite. In fact, he sounded out of sorts. "You hold the winning hand, mister. We'll do things your way."

"I figured you were smart enough to come around," Ford said. "Now climb aboard, 'cause my time is being wasted."

They were rolling again a few minutes later, and when Andy looked back he could see the emerging skyline of Independence. "Gizzard, I sure am glad that we're on our way."

"Me, too. But what are we going to do about all this money I'm carrying? If he finds it, he'll want to keep it."

Andy thought a few minutes, then said, "We could hide it in our shoes."

"Could be he'll ask us to take them off."

"Now, why would he do that?" Andy demanded. "Mr. Ford sure isn't going to worry about us stuffing them with sowbelly or grain."

"Yeah, I guess you're right." Gizzard yawned. "My head is pounding and my eyes feel like they've been scratched by a barnyard rooster. And I'm getting hungry enough to eat some of that sowbelly."

"Best not," Andy cautioned. "When we get to the Kansas border, then we can find something to eat."

"Yeah," Gizzard admitted, "that's true. There's a couple of stores and some places to eat and drink. And I could sure use a drink or two."

"No time for that. Not with Captain Marsh probably waking up about now and starting to look for us."

"I'm going back to sleep," Gizzard decided, ducking under the tarp, where it was nice and dark. "Wake me when we finally get to the border and I'll try and think of some way to hide our roll of money."

"You counted it yet?"

"No."

"Maybe you should."

"Why? It's at least seven thousand dollars. Maybe as much as ten." Gizzard managed a tolerant smile. "Andy, I'm not going to excite you now by telling you what this much money will buy in Old Santa Fe. But let's just say that we can live real well for the next five or ten years, *and* satisfy our hunger for señoritas, frijoles, and tequila."

"What are frijoles?"

"Let's talk about that stuff later," Gizzard said, yawning then closing his eyes.

Andy fell asleep, too, and didn't wake until the wagon ground to a halt that afternoon.

"All right, boys! Wake up! Nap time is over!"

Ford tore the canvas away from them. Andy elbowed Gizzard, and they both sat up, half-asleep, and looked around.

"Is this State Line?" Andy asked.

Gizzard knuckled his eyes and stared. "Hell no, it isn't! It's a damned old homestead!"

"Mine," Ford announced with a grin. "I decided that you boys look like you could use someplace to bunk and hang your hats."

"Now, wait just a minute!" Gizzard said, jumping down from the wagon. "The deal was that you took us to the Kansas border."

"I know. I know. And I will one of these days."

"That's not good enough!"

"Empty your pockets," Ford said, dragging out his pistol, "and don't give me any more lip."

Gizzard was shaking with anger. Andy stepped between him and Ford, saying, "We just want to be on our way, mister. We don't want any trouble."

"Well, you *got* trouble," Ford said. "First there is me, then Julius, who will tear you to pieces, if I say so. Finally, you boys need to look around and then you'll see that we are way out in the country and that this is not a farm."

"I don't care what it is," Gizzard said, voice shaking with fury. "We are free men and we won't be kept where we don't want to stay!"

"Fine. I never meant for you to be slaves. But I still want to search your packs and your pockets. Until I do that, you're going nowhere, unless it's to an early grave. Get my drift?"

Andy sure did. "Let's do what he says, Gizzard."

Gizzard's hand twitched by the pocket filled with Captain Marsh's money. "No!" he said stubbornly.

Ford took a half step forward and pistol-whipped

Gizzard—hard. One minute Andy's friend was standing, the next his eyes were rolling up in his head and he was out cold and sprawled on the ground.

"You might have killed him!" Andy shouted, dropping down to his knees beside Gizzard and seeing blood trickle from his scalp and soak into his collar.

"Maybe I can do a better job with you," Ford said, eyes narrowing. "And I will unless you empty all your pockets right now!"

Andy had no choice. The man was holding a gun on him, and if that wasn't enough, Julius was beginning to growl, lips pulled back from his fangs and hackles raised.

"All right," Andy said, emptying a little change and his own pocketknife and then taking a deep breath. "We have some money."

"I saw that roll in your friend's pocket and figured it wasn't his horse-sized pecker," Ford said. "Take the money out and do it real slow."

Andy removed the roll of hundred-dollar bills and then he flattened them out and counted, certain that Hoyt Ford was about to take his life.

"Ten thousand two hundred dollars," he said, hearing a tremor in his voice and staring at more money than he'd ever expected to see in his entire life.

"What did you do, rob a bank!" Ford exclaimed, eyes wide with surprise, lips split in a huge grin.

"We didn't—"

"Stop!" Ford growled. "Not another lying word or it will be your last. I want the simple truth!"

"All right, we got it off a riverboat captain by the name of John Marsh."

"I know Captain Marsh well and I never took him for being an easy mark. Certainly not one that would allow himself to be robbed by a couple of kids."

Andy wasted no time explaining what had happened

back on the river. He ended up saying, "We never meant to steal from Captain Marsh. In fact, we were celebrating hiring on with the man and hoping to steam on down to New Orleans. Gizzard is good with fixin' most anything and I am a hard worker. We were going to keep right on working for Captain Marsh until next spring."

"But you robbed him instead?"

"Wasn't my idea," Andy said, standing, and realizing that he was taller and probably stronger than Ford. But not tougher. "Gizzard found out that Captain Marsh intended to buy weapons and supplies for the Confederacy. We're Northern sympathizers. My pa joined the Brighton Township Volunteers and was killed at Chickamauga Station, in Tennessee."

Ford glanced down at Gizzard. "How'd you team up with a little snipe like him?"

"An accident."

"So you are on the run from Captain Marsh and his Confederate gunrunners."

"I expect we are." Andy steeled himself to attack. He'd be damned if he'd go down without a fight, but he was scared. "What happens now, Mr. Ford?"

"That depends."

"On what?" Andy asked, feeling a first glimmer of hope.

"On what you and your friend decided to do about taking me on as an equal partner."

"Huh?"

"You're going to buy into the new freighting company we'll call Ford, Gizzard, and—what's your name?"

"Andy. Andy Parmentier."

"All right," Ford said, "we're going to use that money to buy us a couple more freight wagons, along with the oxen teams to pull 'em and a mountain of supplies."

"We are?"

"Yep. Where were you and your thieving friend headed?"

"Santa Fe."

"I'm afraid that's where we have to go," Ford said. "We'll outfit a small pack train, then head for Santa Fe next spring, as the weather allows and the roads dry out a bit."

"Maybe we don't want to be freighters," Andy dared to reply.

"You don't have any choice. I've been waiting all my life for a chance like this and I know that we can at least double our money. I've got the experience and you boys can learn to handle oxen and fix wagons. In just a couple of hard months, we can parlay this ten thousand into a small fortune."

"I can't speak for Gizzard."

"Yes, you can," Ford said bluntly. "You're speaking for him right now. Either take my offer or start walking, but you won't get very far."

"Why not?"

"Because a man like Captain Marsh has a lot of friends and the word will be out with a sizable reward. You boys probably went and told him you where you were headed, right?"

"Yeah."

"Someone would have collected the captain's reward by delivering your bloody heads in a filthy gunnysack."

"We could start off for someplace else," Andy ventured.

"Where?"

"Maybe the California goldfields."

"In the middle of winter and on foot?" Ford laughed humorlessly. "You wouldn't get ten miles. There's a blizzard coming this way. It'll be here in about three hours . . . or less."

Andy followed the man's eyes and decided that he just might be right.

"Give me the money, Andy."

"I thought you said we were going to be partners!"

"We are," Ford said, looking quite pleased as he stuffed the big roll of hundreds in his coat. "But I'll be the banker, the numbers man, and the purchasing agent for our freighting company. When we reach Santa Fe, then you and Gizzard will get your fair shares of our profit."

Andy didn't believe a word ot if, but then it didn't matter what he believed, given the circumstances.

"All right," he said, "we'll trust you."

Ford chuckled and holstered his gun. "Smart decision. Real smart."

Andy was quick to agree. Hoyt Ford wasn't to be trusted, but if he could save them from Captain Marsh and deliver them to Santa Fe, that would be the time to iron out their differences in whatever way seemed right or necessary.

Chapter Eight

Hoyt Ford was both ambitious and enterprising. All winter long he had awakened at dawn, even when it was snowing and blowing a fierce gale outside. Banging a tin cup on the edge of a potbelly stove, Ford ousted Andy and Gizzard from their bedrolls on his cabin floor, then prodded them into cooking breakfast and making coffee while he bundled up and went out to the barn to feed and water their growing number of oxen.

At first, Andy and Gizzard had tried to use that brief time to discover where Captain Marsh's ten thousand dollars was hidden. But after a few weeks Ford laughed at them, saying, "You boys must have turned over every plate and piece of furniture in this poor cabin looking for that stolen money, but I've got to tell you that it just ain't here."

"Where is it, then!" Gizzard shouted in frustration. "It's *our* money! We've a right to know."

"*Was* your money," Ford corrected. "Now it belongs to our freighting company and is being used to buy oxen and supplies for our trip to Santa Fe."

"We'd rather have our shares and strike off on our own," Gizzard said with characteristic bluntness.

"Too bad," Ford replied. "And besides, there is a five-hundred-dollar reward on each of your thievin' heads."

"There is?" Andy asked, shocked at the size of the reward.

"Yep. That's why you boys have no choice but to stay put while I'm off making deals and getting things ready to roll west come springtime. Fact is, I've got to figure out some way to keep you both under cover for the first fifty or a hundred miles. Otherwise, one of Captain Marsh's friends would recognize you for certain."

"Maybe," Gizzard said, "none of what you say is true. Maybe Captain Marsh has given up and there is no reward."

"If you think that," Ford said, "then you're welcome to leave at any time—but you'll forfeit your share of our freighting company. Then it'll belong to just me and Andy."

"That's not fair!"

"Life isn't fair, but I think you already know that, don't you, Gizzard?"

"What do you mean?"

"I mean you've had more than your share of troubles with life and the law already." Ford's eyes narrowed and his voice took on a hard edge. "Gizzard, I'll bet that you are a wanted man in places other than Independence. Isn't that so?"

"Hell no!" Gizzard yelled indignatly.

Ford turned to Andy. "What do you think about the chances of your friend here being wanted for other crimes?"

"I don't know," Andy lied, believing that Gizzard probably had done a lot of thievery and was wanted by the law.

"Well," Ford said, "I think you have figured Gizzard out almost as well as I have by now. He's big trouble, and if he wants to prove me wrong about there being a five-hundred-dollar reward on his head, then that's what he should do."

After that, Gizzard never talked much about either running away or overpowering Hoyt Ford and beating him until they learned where their cash was hidden. All Gizzard would say on the matter was, "Ford wouldn't dare deposit that much money in a bank. That would raise too many questions. I tell you, the man has buried it in a tin can or hidden it out in that big hay-and-wagon-repair barn! All we have to do is find it and light out for parts unknown."

But they never had been able to find it. And after the worst of the winter passed, the month of March was unusually wet and cold. So wet that the roads out of Independence remained a quagmire and it was all their oxen could do to pull their newly purchased wagons laden with Santa Fe–bound supplies across the yard and into the cavernous barn.

To Ford's credit, the freighter did give them a good accounting of how he was spending their company's funds. One afternoon when it was sleeting and too miserable to be outside, Andy questioned Ford about why he was buying the bigger, slower oxen rather than good Missouri mules.

"It's a matter of advantages and disadvantages, Andy. The price of good mules is running nearly seven hundred dollars a span."

Andy was flabbergasted. "They only brought about four hundred dollars back home in Indiana!"

"Well," Ford said, "they're nearly double that much hereabouts because of the high demand for good pulling teams on the Santa Fe Trail, where, with a little luck and lots of hard work, fortunes can be made. But you can see how, at seven hundred a span and six spans to a team, it costs over four thousand dollars' worth of mules to pull each wagon."

"Then our ten thousand wouldn't even be enough to buy three teams."

"That's right. On the other hand, big, dependable oxen

are cheap. I can buy them for a hundred and fifty dollars a yoke. At six yoke to a team, that means that you can buy a good team of oxen and their yokes for about a thousand dollars. Compare that to the over four thousand for a team of mules."

"I see," Andy said, "but mules travel so much faster."

"No so much faster," Ford argued. "Oxen go twelve or fifteen miles a day pulling a heavy wagon; mules or draft horses will do twenty. But speed is more than offset by danger."

"Meaning?"

"Meaning that Indians love to steal mules and horses, which they can ride and trade, but they consider oxen worthless."

"I see."

"And you also need to keep in mind that wooden oxen yokes are a lot cheaper than the leather harness you need for mules or horses. Finally, if everything goes bad on the trail or you have some disaster, a freighter can butcher an ox and feed on him until the meat rots. Ox is far, far tastier than mule or horse meat."

"All right," Andy said, "I'm a believer in oxen."

"And you ought to be," Ford assured him. "There's really only one big drawback to oxen and that's their feet."

"What's wrong with 'em?"

"They get tender real easy," Ford answered. "Some freighters shoe their oxen, but I use leather boots if and when the trail gets hard and their feet start to get tender. Oxen will quit on you if their feet hurt."

Andy learned plenty of other things about freighting as well. For instance, he learned that their two newly acquired wagons were copies of wagons made by a famous St. Louis craftsman named Joseph Murphy. The Irish wagon maker had designed freight wagons capable of carrying three tons, far more than the old Conestogas that had once been the standard both on the Oregon and Santa Fe trails.

"And the three we'll take are all Joseph Murphy 'copies'?" Andy asked.

"That's right. Our wagons are some used and I didn't pay more than eight hundred dollars for any one of them, while a *real* Joe Murphy wagon, new and with the J. Murphy stamp on its side, is worth twice that money."

"Why such a difference?"

"Harder woods and better craftsmanship," Ford said. "Murphy doesn't use anything but maple, hickory, and oak, all very expensive woods. And his workers bore out every bolt-hole with a hot iron, instead of drilling 'em by hand, so they don't crack, split, or rot. These may seem to you like small and piddling details, Andy, but breakdowns on the trail can ruin a freighter. I've seen it happen time and time again. When we leave for Santa Fe, we'll have good stock and good equipment; and even at that it will be risky."

"Because of the Indians?"

"Yes," Ford said, "and the weather and things that a man never counts on, like your stock getting into poisonous plants or stampeding or any one of a hundred mishaps that can, and usually will, go wrong."

"And even with all that," Andy asked, "it's still worth the risks?"

"You bet!" Ford expelled a deep breath. "If we can deliver three wagon loads of the kinds of supplies I know will sell in a hurry for top Santa Fe dollars or pesos, we're going to be financially fixed for life."

Andy thought that he and Gizzard already would have been "fixed for life" if they'd managed to hang on to their ten thousand dollars and maybe invest some of it in a gold mine, but he was smart enough to keep that opinion to himself. And besides, he was beginning to like Hoyt Ford. Andy had a feeling that Ford would do as he'd promised.

*   *   *

April smiled on the prairie. Pale shoots of grass burst up through the soggy earth, a thin green haze that would soon become a sweet, nutritious field of livestock feed. Hoyt Ford had already bought most of their Santa Fe supplies, but there were plenty of things he needed at the last minute to fill the huge freight wagons. Furthermore, the man expected Andy and Gizzard to learn all the prices of every single commodity he'd purchased.

"What will happen just before we reach Santa Fe," he explained, "is that the sharpest buyers will have boys to spy for them out at the town's east edge. Once a freight wagon is spotted, those sharp-eyed devils will alert their buyer, who keeps a horse saddled and ready beside his office. He'll come out to greet the supply wagon and then he'll be trying to get inside to poke around and see what he can buy and resell in a few hours at a profit."

"So what do you do," Gizzard asked, "run them off?"

"No, I sell to them, but at double or triple my cost. That's why you boys need to know the price of every single item that is in your wagon. For instance, if one of these buyers shouts, 'Mister, do you have any muslin, canvas, or black lace in that wagon for sale?' you have to know those items cost us twenty-two cents, fourteen cents, and seven cents, respectively, a running yard. Then, real fast, you triple those prices and that's what you tell him you'll sell them for."

"Sixty-six cents, forty-two cents, and twenty-one cents," Gizzard said, concentrating hard.

"Good! You can do the multiplication figures in your head. Now, Andy, what if they want flannel pants that cost us three dollars and twenty-five cents each, men's shoes at sixteen-fifty each, a tin bucket at ninety-five cents, or maybe those pretty mirrors we packed in straw which cost us two dollars and fifteen cents apiece?"

Andy had to grin. "I can do some multiplications in my head, but not that large of figures."

"Could you scribble the correct answers out on a tablet with a pencil?"

"Sure."

"Then you'll do fine, because I'll also be figuring the costlier items out on a tablet. Boys, the important thing to remember is that we never sell anything unless we at least double our price. Ask triple, try to get something in the middle, but *never* sell for less than double. Is that clear?"

Both Andy and Gizzard nodded, the latter asking, "What about all the money we've invested in oxen, yokes, and the two wagons that you bought with our money?"

"And quite a few dollars of my own money," Ford added. "But I can't answer that question yet. We can either load these three wagons up with whatever supplies we can buy and resell for a profit in Independence or St. Louis, or sell our outfits and recoup most, but not all, of our investment."

"You mean that we'd lose some money," Gizzard said, looking disgusted.

"That's right. Wagons and supplies are worth more here than out west because more go that way than this. But there are freighters that do a real brisk business running goods all up and down the eastern slope of the Rocky Mountains, from Albuquerque to Cheyenne in the Wyoming Territory. They pay good prices for good freight wagons. So don't you worry, we won't get hurt too bad if we decide to sell out."

"Ain't no doubt that I will," Gizzard said, making it clear that he was not much interested in freighting. "I'll take my money and live the good life in Santa Fe."

"What about you, Andy?"

"I may buy a cattle ranch or a gold mine."

Ford shook his head. "You boys need some seasoning

and that's for certain. Gizzard, my guess is that you'd piss away your third of our profits in one or two years and wind up with nothing, just like you have now."

Gizzard's eyes blazed with indignation. "I'm no fool!"

Ford didn't respond to that but instead turned to Andy and said, "I think you'd be wisest to either go back into farming or stick with me in freighting."

Andy didn't much care to be told what he ought to do, but he kept his lip buttoned.

"Either way, boys, if we make it to Santa Fe with these three freight wagons of cargo, we'll be well-fixed."

"Yeah," Gizzard said, "but it still don't seem right."

"What doesn't?" Ford shot back.

"That you took our money and expect an equal share."

Ford didn't say a word as his hand shot out and he slapped Gizzard hard across the face. Gizzard staggered and reached up to touch his bleeding lip. When he saw the blood, he balled his fists and charged.

Andy stood back, not sure what to do. As it turned out, there was nothing he could do to save his friend. Gizzard managed to land one wild, glancing punch off the crown of Ford's skull, but it only made the freighter even madder. In retaliation, he punished the younger, smaller man with an uppercut to the belly and a jolting right cross to the mouth that turned Gizzard's already bleeding lips to pulp and sent him crashing to the floor.

"I'll kill you!" Gizzard screamed, tearing a knife from his pocket and scrambling to his feet with one hand cradling his aching belly.

Andy grabbed his friend's wrist, then twisted it hard until Gizzard was forced to drop the weapon. "You son of a bitch, I thought we were friends!" Gizzard yelled.

"We are," Andy said, "and that's why I just saved you from worse punishment."

"Andy's right," Ford said, his own huge knife balanced lightly in his fist. "I'd have cut you up like a frying chicken. Probably would have saved myself a lot of grief by doing it now instead of later."

Gizzard was really hurting. He sank to his knees, tears streaming down his cheeks, blood flowing down his chin. He rocked back and forth for several minutes, cursing softly under his breath.

"Well," Ford said, sheathing his knife, "I've written out a list of every damn thing we're taking to Santa Fe and I expect you both to *memorize* the prices during the next two days."

"Why so soon?" Andy asked.

"Because we're pulling out of here in two days. We'd leave tomorrow, but it's Sunday and I need to get the last of our money out of the banks."

"Banks?" Andy asked.

"Sure! What'd you think I did? Stash ten thousand dollars in a big bean can and take some of it out every day or two to buy supplies?"

"Well, yeah, kinda," Andy said, feeling foolish.

"Wrong. There are five banks down in Independence and I've been a very favored customer in every one of them since you boys hitched a ride. Still got open accounts in three. There's not much cash left to withdraw, but enough to see us through any emergencies where cash might be useful. Can't think of any out on the Santa Fe Trail, but you never know, and there is a little trading settlement on the Cimarron River. Anyway, I'll be going down to Independence and closing those three accounts. Then, barring a late-season storm, we'll be rolling on west Tuesday. If all goes well, we'll camp about halfway between State Line and Round Grove."

"How long will it take to reach Santa Fe?"

"With luck, sixty or seventy days. Without luck, up to twice that long. With *bad* luck, we won't get there—ever.

Now, you boys get back to business checking inventories and packing the last of the trade goods. Oh, and keep going over the price lists. Call the prices back and forth to each other until you can recite the whole damned list."

"That would be impossible!" Andy protested. "There are over a hundred different items."

"You boys are ignorant but not stupid," Ford said on his way out of the barn. "Get to it!"

"I'm going to *kill* him!" Gizzard swore after Ford was gone, while holding his gut with one hand and his broken lips with the other. "I'm going to kill him *slow*!"

Andy knelt beside his friend. "Once we're out on the trail, a lot of bad things can happen. We'll need Mr. Ford's knowledge and trail experience to get us through. I've been told that it's seven hundred and seventy miles from here to Santa Fe—that's if Mr. Ford decides to take the Cimarron route, which he says is a lot shorter than the mountain route."

Gizzard wasn't listening. "First, I'll shoot him in the knee," he muttered, "then the foot, then the arm, and then I'll blow his balls off."

Andy grabbed Gizzard by the collar and shook him. "Listen to me! We've got a once-in-a-lifetime chance to make a lot of money. After we reach Santa Fe and get our shares, *then* you can face Mr. Ford and try to kill him. But I'll not have you ambushing him and ruining the best chance I'll ever have of making a fortune. Do you hear me!"

Gizzard batted his hand away and swayed to his feet. "I heard you, Andy! But your words don't mean shit! I'll kill that son of a bitch when I want and you had damn well better not try to stop me!"

"If you ambush and kill him, I'll kill you," Andy said, before he had time to think it out. But he knew it was the truth.

"You can't be my friend and his, too," Gizzard hissed,

spitting blood. "It don't work that way. One or the other, you got to choose right now!"

Andy felt his anger suddenly drain away, leaving him cold and empty, but also very sure of his position. "I won't take sides in a fair fight, but it had better be fair and it had better not happen until we've sold these wagon loads of goods and gotten the cash in our hands."

"You fool!" Gizzard ranted. "Do you actually believe that man is going to give us equal shares of anything other than a bullet or his blade!"

"Yes."

"Jaysus Kee-rist," Gizzard spat. "Ford was wrong. You are ignorant *and* stupid!"

Andy couldn't take any more and not explode and wind up beating what was left of Gizzard. So he turned on his heel and marched outside, almost crashing into Ford, who'd obviously been eavesdropping.

"Get out of my way!" Andy snapped, marching toward the pasture where the oxen were grazing.

But Ford followed after him. "I have to tell you that I heard what you boys said after I left."

"So I figured."

"And I also have to say that you are right and Gizzard is wrong. I *will* pay you an equal share after this is finished in Santa Fe. And I'll offer you an equal partnership with me in a freighting company, too."

"I want to find gold. Maybe ranch."

"Fine. Then do it," Ford said, sounding disappointed. "But keep your friend away from my backside and you will be saving your own hide and future. If I didn't need Gizzard's skills at fixing things, I'd have killed him a few minutes ago. He's no damn good."

"Gizzard has his moments."

"Yeah, well, that may be true, but they are few and far between. Sooner or later that boy will get you in a jam that you can't escape, and I'm not talking about a little jail time, either. He'll either kill someone or steal something that will get both of you hanged."

"Mr. Ford, I don't want to talk about any of this anymore."

"I understand," Ford said. "But by covering my backside, I'll do you the favor of killing Gizzard in a fair fight. That way we'll both be done with him and far better off."

Andy didn't know how to respond. Despite what had just taken place, his first loyalty was to Gizzard, not this man. Maybe that is why he said, "I'll just say this once like I said to Gizzard. A fair fight is okay, but don't you try to kill him by surprise."

"Andy, you know that isn't my style."

"I don't know anything about you except what you've told me about freighting. I don't know where you came from, what you have been, or what you think about, other than reaching Santa Fe and making a big pile of money."

"I had a wife and two kids," Ford blurted. "They died of the river fever about three years ago while I was wagon master for a good man named Clyde Matthews. I figured it happened when I was laying over at Fort Dodge and trying to decide whether or not to take the Cimarron route or go up to Bent's Fort and follow the mountain route. You see, the Comanches had just wiped out the wagon train ahead of us. In some ways, I wish I'd have been on that wagon train instead of working for Matthews, because I almost lost my mind when I finally returned here and found the missus and the kids buried. I blew all my profits and wages in a single week. I drank up plenty, some I believe I either gave away or threw in the Missouri River. I don't remember or care."

Hoyt Ford cleared his rough throat. "Kid, do you believe me?"

"Yes," Andy said, seeing the man's deep pain.

"All right, then," Ford said. "Let's talk no more and

get to work. I'm riding off to Independence to take care of some matters, including checking on Captain Marsh."

"Maybe he's shipped off and headed for St. Louis or even New Orleans," Andy said hopefully.

"Maybe. But I'll be back late tomorrow. Keep that 'friend' of yours under control until we reach Santa Fe or I swear I'll kill him."

"You can't," Andy said. "We need him to handle our third supply wagon."

"No, we don't," Ford replied. "We can hitch one wagon to the back of another and both teams in front. It's not a good way to do it, but it will work. I've seen it work."

"Twelve yoke of oxen pulling five or six tons of trade goods?" Andy asked, not bothering to hide his skepticism.

"Out on the trail, a man does what he has to do. He survives and he perseveres against all kinds of bad luck and hardship. And when he's finished and the gold is in his pocket, he feels more like a man than ever he will in his life. You wait and see, Andy."

"I hope to do that," Andy answered as he left Ford and headed back to the barn to work and learn a hundred item prices.

Chapter
Nine

They were on their way at last! On Tuesday, the sun came up warm and bright. Under Hoyt Ford's watchful eye, they'd been instructed how to yoke the oxen, but it had taken them nearly two hours to complete the task.

"Don't worry, boys." Ford said, not a bit surprised or impatient. "The next few days are for learning. However, by the end of the week, I fully expect you to yoke your teams in less than thirty minutes and be ready to pull out at the crack of dawn."

"Thirty minutes?" Andy asked. "That sounds impossible."

"It isn't," Ford assured him. "After a week on the trail, the oxen will practically yoke themselves. They'll know the routine so well that you'll actually find them lining up in the proper order. Wheelers to the hitch, then the pointers, then two pair of swingers with a pair of leaders up front. Every day, you keep them in the same order and give 'em the same commands in the same tone of voice and they'll be fine."

"I sure can't seem to get the hang of using a bull-whip," Gizzard said, his lips still bruised and puffy.

"It takes some practice," Ford said. "But you'll be

good with it by the time we reach Santa Fe. Just remember to yell 'gee' when you want 'em to pull to the right and 'haw' when you go left. These are seasoned oxen who know the drill. That's why I chose 'em."

"I sure would rather ride like a mule skinner than walk like a bullwhacker," Gizzard complained. "I don't much fancy walking nearly eight hundred miles."

"Well," Ford said, making an obvious effort to be patient with Gizzard, "you'll do fine. Remember that we'll only be going twelve or fifteen miles a day. Oxen are slow and they require plenty of rest. We'll be one of the very first wagon trains heading out this spring, so the grass ought to be good, but we might have some soggy ground to pull through."

"What about Indians?" Andy asked. "Wouldn't it make sense for us to team up with another outfit in Council Grove for better protection against attacks?"

"It probably would, but being the needy ones, any big outfit would make us abide by their rules and expect a share of our profits."

"They would?" Gizzard asked.

"Yep," Ford said, "and I don't know about you, but I'm not ready to tie into someone else's rules and regulations. I've worked for the big outfits too long already and they'll bleed us dry."

"Maybe a whole lot better them than the Comanches, Kiowa, Arapaho, or Cheyenne, all of which we might have to fight," Gizzard said, looking worried.

"Well," Ford replied, his patience wearing thin, "if you want to walk out on your share of the partnership, then go ahead and do it now. Andy and me can hitch your wagon to the back of another, double up the teams, and make out fine."

"You'd like that, wouldn't you!"

"Yes, I believe I would. So which is it going to be, Gizzard? Make up your mind right now and then stick to your decision."

"I'm not walking out on my fair share!"

Ford relaxed. "Then maybe you're just a mite smarter than I figured."

Andy asked, "What about Captain Marsh or someone he hired to keep a lookout for us?"

"The captain headed downriver for St. Louis about a week ago. As for someone watching for you, we'll just have to take our chances. Once we get past 110-Mile Creek, I don't think we need to worry about Captain Marsh anymore. From then on, we'll worry a lot more about the red man than the whites."

Ford consulted his pocket watch, then took a small notebook and pencil out of his shirt pocket and made an entry. "It's eight-thirty in the morning and the air is warm and sweet with new grass and spring flowers. Boys, let's roll these wagons and see if we can still make ten miles!"

Ford had instructed Andy to bring up the rear. Andy supposed that was so he could keep a watchful eye on Gizzard. It didn't matter to him whether he was in the middle or at the end of their little wagon train. Because they were starting so early in the season, before the roads were hardly dried, there wasn't going to be much dust.

Just up ahead, Gizzard was already trying to use his bullwhip and the results were comical. He kept snapping the whip, but it didn't stretch out to its full length and sometimes it even caught him in the back of the head, knocking off his hat or lashing his back. Andy couldn't hear him swearing over the lowing of the oxen and the creaking protest of their heavy wagons, but he would have bet anything that his friend was cussing a blue streak.

The morning passed easy enough and the road was good. Andy knew that they would not really be in danger from Indians until they were quite a bit deeper into Kansas. He still worried about Captain Marsh. Would Marsh go so far as to send a man all the way to Santa Fe next spring in the hope of finding them and his money? Andy thought the riverboat captain just might. With that in mind, he'd decided to leave Santa Fe with his share of the freighting profits and head off for someplace like the Colorado Rocky Mountains, where there was plenty of gold and silver to be found.

Just be smart, he told himself. And cut loose of Gizzard before he gets you into a real bad scrape—if Hoyt Ford doesn't kill him the moment we reach Santa Fe.

Forcing his mind onto other things, Andy began to recite goods and prices, going down Mr. Ford's list as best he could remember.

"Nails, eight dollars and forty-five cents a barrel; writing paper, one dollar and twenty-three cents a ream; fine-toothed combs, twelve cents each; ink, nine cents a bottle; axes, two dollars and twenty-three cents; hoes one dollar and seventy-eight cents; pocketknives, one dollar and twenty-seven cents; sewing needles, four cents apiece."

Reciting prices helped make the time pass faster. When he wasn't memorizing prices, he was looking around, waiting for the country to change, going from heavy woodlands to more open rolling hills.

"You boys are doing just fine," Ford said that evening when they stopped and made camp near a stream. "If you ever decide to turn into bullwhackers, I'll probably be able to give you a recommendation by the time we reach Old Santa Fe."

"Not me," Gizzard said, rubbing his stockinged feet. "I prefer riding to walking. If I was to become a freighter, I'd hire onto a wagon with mules or horses. How many miles do you reckon we traveled today?" he added.

"About eleven. I'm happy with that."

"I'm not," Gizzard said. "If the trail is seven hundred and seventy miles long, give or take a few days, that means it will take us seventy-seven days, more than two months."

"Yep," Ford said, "that's about right. We'll be leaving every morning at daybreak and stopping at mid-morning for rest and so the animals can graze and drink. Then, about two o'clock in the afternoon, we'll reyoke the teams and push on until near sundown."

"That way we have to yoke 'em up twice every day!" Gizzard protested.

"Can't be helped," Ford said. "The oxen need a mid-day break. If you try to push them straight through the whole day, they'll get contrary and slow down to a snail's pace. Not much to be gained that way and they'll start to weaken."

"I been on this trail before and mules don't stop for that long a rest."

"That's right," Ford said, "but I already explained how, even with the captain's money, we couldn't afford mules."

Andy yawned. "We ought to hit State Line and be in Kansas tomorrow, right, Mr. Ford?"

"That's right. If the road stays firm and this good weather holds, we'll be in Council Grove a week later."

"When do we start worrying about Indians?"

"After crossing the Neosho River at Council Grove, we are pretty much on our own, because the United States Army forts and posts are few and far between. We'll have to stand watch every night."

"Huh?" Gizzard asked with surprise.

"We'll each take turns every night keeping watch. We'll also have to take turns cooking. I think it will work out best if we trade off doing that every three days."

"I can't cook and I never had to stand night watch before!" Gizzard protested.

"That's because you were probably with a lot of men

and wagons. They would have had a night herder, maybe several. Besides, Indians won't often attack big trains, only small ones, and they don't get much smaller than ours."

Ford's voice took on an edge. "We'll each do our watches if we want to get through the Indian country. That being the case, maybe you better get your beauty sleep right now while you can, Gizzard."

Gizzard grabbed his bedroll and stomped off. At the edge of the camp, he hurled it to the ground, kicked off his shoes, and climbed inside to sleep.

"Andy, I don't know how you ever teamed up with such a bad one as that."

"Gizzard has his good points."

Ford raised his eyebrows in question. "He does?"

"Sure."

"I'd like to hear them."

"He's . . . he's a true friend."

"How do you figure that?"

"Well," Andy finally decided out loud, "when we got caught in Brighton for being drunk and stealing chickens, he didn't try to put the blame on me. In fact, he admitted that it was his fault that we got in trouble. And when he cracked Captain Marsh over the head and took his money, he woke me up and told me half was mine."

Ford shook his head and gazed into their campfire. "And you think *that* was a kindness?"

"He could have left me behind."

"You'd have been a sight better off."

"Maybe. All I know is that I left Indiana with nothing and now I have a third ownership in this supply train, which makes me a man of some substance."

"It does if we deliver the goods to Santa Fe. Until then, well, you shouldn't be counting your money."

Andy studied Ford, then decided to be frank. "How big a chance *are* we taking?"

"A damned big one."

"Because of the Indians?"

"Yes, and the weather and things we can't predict."

"Yet," Andy said, trying to find hope, "I've the feeling you like our chances."

"Damn right I do! And if we can pull this off, I'll outfit a wagon coming back this summer and then maybe even another returning to Santa Fe early in the fall. But it'll be much bigger than this one and, therefore, a lot safer."

"You're starting to make me worry."

"You'd best be real worried. This is a big gamble, but there's a big reward waiting in Santa Fe. I told you to ask triple the price we paid, right?"

"Yes."

"But take double."

"That's what you said."

"Well," Ford mused, "I've been giving that a good deal of thought and I reckon we can do even better—if we are the first supply wagons to arrive in Santa Fe this spring. Are you a Christian?"

Andy blinked. "Huh?"

"Were you raised to love the Lord?"

"Yeah," Andy said, confused by the question. "I guess so. My ma read us the Bible after supper and we went to church pretty regular before Pa died."

"Then say your prayers every night that things go smooth the next day," Ford told him gravely. "And just remember, if Gizzard gets me when my back is turned, you haven't got a prayer of reaching Santa Fe."

"He knows that as well as I do!"

"I hope so," Ford said. "Everything is depending on it."

"He won't try to hurt you, Mr. Ford. Leastways, not until we make it to Santa Fe."

"I'm depending on you to see that is the case," Ford

said, coming to his feet. "Guess I'll take a walk around the herd and then sit up a while and talk to the man in the moon. Andy, get some sleep."

"Yes, sir."

That night, Andy went to bed feeling more worry than he'd felt in some time. Hoyt Ford had confided his considerable fears. Fears of the Indians and fears of being jumped or shot from behind by Gizzard. In so doing, he'd asked for Andy's friendship and trust, only not exactly in those words. That meant that Andy had even more responsibilities than he'd thought. And more to be concerned about.

"We'll get to Santa Fe," Andy whispered to the stars above, "and we'll make our fortunes, then all go our separate ways. Mr. Ford to outfit more supply trains, Gizzard to find himself a señorita, and me to travel to the goldfields, wherever they might be."

An owl sailed silently across the soft halo of the moon and one of the oxen bawled low and mournful. Andy closed his eyes. He was worried. He was even scared. But he was damned glad finally to be heading west, to the land of his dreams, where unknown dangers and great adventures awaited a poor Indiana farm boy.

Chapter Ten

Andy was disappointed in Council Grove, and the Neosho River was even less impressive. He'd expected some big Western frontier town full of colorful old mountain men telling amazing stories, and wild-eyed frontiersmen swaggering up and down the main street. Instead, he saw a community that, at least from a distance of half a mile, was as placid as the hometown he'd left in Indiana.

"It's a little wilder than it might first appear," Ford warned him and Gizzard. "There are a couple of pretty rowdy saloons and houses of ill repute, not to mention the gambling establishments."

"Yeah, they got some pretty whores in Council Grove," Gizzard said, lust burning in his eyes. "Leastways they did when I come from Santa Fe."

"Well," Ford said, clearly wanting to dissuade Gizzard from partaking of the pleasures, "you have no money and I'm not about to give you any, either. I'm the only one of us that is going into town."

"Dammit!" Gizzard swore. "We got a right to have some fun, too."

"I'm not going to have fun. All I'm going to do is walk into town with Julius and maybe a hundred dollars. I'll buy what we need and walk out with fresh provisions. That's not what any man would consider fun."

Gizzard wasn't convinced. "If it ain't fun, then why can't *we* do it!"

"Because I know what we need and you don't."

"Then write a damned list. We're not slaves and we ain't stickin' here while you go into town."

"You *have* to," Ford said in a hard voice. "You and Andy have to protect our livestock and supplies from thieves."

"What thieves!"

"Gizzard, don't you think for even a minute that the folks in Council Grove haven't heard about our arrival. And don't think either that they don't know we're loaded with trade goods and supplies bound for the Santa Fe market. One man isn't enough protection."

"Fine," Gizzard said. "You and Andy can stay and I'll get the supplies. Give me the money and a list."

"No," Ford said, fists balling at his sides. "I wouldn't trust you with an old dog bone. I'm ordering you to stay!"

Gizzard had a reply. Yanking a gun out from under his coat, he cocked back the hammer, pointed it at Ford's gut, and said, "I guess I'll be taking the money and the list into Council Grove. Either that, or I'll be taking your corpse into the funeral parlor. Now, which is it going to be?"

Ford turned pale. His dog, Julius, came off his haunches with a rumble way down deep in his throat.

"Call him off or he's a dead dog," Gizzard warned.

"It's okay," Ford said, getting control of his temper and making a hands-down motion to his dog. He was still pale, but Andy knew it was more from anger than fear. What he didn't know was if Ford realized Gizzard wasn't a bluffer.

"Gizzard," Andy said, "why don't you put that gun away and we'll talk this out?"

"Nope. Our talking is over. The last time I was through, I met a whore in Council Grove and I remember her very, very well. She said to come back and pay her a visit, and by gawd, that's what I mean to do."

Andy looked to Ford. "I think we'd better give him some money and a list of the provisions we need."

"Andy, if we do that, we'll never see him or the supplies again."

"Oh, yes you will," Gizzard countered. "A third of this wagon train is mine and I ain't about to throw it away. I just need a couple of drinks and a tumble with Molly. I'll be back with the supply before midnight."

"I think we'd better trust him," Andy said to Ford. "It sure won't do any of us any good if he shoots you. We'd *all* lose out if that happened, wouldn't we, Gizzard?"

Andy was hoping that truth would be self-evident, but Gizzard chuckled and said, "I think we could make it to Santa Fe without Mr. Ford. The trail is wide and deep. We know the oxen now and the daily routine. I've put some thought to it and I don't think we need Mr. Ford anymore."

"Oh, yes you do," the freighter argued, eyes burning into Gizzard. "You'd never make it even to the Little Arkansas River, much less to the Cimarron. If the Kiowa or Comanche Indians didn't wipe you out, thieves sure as hell would. Your bones would join those of a lot of other fools that underestimated danger on the Santa Fe Trail."

"He's right," Andy said.

"How do *you* know!" Gizzard screamed in rage. "I'm the one that has been to Santa Fe. Not you! Andy, you just swallow everything this son of a bitch says as if it were gospel! 'Mr. Ford says this. Mr. Ford says that!' Well, he can eat my bullet if he don't give me a list and some money!"

"Do it," Andy said. "Give him what he wants."

"All right," Ford said, expelling a deep breath and then going back to his wagon.

"He might come back with a gun and kill you," Andy said, realizing that he did not even care if Gizzard met his end in the next few minutes.

"No, he won't. Ford needs *both* of us." Gizzard let his gun hand drop to his side. "That story about hitching two wagons and teams together is bullshit!"

"Meaning you've never seen it done?"

"Yeah, I have. But it only works on flat ground and not for long. You'd never make it double-hitched clear to Santa Fe. Ford knows that as well as I do. That's why he won't come back with a gun to kill me."

"Be careful in town," Andy said. "Buy the supplies first. Pay for them and have them waiting for you after Molly. Otherwise, she might steal your money."

Gizzard swore softly. "Andy, are you trying to tell me what a whore will do or not do?"

"No, but—"

"You are a real pisser, and that's for sure!" Gizzard shook his head. "You don't know nothing about nothing except raisin' corn and hogs, but when push comes to shove, you suddenly make yourself an expert on freighting and whores."

"Just buy the supplies *first*," Andy insisted. "That's all I'm asking. Will you do that?"

"I will."

"And watch out for trouble. Don't tell anyone our names or it might get back to Captain Marsh."

"He left for St. Louis!" Gizzard brought the pistol up and jammed the barrel into Andy's chest so hard he took a backstep.

"Don't do that!"

"You sure are a champion worrier, Andy! You sure worry a lot for a man that knows everything."

Andy could feel himself going cold with anger. He figured he could probably grab Gizzard's wrist, shake the

gun loose, and beat him like a rug, but he didn't want to take
any chances. Guns were too dangerous and they sometimes
caused terrible things to happen. So Andy turned on his
heel, heading back to his own wagon and team.

"Andy!" Gizzard called. "Ford isn't God! And I'm no
fool, either!"

Andy thought different, but he knew that saying so
wouldn't help matters. So he kept quiet, not even turning
to watch when Gizzard had his money, his list, and was set
to have his evening on the town.

Gizzard was seething but, at the same time, feeling
pretty damned pleased with himself. He'd gotten the drop
on Ford and then given both him and Andy a good piece of
his mind. Ford was a pure son of a bitch, but at least he was
open about it. Andy, on the other hand, had betrayed their
friendship. He'd sucked up to the freighter from the minute
they'd been caught under his tarp leaving Independence.
And the sucking up had gotten only worse during the long
winter while they'd both slaved under Ford, after having
their money stolen.

Sure, it was really Captain Marsh's money . . . or the
Confederate army's money. Who the hell knew or cared?
Gizzard had taken the money, and if he had it to do all over
again, he'd have left Andy to sleep off the rum and take his
beating from Captain Marsh while he ran away a very rich
man. Sharing money with someone he'd thought was his
friend was a big mistake. At the time he'd actually worried
that Andy would be partially blamed for the theft. Captain
Marsh, for all his friendliness, had been a spy and a gun-
runner and he'd have peeled Andy's hide like the skin from
an apple.

I learned a lesson there, Gizzard thought as he tromped
into town, feeling the thick wad of money resting in his
pants pocket. He'd made sure that there was enough for

buying all the provisions with some remaining for pleasures. And when the night was over, he'd rent a burro or a pack animal to carry the provisions, because damned if he would carry them a half mile like a plantation slave.

Just to prove that he was a man of honor and his word, Gizzard went to the general store first and handed the owner the list that he'd been given. "Tally it up and give me the full price right now," he ordered.

The fiftyish and aproned proprietor studied Gizzard over his wire-rim spectacles and then cleared his throat. "This is going to come to a considerable amount of money."

"I reckon it will," Gizzard said, knowing the man wanted to see his money without having to ask.

"Ahem," the storekeeper rasped, clearing his throat, "I'm afraid that I'll have to see the color of your money."

"Are you saying maybe I don't have it?" Gizzard asked with a sneer.

"Well . . . I . . . I don't know."

Gizzard pulled back his coat and let his hand drop on the handle of his pistol. He retreated a step as if he'd just seen a ghost.

"Maybe you think I'm fool enough to try and rob you in broad daylight and take off on the run," Gizzard taunted. "Is that what you think?"

The man was turning gray. "I . . . I hope not!"

"Well," Gizzard said, wondering if this fool was going to have heart failure and die. He decided that would not be in either of their best interests. "I guess I'll show you my money."

And he did. Gizzard slapped it right down on the counter next to the pickle jar. "Now, are you going to tally up my list or do I go to the next store?"

"No, sir!" The man snatched up the list and a pencil. Before Gizzard had time to devour a second pickle, he was told, "The total is eighty-seven dollars and ninety-six cents."

"I've got a hundred," Gizzard said. "Count out your money. How much are these dill pickles?"

"Two cents each."

"Then I'll have another couple," Gizzard decided out loud. "That will bring my bill up to eighty-eight dollars. Eighty-eight dollars subtracted from a hundred is . . . is twelve dollars comin' back to me in change. Right?"

"Yes, sir!" the storekeeper said. "Young man, you've an excellent head for figures!"

"I'm no fool, that's for certain," Gizzard bragged. "Say, does Molly still work at the Red Onion Saloon?"

"I'm afraid I wouldn't know," the man said, making change. "I don't patronize that establishment. I've a wife and kids. Grand-kids, too! Jimmy is seven, and—"

"I'll be back about ten o'clock for my supplies. Have 'em sacked and ready."

"But I close at six!"

"Not tonight you don't," Gizzard yelled on his way out the door.

The Red Onion wasn't very busy. There were maybe a half-dozen men at the bar and about the same number seated at tables, some playing cards, some just nursing a drink and a conversation. When Gizzard walked in the door, all heads turned, which was normal. He wished that he had some better clothes, for he looked almighty poor, but his money was as good as anyone's, so he ordered a double shot of rye whiskey.

"You new in town?" the bartender, a pudgy man with a black vest, white shirt, and red tie, asked.

"Just arrived."

"Yeah," the bartender said, "I heard that there was a new supply-wagon outfit come in from Independence. You must be the wagon boss."

Gizzard liked that. Liked it a lot. "As a matter of fact, I am," he lied. "I just bought us some supplies at your general store. We mean to push on for Diamond Spring first thing tomorrow morning. That'd be about ten or eleven miles, wouldn't it?"

"Fifteen is closer," the bartender said, pouring. He smiled, a congenial man hoping for a tip, and took Gizzard's money. "You got three wagons, right?"

"Yeah."

"How was the road over from Independence?"

"Pretty long; but dry."

Gizzard tossed his rye down like a man and felt it burn all the way to his toes. He grinned and slapped the empty glass down on the table, burping. "Pour me another."

"Yes, sir!"

Gizzard had two more rounds and felt good. So good that when he saw himself in the back-bar mirror, he was grinning, although he couldn't think of anything funny. So both he and the bartender grinned at each other whenever the latter poured another round of rye.

"My name is Walter," he finally said, offering his soft, white hand. "And you must be awful thirsty."

"I am," Gizzard agreed, nodding hard. "I'm damned itchy for a whore, too."

He swiveled around, putting his back to the bar and trying hard to focus. "Where is Molly?"

"Who?"

"A whore with black hair and eyes. You must remember her. She was everybody's favorite. Especially mine."

"Molly! Oh, yes, but I'm afraid she's gone. Ran off with a gambler named Bert. They joined a wagon train headed for Santa Fe last October. I heard that the gambler made her pay their passage on her back then left her when they reached Santa Fe."

"Doesn't sound like much of a man to me," Gizzard said. "What'd a beautiful woman like Molly see in that son of a bitch?"

"Oh, Bert was a dandy. Tall, good-looking fella with quite a line for the ladies."

"Shit," Gizzard swore bitterly. "Maybe I'll look her up in Santa Fe and marry her . . . or something."

"She'll be easy enough to find, I expect. From what I heard, she's back to her old profession."

"Then I'll sample her in Santa Fe and maybe make her an honest woman."

"That'd be the honorable thing to do. Well, like I said, my name is Walter. What's yours?"

"Gizzard, 'cause I love chicken gizzards."

"Unusual name."

"Just a nickname," Gizzard said, thinking too late that maybe he ought to go by his Christian name until he reached Santa Fe, just in case. "Who's your prettiest whore now?"

"Sally," the bartender said. "But she's always busy upstairs. In fact, she's with a customer right now."

"Well, how long can he go?" Gizzard demanded, gripping the edge of the bar and trying to look important.

"Not too long, I expect." Walter smiled. "Tell you what, Gizzard. I'll send someone up there to find out. Sally might even let you into the room to watch her, if you want."

Gizzard shook his head and made a face. "What'd I want to do a thing like that for!"

"No offense meant," Walter said, looking repentant. "And just to prove it, I'll pour you another drink—on the house."

"Well, you damn well ought to!" Gizzard snapped. "Hell of a suggestion. Anybody else ever do that?"

"Lots do." Walter leaned closer and whispered, "In fact, we have holes in the walls to peek through so a man can see our girls in action. That way they can pick out the one that is just right."

"Hmm," Gizzard said, mouth going dry, so that he lubricated it with another gulp of rye. "Kinda makes sense, when you think about it."

"Sure it does! And it gets the juices working, if you know what I mean."

He winked and Gizzard tried to wink back but only crossed his eyes, causing him to giggle, then say, "Walter, maybe I'll watch this Sally at work through a peephole. Does it cost anything?"

"Two bits . . . but you'll get your money's worth!"

"All right," he said, taking his newly poured drink. "Let's go see Sally gettin' humped!"

Walter signaled for a man to take his place at the bar, then headed for the stairway that led to the rooms upstairs. Gizzard tripped going up and landed hard on his chin, breaking a tooth because he bit down so hard.

"Dammit!" he stormed. "Why'd you put the rooms upstairs!"

Walter helped him up and replied, "Just a little farther, Gizzard"

"My real name ain't Gizzard."

"I'm sure that's true," Walter said, helping him inside a little room with a bed, nightstand, and washbasin.

"Where's the peephole?"

"Just lift that little picture off the wall and you'll see it," Walter promised.

It was a small ink painting of a vase and flowers. Ugly as anything. Gizzard lifted it up to stare at a blank wall. "Hey, there's no—"

Searing pain drove him down, and then Walter's knee was pressing his chest to the floor and his hands were yanked up behind his back and tied. Gizzard knew all this but was powerless to offer any real resistance, because the blow to the back of his head had left him stunned and floundering helplessly in a raging ocean of red pain.

"Where is Andy Parmentier," Walter asked when he'd finished hog-tying Gizzard and then rolled him over. "And where is the money?"

Gizzard tried to think of a clever lie but couldn't. In fact, he could barely talk, because his tongue felt like a huge, burning sausage, and when Walter slammed the heel of his boot down on his solar plexus, it made him gag and toss up a most hideous mix of pickles and rye whiskey. Gizzard's eyes burned with tears and he kept heaving until his belly burned.

He didn't even feel the knife's blade pressing down on his throat. Not at first he didn't. But then the blade cut a little deeper and he screamed.

"Don't kill me!"

"Where is Andy Parmentier and the captain's money!"

"Oh, sweet jaysus!" Gizzard cried, realizing his worst nightmare was unfolding.

Walter leaned closer. "He's with them three wagons camped south of town in the trees, isn't he!"

Gizzard nodded.

"And you spent the entire ten thousand dollars of Captain Marsh's money on Santa Fe supplies, didn't you?"

"Yes!"

"Who else is there?"

"Nobody!"

It was a stupid lie. Gizzard knew it was stupid the moment it left his lips. Three ox-drawn wagons needed at least three bullwhackers. Maybe more. And the lie brought instant pain as the knife pressed deeper, cutting through flesh to his windpipe until he screamed, "Mr. Ford. Mr. Ford! Mr. Ford! Please, don't cut my throat, Walter!"

The blade's pressure diminished. Crying and nearly

insane with fear, Gizzard couldn't see the bartender's grim face when he said, "When were you supposed to be back?"

"Now! I swear it!"

"You stupid bastard," Walter said, going to the washbasin and wiping his hands clean. "If you don't do as we say, you're as good as dead.

"Anything! I'll do anything!"

"Yeah," the man said with contempt, "I expected you would."

Walter left the room with a warning to Gizzard not to make a sound. After the door closed, Gizzard made a feeble attempt to break loose of his bonds, but he hadn't the will or the strength. So he waited until Walter and two others returned.

"What are you going to do now, Walter?"

"You're the bait. Hoyt Ford is no stranger to us. Sooner or later he'll come to find you."

Gizzard looked up at the three men and tried to draw them into focus. "What . . . what about Andy?"

"The farm boy?"

"Yeah."

"Captain Marsh said to bring both your heads back in gunnysacks if we want the reward."

Gizzard opened his mouth to wail, but the scuffed toe of a work boot cemented his silence.

Chapter Eleven

"Something is wrong," Hoyt Ford swore, pacing back and forth beside their little campfire. "It's past midnight and Gizzard must be in big trouble."

"We don't know that for certain," Andy said, although he was also pretty certain that Gizzard was in serious trouble.

Ford paced another few minutes and then stopped. "Did your friend say where he was going when he got to town?"

"He talked about a whore named Molly who worked in the Red Onion Saloon."

"Well, let's just hope that he's still with her," Ford said. "But we have to find out."

"Maybe we should wait until morning," Andy offered.

"I don't think so. At least we have the cover of dark. And come morning, the oxen will become restless and won't stand being left alone."

"Are we both going into town?"

"Yeah," Ford said. "Only you stay far enough behind me that we aren't seen together."

"Then what do we do?"

"I don't know. I'll go to the Red Onion looking for Gizzard. If there is skulduggery afoot, Andy, you'll be my ace in the hole. Arm yourself well."

Andy watched Ford stuff an extra pistol into his waist-band and he couldn't help but shiver with anxiety. "Mr. Ford, what exactly do you think happened to Gizzard?"

"It's anyone's guess."

Ford threw his head back and gazed up at the stars as if searching for an answer. Finally, he looked back down at Andy. "What I *do* know is that the Red Onion is a hangout for muggers, cutthroats, and all kinds of riffraff. Gizzard couldn't have picked a worse place in Council Grove to get drunk, and I'm sure that's what he did before he sought out his whore."

"I guess I should have told you, huh?"

"It would have been a real good idea. Although, with a gun pointed at my gut, I doubt I could have stopped him ex-cept with a rifle bullet."

"You'd have done that?"

"No," Ford admitted. He marched over to his dog and Andy heard his sharp command. "Stay!"

Ford came back, looking grim. "Andy, are you ready?"

"Yes. Will Julius really stand up against anyone that tries to steal our supplies?"

"Damn right he will," Ford said with pride. "But a dog is no match for even one man with a loaded gun in his fist."

"No, he isn't."

"Let's just hope it doesn't come to that," Ford said, sounding as if he were trying to convince himself. "And it won't—unless we are being watched and baited."

Andy spun around in a full circle. "You mean that someone might be watching us right now and waiting to steal our outfit!"

"Could be. Worse happens out here. A lot worse. And it could be the other thing."

"What . . ."

"Captain Marsh probably left a description of you and Gizzard at the saloons and whorehouses in Council Grove.

He'd also have promised a hefty reward. That, coupled with our wagon train, would be quite an incentive to a pack of thieves and murderers, wouldn't you agree?"

Andy nodded.

"Like I said, you're the hole card. If Gizzard was recognized and then taken captive by one of Marsh's friends, he becomes the bait."

"Maybe they don't know how strong we are?" Andy said hopefully.

"Oh, they know all right. Gizzard would have told them there are only two of us left to guard this wagon train."

"But won't they be expecting me to stay here?"

"Yes," Ford responded, "they'd expect you'd have to guard our livestock and wagons. That's my hope, anyway."

"We might have to kill them, won't we." It wasn't a question. Andy knew they would.

"If Gizzard is in their hands and not just passed out drunk or screwing Molly, I expect we will have to do some killing. Are you up to that, Andy?"

"I don't have any choice."

"No, but I'd like to think that you won't freeze or panic. You wouldn't do that, would you?"

"No. Not ever."

Ford clapped Andy on the shoulder. "That's what I figured. I'm leaving. Wait a couple minutes until I'm almost out of sight, then follow. When I get into town, I'll stay out on the boardwalk and you'll have no trouble seeing and following me in lamplight."

"Should I come inside the Red Onion?"

Ford considered this for a moment, then shook his head. "Go up to the window and try to peek inside. Stay ready. If I go upstairs where the whores work, slip inside. If you hear shots or me yelling, come on the run and have your gun in your hand."

Andy nodded. He was grateful for the darkness; otherwise, Mr. Ford would have seen that he was so nervous he was perspiring in the cold night air.

Andy had no trouble following Mr. Ford into Council Grove. As promised, the man stayed on the boardwalk until he reached the Red Onion Saloon. Then Ford turned and looked back for a moment before entering the saloon, while Andy remained lurking in the shadows. But the minute Ford was inside, Andy stepped out onto the boardwalk and strolled down to wait outside the saloon. He was disappointed that the saloon's front window was too grimy to see through.

What should he do now? Andy paced back and forth for a couple of minutes, then got lucky and was able to join three tough-looking men who entered the saloon. It was his intention to blend in with them and avoid attention.

It worked. No one seemed to notice as Andy sidled down the bar as if seeking a place to plant an elbow and order a drink. Mr. Ford, however, already had his whiskey and was talking to the bartender, an innocent-enough-looking man. Andy had been in only a few saloons, all of them while traveling with Gizzard. But now on his own, he felt ill at ease and conspicuous.

"Yeah, Molly is her name," he heard Ford say in a loud voice that was both strained and impatient. "So I'm asking you again, where is she?"

Andy didn't hear the bartender's reply, but he did see Ford slip the man a few greenbacks and then watched the bartender signal for a replacement. A moment later they were both heading up the stairs. But no sooner did they disappear into a little room at the top of the landing than the same three toughs that Andy had joined outside went up the stairs, too!

Andy realized there was no time to lose and that Ford wouldn't have a chance upstairs. Taking long, swift strides, he crossed to the stairs and mounted them three at a time while drawing both his pistol and pepperbox. Outside the door he heard a shout and then a loud thud that sounded like a falling body.

Andy threw the door wide open to see both Ford and Gizzard writhing on the floor. There wasn't time to see anything else, because the bartender shouted a warning and men started reaching for their guns.

Andy opened fire with both pistols, but it was the pepperbox that reaped by far the greater destruction. It sounded like a cannon and it indiscriminately issued smoke and death in massive doses. Andy kept squeezing the triggers of both guns as fast as he could, not bothering to aim, not even aware of any conscious thought as men howled and died. He kept firing until they were all knocked down, then he shoved his pistols into his coat pockets, choking on gun smoke as he dragged Ford erect and then cut free the ropes that bound Gizzard.

Moments later they staggered out of the room in a cloud of blue gun smoke. Andy didn't remember much else after that, except that some fool downstairs shot out the lanterns and everyone stampeded for the front door.

"There's a back way," Gizzard wheezed. "Down at the end of this landing!"

"You stupid son of a bitch!" Ford shouted, half dragging him to the second-story exit.

Andy had the impression of painted women shrieking and naked, and of curses erupting out of the upstairs cribs like fleas bailing off a dying dog. Everything was crazy and he couldn't wait to get outside and breathe some clear, fresh air.

Gizzard was in terrible shape. They had to carry him down the stairs into an alley and then they each took one of his arms and threw it over their shoulders and mostly dragged him up the alley, heading for their camp.

"What about the authorities!" Andy wheezed when they reached the wagons. "Won't they come to arrest us!"

"The only authority in Council Grove is the gun in a man's hand," Ford answered. "But all the same, we're breaking camp and heading out before daylight!"

That was fine with Andy. He didn't care if he never saw this town again.

They didn't stop pushing the oxen for another week, even though Gizzard looked and probably felt like death. He had taken a savage beating and rode in his wagon instead of walking beside it. They camped wherever they found water, at places named Diamond Spring, Lost Spring, Cottonwood Creek, and Turkey Creek. They did not even take the normal midday rest stops until they finally reached the banks of the Little Arkansas River, which Mr. Ford reckoned to be 230 miles from Independence.

"We're a third of the way to Santa Fe," Gizzard quietly informed them late in the afternoon.

"Yeah, but we've only come the easiest and safest third," Ford answered. "From now on we are in Indian country and we'll start keeping night watches."

Ford shot a hard look toward Gizzard, no doubt expecting an argument but not receiving one. That told Andy what he'd already begun to suspect—that Gizzard was a changed man. He had lost his defiance and his smart mouth. Now Gizzard took Mr. Ford's orders without complaint and the brag was missing from his battered lips. His eyes seemed to have lost their luster, but Gizzard did his job and healed enough to take his turn at cooking, gathering cow chips and wood for the fire. He didn't laugh anymore, though, and that was something that Andy missed. Gizzard had lost his zest for living and plodded through each long day with no more enthusiasm than his team of trail-worn oxen.

For some reason, Gizzard's lethargy bothered Andy more than it should have. He said, "What happened back in Council Grove is past. We got out of the scrape and Mr. Ford says that there probably won't be any more men waiting to collect a reward from Captain Marsh."

"We don't know that," Gizzard said as he pitched little stones into the sluggish river. "Andy, there may be men waiting to kill us for a reward all the way to Santa Fe. Ain't no way of knowing. And sooner or later someone is going to put us in their rifle sights and it'll all be over."

"That's an awful way of thinking. No wonder you're still acting so punk and puny!"

"We ain't going to make it," Gizzard predicted, still pitching pebbles. "I had a dream the other night. We all got killed by Indians. We were scalped and Julius looked like a pincushion with so many arrows sticking out of his body."

Andy's scalp suddenly tingled with fear and he jumped to his feet. "I won't be hearing any more of that talk! You got to stop thinking about it and acting like we used to act. Remember?"

When Gizzard didn't answer, Andy got even madder. "What about the Santa Fe señoritas? Have you forgotten how beautiful they are and how you vowed to someday marry one!"

"No, I ain't forgot 'em. But remembering them makes me even sadder now."

Andy crouched beside his friend. "Listen, what you did is in the past. We lost a hundred dollars in Council Grove by not stickin' around to pick up those supplies. But Mr. Ford says we can live without 'em and things are going pretty well for us now."

"You *killed* four men up in that saloon," Gizzard said, looking Andy right in the eye. "Don't you think about that sometimes? Or is killing real easy for you since you done it so often?"

Andy balled his fists, and if Gizzard's poor face hadn't already been such a sorry sight, he'd have clobbered him good a time or two. But Gizzard just stared at him like a walking dead man and it took all the fight away, so Andy took a deep breath.

"I don't know what those men at the Red Onion Saloon did to you, Gizzard, but I do know that it must have been pretty awful the way they beat you so bad. And I figure you must have thought your life was over while laying hogtied up in that little room with your throat bleeding. But we didn't get killed, so maybe we just got real lucky."

"It wasn't 'lucky' the way you killed those four men, Andy. I saw how easy you did it. Mr. Ford saw it, too, and he won't talk about what you done but . . ."

"But what?" Andy demanded.

"I have seen him looking at you when you don't know it and I can tell by his expression that even he can't quite get over the way you cut down all those saloon fellas."

"Gizzard, they were going for their guns! You told me they were going to cut off our heads and stuff 'em in gunnysacks for delivery to Captain Marsh!"

"That's what they were going to do, all right."

"So what choice did I have?"

"None, Andy. But I can say for certain that you've earned a reputation as a shooter and killer."

"The hell you say!"

"Oh, you have," Gizzard insisted. "Mark my words, there's folks that are going to come gunning for you."

"Why would anyone want to do that?"

"Because of your reputation! Whoever kills you kills the man that gunned down four others at the Red Onion Saloon."

Andy was getting upset. "I think that you took a bad punch in the head and it has affected your thinking."

"That's because you've never been to the West. But I

have and I know how folks out here think. Like it or not, Andy, you're a gunfighter with a reputation you'll never shake."

"Well," Andy said cryptically, "if your dream about us getting killed and scalped by Indians comes true, then I guess this whole discussion has been a big waste of words, hasn't it?"

"Maybe we will make it to Santa Fe somehow," Gizzard answered. "I just don't know."

"Nobody knows about the future. You dream we get scalped, I have always dreamed of finding gold in the mountains and getting rich. If I were a betting man, I'd sure as hell bet on my dream over yours."

"Maybe you're right and it is your dream that'll happen and not my own. Fact is, I might just as well think that as the other."

"Now, you're making good sense," "Andy said, encouraged by those words. "You been acting like a man facing the gallows instead of one that has a pretty good chance of becoming wealthy in about two months' time."

"I'll buck up," Gizzard promised. "And I'll carry my share. I already told Mr. Ford that he can deduct that money I lost in Council Grove from my share of the profits . . . if we make it to Santa Fe."

"You did?"

"Yep."

"What did he say to that?"

"He said that was only fair and would be fine. Mr. Ford also said that if we all worked hard and had some luck, we'd do real well."

Gizzard paused. Still looking worried, he said, "Andy?"

"Yeah?"

"If I was you, I'd start getting real familiar with a six-gun. I'd start practicing with one whenever I had the chance."

"Well, I don't have the chance," Andy shot back as he climbed up the riverbank and started to return to their wagons. "Like you and Mr. Ford, I'm nursing a team of oxen all day and, starting now that we have to take watches, a fair share of the night."

"Just a suggestion," Gizzard said in a voice full of disappointment.

"I do think your head has been damaged," Andy said, walking away.

They continued, sometimes getting rain and bad weather, but mostly running smooth with few problems. They followed the Big Bend of the Arkansas River along its northern bank and purchased a few provisions at Fort Zarah, where they learned that the Comanche and Kiowa had attacked and wiped out a large wagon train only two weeks earlier. There had been no survivors, only ashes and bones already picked clean.

A few days later they saw Pawnee Rock. Being a farmer, Andy was aware of changes in the soil and that they left the tall grass prairie to enter the buffalo-grass plains, which were marked by occasional high mesas, buttes, and crumbling outcroppings of mostly brown and red rock. Since he was the best shot of the three, it had become his job to walk out onto the prairie just before sunset and try to shoot some fresh game. And although tired after a long day of bullwhacking, he came to treasure these few hours alone. Often it was just Andy Parmentier, his rifle, a forever sky, and a waving ocean of buffalo grass. A couple of times he was able to shoot antelope, but since they had no horse to carry them, it was hard work bringing in so much meat. Andy usually shot smaller game like wild turkeys, sage hens, and rabbits, all of which were plentiful.

"When I first came out here you could still see huge buffalo herds," Ford said. "But they've mostly been wiped out by the Indians, and mountain men who turned hide hunters."

"I'd give anything to see buffalo," Andy said.

"They're a sight and that's for sure. We may see some yet, Andy. Last time I was through, I saw a couple of small herds west of Pawnee Rock, not more than ten miles away."

"Maybe I shouldn't try to shoot one if they're that scarce."

"No," Ford decided, "if you get the chance, kill a small cow. We'll butcher her and smoke a couple hundred pounds of meat. Nothing tastes better than smoked buffalo tongue. But right now we have to make a tough decision."

"We're both listening," Andy told the man over his cup of steaming black coffee as Gizzard came over to join them.

"A short ways on, we have to decide to either take what has long been called the 'Wet Route' or the 'Dry Route.' " Ford frowned, making it clear this was a real quandary. "The Wet Route stays more to the Arkansas River, while the Dry Route will swing us to the southwest a piece. It's easier to travel because the road hasn't much sand, but it hasn't much, if any, water."

"For how many miles?" Andy asked.

"About sixty. The Mexicans call it the Journey of Death, but we're early in the season and I believe we can find water holes enough to get us through the Cimarron desert."

"Which is faster?"

"The Dry Route," Ford said without hesitation.

Gizzard ran his fingers through his long, straight hair. "Which route is the least likely to have Indians?"

"Now, *that,*" Ford replied with a wry smile, "is the right question but . . . one that has no answer. We're deep in Indian country. Comanche. Cheyenne. Kiowa. Arapaho.

Even some eastern Apache hunt and raid in this country. There's also Comancheros and they might just be the worst of the whole bloody lot."

Andy had heard of them all the way back to Independence. Comancheros were outlaws of many bloods but of only one loyalty, and that was profit and pleasure. It was said that some came up from Mexico to raid and kill whites and trade with the Indians. Others said that most comancheros were Indians themselves, or godless half-breeds filled with hatred and blood lust. No one seemed to know because no one lived who met up with them on these plains.

"There's a hard storm coming," Andy said. "I say we fill our water barrels to their brims and strike out for the Cimarron River. In cool weather, our oxen can live off the rain for a few days even if we didn't find any water holes."

"You sure of that?" Ford asked.

"Pretty sure."

But Gizzard shook his head. "Andy, you never had oxen at your Indiana farm, so you don't know what you're talking about."

"I've been with them long enough to form some opinions, and I'm willing to stake a bet that even with one good rain, we can pull the Cimarron desert and save ourselves time. We've cut through some sandy country and you know what a toll that takes on the oxen. Given that our odds of running into hostiles are about even either way, my choice is to take a hard, fast run to the Cimarron River."

While they sat musing over their words, they heard the approaching rumble of thunder and the wind freshened.

"All right," Ford decided out loud, "we'll take the Dry Route."

"Which one was that wagon train that got wiped out last week taking?" Gizzard asked.

"I didn't ask," Ford replied.

"Why not!"

"Because these Plains Indians never stay in one place for long, so it didn't seem to matter."

That made sense to Andy, so he carried his bedroll to his wagon and burrowed into it for a few short hours until it was his turn to take the watch.

Gizzard had taken the first watch, and when he woke Andy, it was raining hard and the wind was blowing something fierce.

"Andy, it ain't fit for man nor beast out tonight!" he yelled into the wind. "It don't make any sense to be out in this weather. No self-respecting Indian or Comanchero is going to be out, either!"

That made sense to Andy, but he didn't want to risk incurring Mr. Ford's wrath or taking any chances, so he struggled out of his blankets, pulled on his slicker and hat, then went outside. It was miserable and cold. Andy lowered his head and trudged out to circle the oxen, who looked at him as if he were a stranger or a damned ghost.

Even worse, every time the lightning scored the sky and thunder boomed, the oxen shivered. That told Andy that he needed to be out among them talking and calming the huge animals. Somehow, he lasted until about four o'clock in the morning and then the storm passed and he woke Mr. Ford.

"You look awful," Ford said, shaking out of his own blankets. "Long night, huh?"

"Real long."

"Well, at least we'll have all the water we need for the Dry Route. Now all we have to worry about are the damned Indians."

Andy didn't have any comment about that. His teeth were chattering and he was desperate for hot coffee. But that would be Mr. Ford's job, because he had the last night watch.

"Wake me when it's ready," Andy mumbled as he tromped through mud and climbed into bed.

Breakfast was the same as usual. Dutch-oven biscuits, sowbelly and beans, and coffee. But the food was hot and no one complained because it had turned into a beautiful morning. The long buffalo grass was bent with rain, and as the sun warmed the horizon, the earth steamed like their coffee.

"It's good to be alive, isn't it?" Ford said, not taking his eyes off the glistening horizon.

"Yes, it is," Andy agreed, finally getting warm but still a long way from being dry.

"Let's hope we stay alive," Gizzard said darkly.

Andy started to say something sharp to his morose friend but caught Mr. Ford's shake of the head, which told him it was better just to leave Gizzard alone.

"Well, boys," Ford said, downing his coffee and shaking out the dregs, "it's time to yoke the oxen and see if our luck will hold for another sixty miles until we reach the Cimarron."

"It will," Andy said with all the conviction he could muster.

"We'll see," Gizzard replied, again looking like a man headed straight for the gallows.

Chapter ____ Twelve

Because of the rain, the Dry Route wasn't proving to be dry at all. There were no big springs, creeks, and certainly no rivers, but the buffalo wallows that dotted this country were filled with rainwater and the grass was so juicy the oxen were plenty content.

"Our luck is holding," Ford announced late one breezy and cloudless afternoon when they stopped to make camp on the lee side of a broken outcropping of rock that effectively blocked a persistent north wind. "I've got a wagon hitch that needs fixing and the axles could stand some grease. That'll be *your* job, Gizzard."

"Fair enough."

"What do you want me to do?" Andy asked.

"Why don't you hike off to the north?" Ford said, pointing in that direction. "That's where I saw buffalo on my last trip through. Now, that was a long time ago and I don't expect the same ones to be grazing there, but you never can tell. I've talked to buffalo hunters that say a herd will stake its territory. It's worth a try."

Andy went to collect his rifle and a full canteen.

"I'd sure rather go with Andy than repair hitches and grease axles," Gizzard complained.

"I know," Ford said without a hint of sympathy, "but

you're a lot handier with fixing things, while Andy is our best rifleman. So let's not talk about it any longer and make camp. We got a half-dozen oxen that are a little sore on their feet and they could use the extra rest."

So it was decided. Andy couldn't help but feel lucky that he wasn't going to be working around the camp but instead got to go off hunting. And the very suggestion that he might actually see buffalo was cause for excitement.

As always, Julius wanted to go off hunting, but Ford didn't allow that, because the big dog got too excited and would scare off game.

"Sorry, Julius," Andy said, "but you can have the scraps."

Since the day was cool and blustery, Andy took his heaviest coat and a sharp butcher knife. If the best he could do was kill small game, at least he could dress them out on the prairie and make his load that much lighter.

"Lucky bastard," Gizzard said, coming over to join Andy. "I'd sure rather go strolling around out there than work like a dog around this camp."

"I don't figure you *ever* had to work like a dog."

"I never seen a buffalo either," Gizzard said, "and I been over this Santa Fe Trail twice."

"Do you wish you'd have stayed in Santa Fe?"

"Naw," Gizzard said, "because we're going to be worth a lot of money when we sell all the goods that are in these three wagons."

"What about that showdown you threatened to have with Mr. Ford?"

Gizzard toed the soft, green grass. "Well," he said, "I've had some changes of thought since you two saved my bacon back in Council Grove. I guess I owe Mr. Ford my life, same as I owe it to you."

"You don't owe me a thing."

"Yes, I do," Gizzard insisted. "I got us into a pack of

trouble and lost a hundred dollars. Those bastards in the Red Onion Saloon were going to cut off our heads, Andy! But you and Mr. Ford saved my bacon and that's not something I'll ever forget. Mr. Ford is a good man. You saw that a long time before me."

"I can't believe I'm hearing this," Andy said, "but I'm glad that I am. I've been worried what would happen when we reach Santa Fe. It sounds like the next thing you'll be telling me is that you've decided to stick with Mr. Ford and become a Santa Fe Trail freighter."

They both laughed, but then Gizzard shook his head. "No, I'm going to marry a pretty señorita, eat chicken gizzards and frijoles, and have lots of kids. If I stay out of the saloons and don't gamble, I expect that my share of the profits from this job will last me quite awhile. I might even use some of it to buy me a blacksmith or wagon-repair shop."

"You'd be successful at either one," Andy said, delighted at this change of attitude. "You could teach your children to follow in your footsteps and take over the business."

"Yeah," Gizzard said, looking somewhat embarrassed. "I've thought of that, too."

"Well," Andy said, pulling down the brim of his hat tight against the rising wind, "I'd better go hunting. It'll be dark in two or three hours and I'd like to shoot a buffalo and have the pleasure of eating a few pounds of roasted steak."

"The old mountain men favored their guts and tongues," Gizzard informed him. "I listened to them tell me how they'd yank out the gut and funnel it down their gullets like a bird does a worm."

Andy made a face and set off walking. "I sure won't do that if I manage to kill one," he called back to his grinning friend.

After that, Andy was alone, striding north across the spring grass after skirting the rocky outcropping. The ground to the north was rolling prairie and he couldn't see a living thing. But that didn't discourage him, because when the wind came up, game tended to move down into the low places. And this country was so immense that it could hide a couple thousand buffalo. Shoot, you could pass within a half mile of a herd that large and never see them.

"I'll climb a few taller hilltops," he decided out loud as he judged the set of the sun and decided that he had about two hours of daylight remaining.

Andy was a fast walker. With his height and long, muscular legs, he figured he could walk a steady five miles an hour. Oxen moved about half that fast. It often made him wish that they were horses or mules.

Andy walked at least five miles without seeing anything. He started to turn around and spotted a single dark animal standing motionless on the crown of a hill about a mile to the west. The sunset's glare was so intense that he figured he was seeing an illusion, but he pulled the brim of his hat down low and squinted hard. Nope, it was an animal all right and it was huge.

"By gawd, it's a buffalo," he whispered. "It's a great big old buffalo!"

Andy was in such awe of the creature's great size and majesty that he couldn't move! Finally, he took a deep breath and started trotting toward the great beast. If his eyes were playing tricks on him, Andy knew that the buffalo would vanish. If not, he knew that he wouldn't be seen because buffalo couldn't see worth spit. He was in luck because the wind had shifted and was now coming in from the northwest. The buffalo wouldn't catch his scent. He could probably move to within fifty or sixty yards of the beast before it became aware of his presence.

Andy was so excited he broke into a run. He was in fine shape and fairly flew across the grass, thinking that if there were one buffalo, there might be a bunch more hiding down in a draw just behind that hill. That being the case, he ought to circle back a little to the north so as to come around that high hill so he could creep up on a herd and take his best shot. He didn't want to kill the huge buffalo because it was special, being the first he'd ever seen and so large. Be a sin to kill such a big bull.

It took Andy quite a bit longer than he'd expected, but it was worth the effort because there *was* a small herd hiding behind the hill out of the wind. Not many. He counted fifteen—no, sixteen. There were eleven big ones and three calves. Cute little buggers that stayed close to their mamas. So cute that Andy couldn't muster up the gumption to shoot them or their mothers. So he chose what he thought was a very old bull. It seemed old because it was lame and stiff in the hindquarters. Andy told himself that he'd be doing the old fella a favor. Better a quick death by a bullet or two than to be dragged down and eaten alive by wolves.

Andy crawled in for a close shot. So close that he could see the shine in the old bull's eyes. He took aim and fired.

The bull shivered and started to walk off, so that Andy figured he must somehow have missed. It didn't seem possible given his marksmanship and the size of the target. Why, he could have shot the ear off a rabbit at this range and . . . the bull suddenly collapsed with a sigh and then its hind legs began to kick.

Andy reloaded and fired again, aiming for the heart. This time the bull stopped moving. Now what? The other buffalo weren't scattering. They weren't doing anything! It was as if they didn't care that one of their numbers had just been killed.

It was a predicament, all right. Andy glanced upward to watch salmon-colored fingers curl around the last of a pale blue sky. It was almost sundown and he was a long way from their camp. Still, he really wished that the other

buffalo would move on so that he could go down and in-
spect the bull up close. It was so big! Biggest damn animal
by far that he had ever seen and he'd seen some mighty
large mules and oxen crossing Missouri.

And it didn't seem right to shoot something that magnificent and then abandon it to scavengers. And so, over-
whelmed by a massive case of indecision, Andy lay on the
grass and watched the dead bull and the other buffalo until
the sun went down and it got cold.

Well, he thought, I'd better get back to the wagons. No
worry about not finding my way because the moon is full
and I can put the North Star at my back. If I hurry, I can be at
camp in well under two hours.

So Andy crabbed back up the hill on his hands and
knees then trotted down the other side. First thing in the
morning, he and Mr. Ford would come back here with a
wagon. Maybe they'd bring all three wagons and spend
most of the day butchering the old bull and smoking fresh
meat. They'd gorge like heathens and have themselves a
wonderful time.

And why not, everything was going so well!

But an hour later the bright, orange glow of a huge
bonfire where their camp ought to be told Andy that things
were *not* going well. The glow lit up the sky like sundown.
It was a fire that could be seen for miles and the kind they'd
purposefully avoided because it might be seen by Indians.

"Indians!" Andy stopped and stood staring as his
heartbeat jumped dramatically. "Oh, my God!"

Maybe it wasn't Indians, but Andy couldn't think of
any other explanation for the bonfire as he took off running
south again. He ran until the light was bright in his eyes and
then he dropped facedown on the grass and listened.

Although the wind was carrying sound away, Andy
could hear the Indians screaming like demons. His blood
ran cold and his perspiration turned to ice. His breath came

faster than when he'd been running and he pressed his cheek to the grass and dug his fingernails deep into the rich dark earth.

What am I going to do!

For at least an hour Andy lay twisting in torment, one minute determining that he had to climb the outcropping and shoot as many of the heathens from that high vantage point as possible before they could kill him, but the next telling himself to run away. Run with all his strength until he was so far from this terrible place that he would never be discovered and scalped.

Finally, Andy crawled up into the outcropping and gazed down on what was left of his friends and their little supply train. He wished he had run away instead, because the wagons were all ablaze and the oxen shot to death. The scalped and violated bodies of Mr. Ford and Gizzard gave Andy the dry heaves and he had to clamp his hands over his mouth, even though the hideous Indian screams made it impossible to be heard.

They'd even killed poor, valiant Julius, pincushioning the dog with arrows. Andy saw that the Indians had sacked their wagons before putting them to the torch; overturned boxes and goods were scattered in every direction. He counted twenty-seven Indians and was sure that he'd missed some. They were laughing, howling, trying on the new hats, shirts, and shoes. Some had unrolled the muslin and wrapped themselves up like the ancient Egyptian mummies he'd read about in school. One pair was laughing and admiring themselves with mirrors, and quite a few were roasting ox meat over the three great wagon fires. Their bodies weren't painted, but their faces were twisted and glistening in the firelight.

Andy lay among the broken rocks and watched in horror as two Indians began to take turns shooting Gizzard and Mr. Ford in the head until their faces were featureless.

I've got to get out of here now!

Inching away with violent cramps constricting his belly, Andy finally got up and ran down the hill's north slope. He had the presence of mind to hang on to his rifle and canteen, but he had no idea where he was going. This was wild, unsettled land. Indian land.

Andy figured he could run until hell froze, but he was still a doomed man.

There was something in him that demanded familiarity with the past and never mind that it turned out the only thing left in his past was that little herd of buffalo. So without actually thinking about it, Andy staggered to a gasping halt and found his meager comfort in the simple, magnificent animals. They hadn't moved and, in fact, most were resting on their sides down in the low land out of the wind.

Andy went down to be near them. He was chilled and shaking with cold or fear, probably both. Buttoning his coat, he sat down and cradled his face in his hands and sobbed. The buffalo heard him and snorted with apprehension. A few of the bulls tossed their massive heads about and pawed the earth, but Andy paid them no attention. He wept for Gizzard, Mr. Ford, and even for Julius. He also wept out of naked fear.

What was he going to do now? Where could he go that he would not eventually be seen and killed by the Indians? There was no place to hide out here in the wilderness and no nearby fort or sanctuary where he could be saved. He was . . . was as doomed as these poor, dim-witted, half-blind buffalo. Sooner or later someone was going to exterminate them just as he would be found and exterminated.

"Oh, Mama," he choked, feeling overpowered with desolation, "what I wouldn't give to see you again and be safe on our Indiana farm!"

When he could cry no more, Andy finally raised his head and smeared tears across the back of his sleeve. He watched the huge silhouettes resting in the moonlight. They were blessed not to know their sad and inevitable fate the way Andy knew his own. Mr. Ford had told him that the buffalo once covered this land, as many as the leaves on the cottonwood trees. Stupid, simple, and gentle giants, they had been created for a time before man, or at least before man on horseback could overtake and kill them almost at will.

It occurred to Andy that perhaps the Indian and the buffalo were in the same sinking boat. Both were being eliminated by forces neither could begin to comprehend or survive. But that didn't make Andy feel any sympathy toward the Indian. Not after just witnessing their butchery and barbarism.

When they find me, I will shoot as many as I can and then I will kill myself.

Andy sat up all night watching the buffalo. He was afraid to go to sleep, afraid that they would leave him alone, and if they did, he would go crazy.

The buffalo did leave him early the next morning. The exodus began by the simple act of a cow starting off to the northwest as if it had a good plan in mind. The others dutifully followed, all filing behind until they were mere dark specks on a vast, green tablecloth. Now only the dead bull remained.

Andy felt an overwhelming compulsion to follow the doomed buffalo and he would have had he not clenched his fists and reminded himself that he was, after all, a man and a Parmentier. He was his father's son and he wasn't going to resign himself to a pathetic, wandering death. So he picked himself up, checked his rifle, and drank from his canteen. The water revived his appetite and he splashed some of it across his face, glad for the cold shock upon his skin.

The old bull had grown stiff in the night. Its small, dark eyes were glazed, and when Andy touched its massive shoulder, he felt the rock hardness of muscle. He would have to cut himself meat, as much as he could stomach, and then as much as he could carry to whatever lay to the north. The Indians were to the south, but he knew they would not remain long at the site of their destruction.

Andy used the butcher knife to saw at the shoulder, but the hide was so thick he made little headway. Giving that up, he attacked the animal's belly and found it much easier. Andy was no stranger to slaughtering animals for meat. He'd helped his father slaughter hogs and he'd dressed his own game for many years.

This was no time to be squeamish. He sliced into the already bloated belly and then clenched his teeth and went for the heart and the mammoth liver. It was easy enough. Encouraged by his progress, he sliced meat and white fat from the ribs. Hands covered with gore, he ate the dark flesh and organs, choking down as much as he could without getting nauseated. Andy was glad that he did not have to make a fire and roast the meat because that might have given him away. But oh, how fine it would have been to roast this cold, tough meat until the juices flowed and he felt a fire in his belly again.

He stayed beside the buffalo all the next day, eating as much as he could without getting sick. Then he cut huge hunks of meat and liver, wrapped them into a heavy bundle with his shirt, and started north to find the Wet Route that he wished their wagons had taken. Andy had no idea how far it might be and it wasn't until he'd walked far into the afternoon that he realized with a jolt that his most immediate peril was dying of thirst, not getting scalped by Indians.

The buffalo wallows that had watered their oxen only a few days before were now dry. There were no streams and no rain clouds on the horizon. Andy gulped hard and kept walking. He would walk and sip water only when the thirst became unbearable. If he could find a spring or a wagon train crossing the Wet Route somewhere up ahead, maybe he could yet be saved. He'd lost everything of value except his clothes, the canteen, and his rifle, but he was still young.

"I'll make it," he vowed over and over as he trudged north, "and when I find the high mountains, I'll strike it rich and put the past forever behind!"

Chapter Thirteen

So what was an Indiana farm boy to do all alone on a frontier crawling with savage Indians? That was the question that Andy kept asking himself over and over that long first day after seeing Gizzard and Mr. Ford scalped and shot to pieces.

For the first time in his life, Andy really considered how fleeting life could be and how his own might soon come to a premature and violent end. He was not ready to die and certainly not prepared to face Judgment Day after having committed far too many sins, the greatest being a number of killings. Would he fry in hell tomorrow? Andy believed that was an awful probability. Should he pray to God asking mercy for his soul? Would it even help, given the magnitude of his sins, or was he already lost, completely beyond redemption or divine forgiveness?

Andy prayed long and prayed hard. He had been taught that God forgave everyone of almost anything . . . if they truly repented their sins. But he had killed many men and never mind that all of them were at least as unworthy of God's forgiveness as himself. Andy repeated the Lord's Prayer over and over until dark and then he collapsed on the cold green grass and gazed up at the moon and the stars. Never before had they seemed so distant and unforgiving.

He remembered that Gizzard had believed that after a person died, their spirit went up into the sky to wander about in the universe, happy and free. But then Gizzard had been full of strange ideas, and besides, Andy wasn't sure if he wanted his soul to fly around in the sky like some lonesome thing looking for other spirits in a universe so vast it was unlikely to ever find them.

Andy pointed his rifle at the North Star and then he closed his eyes and slept. The sun was shining brightly when he opened his eyes. He sat up and looked all around at the endless grasslands, feeling as small and insignificant as ever a human had felt. The air was still and he saw neither clouds, nor buffalo, nor birds, nor any other living creature. Just grass and a forever blue sky. It was as if all things except himself had been removed from earth so that he could wander first into insanity and then stumble into a dark and hellish death.

Andy shook his canteen and was disheartened to feel how little water remained. He uncorked and drank a swallow, which made him feel thirstier than ever as he stood up, noting a surprising stiffness in his muscles. He was unable to eat, having no appetite for the cold, uncooked buffalo meat. Taking careful sight along the butt of his rifle, he headed south for the second day, keeping a close eye on his surroundings in the hope of avoiding detection by the Indians and also perhaps finding a stream or a buffalo hollow still holding rainwater.

But he found no water that day or the next, and by then his canteen was dry, his tongue was swollen bigger than a Polish sausage, and his brain was rattling around in his head like chickpeas in an empty pail. By noon, he was reeling around in circles, and finally, he collapsed to stare up at the sun, which burned so fiercely he could hardly breathe.

This is it, he thought, throwing his arms and legs out wide, as if to offer his body in sacrifice first to the scavengers of this vast and merciless land, then to the universe of wandering spirits. *This is where and how Andy Parmentier of Brighton, Indiana, finally died.*

Much, much later, he awoke to the sounds of strange and guttural voices that he was sure belonged to wild Indians. Andy tried to remember what had become of his rifle so that he could shoot himself, but failing that, he steeled himself for the blade of a knife lifting his scalp or sawing across his parched throat.

Instead, he felt the touch of a gentle hand and then the coolness of water that bathed his sunburned face. Andy tried to open his eyes, but could not. Tried to speak, but his tongue filled his mouth and he choked and again struggled to breathe. He wanted to be left alone to die, but the strong hands lifted and carried him into the shade of a two-wheeled cart. His eyes were bathed so that he could open them and he saw what he judged to be a Mexican, who had a gourd filled with water.

The Mexican was saying something that Andy could not understand. His eyes were kind, but his face was lean and badly scarred, the nose twisted and fist-broken. Andy opened his mouth and tried to swallow, but could not. Finally, he felt the coolness of water trickling down his parched throat and was able to swallow.

The Mexican grinned and glanced aside. Andy followed his gaze and saw that there were many other Mexicans, all of them wearing the same wide-brimmed hats with conical crowns as well as brightly colored and strange-looking blankets with neck holes. Some were tending a large band of sheep and goats with the help of dogs. Who were these people and why were they camped out here in the middle of this waterless, treeless prairie?

The friendly Mexican attending Andy left but soon returned with more water and a thin, plate-sized piece of pancake rolled up like a cigar and stuffed with beans.

Andy ate. Slowly and with great pain and difficulty at first, then with more water and ease, until he was gobbling up the food and motioning for more.

"So, gringo," a large, handsome Mexican with a thick accent said, "you will live after all!"

"Who are you?" Andy asked in a voice he did not recognize as his own.

The Mexican leader was in his thirties and one of the most impressive individuals Andy had ever seen. He wore two pistols in a pair of beautifully carved holsters, one on each of his narrow hips. Instead of a colorful blanket draped over his body, he wore a handsome leather jacket decorated with many pretty beads and with fringes on the sleeves. And unlike his companions, he did not wear simple sandals but instead a pair of handsome boots to which were affixed the finest pair of silver spurs Andy had ever hoped to see, their rowels bigger than silver dollars and very sharp.

"Gringo," he boomed, "I, Miguel Fernando Diaz, will ask the questions. Who are you!"

Andy tried to reply, but his throat still felt as if it had been scoured by burning sand. "More water, please," he croaked.

The same gentle soul who had first brought him water reappeared and the gourd was passed to Diaz, who tipped it to Andy's open mouth. Andy drank, noting at least a dozen heavily armed men. Some of them looked like . . . like Indians!

Shocked and recoiling, he stammered, "Mr. Diaz, who—"

Diaz raised a thick finger and cocked his head a little sideways in warning.

"I am sorry," Andy apologized, gathering his wits. "I have no right to ask anything of the men who saved my life."

"It is not yet saved," Diaz informed him.

Andy swallowed hard because the Mexican leader's meaning was chilling . . . and clear.

"Again, gringo, who *are* you?"

"My name is Andrew Parmentier," he began. "I am from Indiana."

Diaz frowned in puzzlement. "Where is that place?"

"Far away to the northeast," Andy replied. "I am the son of a farmer."

"Then why did you come here?" Diaz asked, making a sweeping gesture toward the immense prairie surrounding them.

"I killed a man," Andy admitted, still not thinking very well. "He was a bad man and I killed him to protect my family."

"Then why did you go away if this bad man was dead?"

Andy noticed that all conversation had died among the Mexicans and the few he believed to be fierce Indians. "Mr. Diaz, are those *really* Indians?"

"You have not answered my question!"

"I am called Andy. I left my family because I wanted to find gold."

"Gold?" Diaz chuckled and opened his mouth to show Andy that he had a big gold front tooth. "Like this?"

"Yes."

"And there is no gold in that place called Indiana?"

"No."

"What did you grow on your farm?"

"Mostly corn."

"Ah," Diaz said, finally allowing himself a smile and a nod, "In Mexico my people grow much good corn! Sometimes, when a man is hungry, corn is far better than gold, eh!"

"Yes," Andy readily agreed, feeling such a heavy wave of lassitude wash across him that he could not keep his eyes open.

"We will talk more tomorrow or the next day," Diaz decided, climbing to his feet.

Andy hadn't realized how tired he was and how much his body had suffered from lack of food and water. He'd also lost his canteen and all his weapons somewhere out on the prairie. Right now he missed them sorely.

"Yes, talk, Mr. Diaz," he managed to say.

"*Señor* Diaz!" the leader corrected, before marching off with his big spur rowels jingling like sleigh bells.

During the next few days Andy mostly slept, waking only to eat, drink, and relieve himself. The Mexicans that he was certain were Indians did not seem to be in any hurry to move. Andy couldn't fathom why these people would camp out in the middle of nothing for no apparent reason. They seemed to be enjoying their leisure, however, and kept a fire going with enough smoke to be visible for miles. Weren't they afraid of being seen and slaughtered by hostile Indians? Andy tried to warn the friendly one, but he only smiled while his jovial friends were mostly busy frying those thin, flat, and almost tasteless pancakelike things in heavy black skillets.

"Tortillas," Julio, the quiet, scarred-faced one, told him one afternoon after he'd eaten seven or eight and belched with appreciation.

Andy didn't care what they were called because they were so delicious when stuffed with beans, fiery peppers, and probably goat meat.

By the third day, Andy was feeling well enough to stand and walk around a bit. He soon learned that Diaz was not the only member of the party who could speak English. They could all understand it pretty well and speak it, although their English was mostly broken and uneven. Even the half-dozen Indians knew a few words and maybe a whole lot more. Andy was fascinated by these people, yet a bit apprehensive because they were so heavily armed while he was virtually defenseless and completely dependent upon their charity.

"In a few days, when I am stronger," he said to Diaz that afternoon, "I will leave and try to find the Wet Route to Santa Fe."

"If you leave, you will go as we found you, that being without food, a canteen, or a gun."

"I understand that."

"Then why would you choose to leave and die?" Diaz asked with genuine puzzlement.

"Because I do not wish to burden you."

"You do not! And besides," the Mexican assured him, "the time will come when maybe you can repay us."

"How?"

Diaz shrugged, making it clear he had no answer.

"Señor Diaz," Andy asked, looking at all the sheep, goats, and the thin cattle he supposed that these wandering people used to haul their two-wheeled carts, which he learned they called *carretas*, "there must be water nearby."

"*Sí,*" the leader replied, "just over the hill there is a big spring."

Andy shook his head in amazement. "And I would have died of thirst within a few hundred yards of it."

"This is true," Diaz agreed, chuckling as if the prospect were somehow humorous. "When I was a boy herding sheep with my father and his friends, there were many big trees around that spring."

"What happened to them?"

Diaz shrugged. "We cut them down for firewood a long time ago. Now we must use buffalo chips and the shit from our sheep, goats, and cattle."

Andy decided that these Mexicans had indeed been very shortsighted about fuel, but he was wise enough not to say so to this man. Instead, he muttered, "That's too bad."

"It is all right," Diaz replied. "We did not want every-one to find so much good water anyway."

"Why not?"

Diaz grimaced at the question, as if it were the height of stupidity, and snapped, "Gringo, anyone who would ask such a question does not deserve a good answer."

"I'm sorry," Andy apologized. "But I don't under-stand."

Diaz sighed and drew a cigarillo from his fancy leather jacket, bit off the tip, spat it onto the grass, and then lit his smoke with a sigh of contentment. Finally, he opened his eyes and studied Andy for a moment.

"Gringo," he replied, voice hardening, "all this coun-try once belonged to Mexico. It still does, but you *ameri-canos* think it was given away by that bastard General Santa Anna at the Treaty of Guadalupe Hidalgo."

Miguel Diaz turned away and spat to show his dis-gust. "Santa Anna was a fool, a coward, and a traitor to all of Mexico! This land does not belong to you!"

"I . . . I don't want it!" Andy exclaimed, suddenly fear-ing for his life. "Honest, Señor Diaz! All I want is to find some gold in the Colorado Rockies!"

"*That* was also stolen from the people of Mexico!"

"Then California!"

Diaz's face mottled with fury and he sputtered with rage, crying, "California is still Mexico!"

Andy skidded away, throwing up his hands and yell-ing, "Of course it is! You are right, señor! Forgive me. I am just an ignorant corn farmer!"

Diaz was trembling and nobody in camp was speak-ing. Andy wondered if he was about to be killed for the sins of General Santa Anna.

But suddenly Julio, with his crooked nose and scarred face, hurried over to rescue him. Pushing in between him and Diaz, Julio spoke in a low, hushed voice, then pointed to the south, where the dogs had began to run and bark.

Diaz immediately jumped to his feet, shouting orders. Men grabbed up their weapons and formed what Andy could only describe as a skirmish line facing to the south.

"Julio," Andy said, grabbing the Mexican before he could also take his place in the line, "what is it!"

"Comanche," the Mexican replied, making a hurried sign of the cross in front of his serape.

Just having survived Diaz, Andy took this news hard and was sure that he was about to meet his Maker. "Give me a gun," he pleaded. "Let me fight beside you as a friend."

But Julio was already hurrying away to leave Andy by himself. Spotting a hatchet by the fire, Andy snatched it up and followed his rescuers, repeating the word "Comanche" over and over as if it were his personal death knell.

There were exactly twenty-seven Comanche and they had plenty of goods to trade—all of which had quite recently been the sole property of Andy, Gizzard, and Mr. Ford. Sick with fear and outrage, Andy choked the wooden handle of the stubby ax until his knuckles were white. He stared at the proud and noisy Comanche on their fine ponies as they dismounted and walked forward as if they were princes instead of butchers.

Miguel Diaz and a few of his senior lieutenants left the skirmish line and strode forward to meet their haughty visitors, upon whose hands the blood of two innocent men could barely have dried. Tears came to Andy's eyes when he noticed that many of the Comanche wore the very same hats, shirts, boots, and other trappings that Mr. Ford had so painstakingly purchased with Captain Marsh's stolen ten thousand dollars. Then other Indians began to unload other precious trade items whose prices Andy knew by heart.

Axes, $2.23; muslin, twenty-two cents; canvas fourteen cents; and black lace, seven cents a running yard. Flannel pants, $3.25 each; men's shoes, all black, $16.50 each; tin buckets at ninety-five cents apiece; and pretty mirrors, many now cracked, originally costing $2.15 apiece.

Triple those prices and there had been a surefire fortune. But all gone now. Washed away in the blood of his horribly mutilated and defaced friends.

Andy began to shake as if he had been struck by lightning when his eyes came to rest on an Indian wearing Mr. Ford's hat, then another with Gizzard's red flannel shirt. It was more than he could endure and his mind must have cracked like the trade mirrors the Comanche were displaying to the Mexicans, because he let out a yell, raised his ax, and attacked the Indians.

"Murdering sonsabitches!" he howled in demented fury as he sprinted forward, waving the dull ax.

In the dim, murky recesses of his rational mind, he realized that he was probably committing suicide, but he no longer cared, for he could not bear to breathe another moment with the torment he felt churning inside.

"Murdering bastards!" he cried raggedly.

The Comanche stopped hooting and yipping. They saw Andy and the deadly craziness contorting his haggard face. Wordlessly, they raised their weapons and prepared to shoot him with no more compunction or compassion than if he had been a rabid animal, which was what he most closely resembled.

Julio jumped at Andy, pistol sweeping down in a vicious arc that terminated against the side of Andy's skull, almost tearing off his ear before dropping him to the earth, more dead than alive.

After that, Andy remembered nothing for a long, long time.

_____ Chapter _____
Fourteen
_____

A ndy finally awoke with dried blood filling his ear
and thunder and lightning playing games in his head.
Over all that, he could still hear the shrill, shrieking
protest of a *carreta*'s grease-starved axle and feel the rough
thumpity-thump of the large and unevenly worn wooden
wheels. Andy feebly raised his head and noticed a dramatic
change in the landscape. Instead of the rolling grass plains,
they were now surrounded by a scattering of tall, conical
hills, while varieties of small cactus now dotted a sea of
stem-cured prairie grasses.

Far off to the west Andy saw a low-lying string of
white clouds and he focused on them for the next two days
as he bounced along in Julio's humble *carreta*. Sliding in
and out of consciousness, he took food and water from the
gentle Mexican and sometimes even understood a few of
Julio's words, but not very many. He had no idea where he
was or how long he had been riding in the *carreta* but
guessed it might have been for days. What he finally did decide was that the low string of white clouds off to the west
were stationary. That seemed very odd to Andy; he'd never
seen clouds before that did not move this way or that with
the wind.

"They are not clouds, señor, they are *mountains*," the Mexican told him.

"White mountains?"

"No! They are covered with . . . I do not know the word in English."

Andy tried to think. "Trees?"

"No."

"White rocks?"

But Julio shook his head.

"Snow!" Andy exclaimed. "Those mountains must be covered with snow!"

"*Sí*. Snow."

To make sure that they understood each other, Julio hugged himself with both arms and grimaced, rattling his teeth.

Andy almost laughed. Almost, because he knew laughing would send a hot spear of pain lancing through his battered brain. "They must be very tall mountains," he managed to say.

Julio nodded, flicking the cattle whip in his fist. "Andy," he said, "you go loco with the Comanche. Why?"

"They were the ones that scalped and shot the faces off my dead friends, Julio. Those trade goods you got once belonged to us."

"Ah, *sí*! I told Miguel this was why you went loco." Julio made a circular motion around his right ear. "You must be careful because he is very angry."

"With me?"

"*Sí*, Andy, Miguel Diaz will kill you himself if you ever do that again."

"I could not help it, *amigo*."

"This very bad," Julio said, shaking his head and looking sorrowful. "If there was a big fight, maybe we all die. Maybe I never see my family again."

"I am sorry," Andy said, meaning it. "I had no right to put your lives in danger. If you had killed me, you would not have shamed yourself."

"Very bad," Julio muttered again before he patted Andy on the arm and walked up beside his plodding cattle to give them the sting of his whip, which, as far as Andy could tell, did not make them move any faster.

What mountains could be so tall that they still have summer snow? Andy wondered. Surely not the Rocky Mountains.

But even as he labored with this puzzling question, Andy realized that they could be no other.

"They *must* be the Rockies!" he whispered aloud.

That evening, Andy's suspicions were confirmed by Miguel Diaz. "The Rockies, yes," Diaz told him, "that is what the gringos call them."

"Then I must have been unconscious for a long time."

"That is true. I told Julio to leave you behind, but he would not, and he is too good a man for me to punish. You owe him your life, stupid Indiana gringo."

"I know," Andy said, "but maybe, if you had seen your friends scalped and—"

"I have," Diaz growled, "and also my family."

Something told Andy not to say that he was sorry. Something told him not to say anything more to Diaz that might provoke his wrath.

"Maybe you should not say so much," Julio told Andy when they were alone.

"I think that you are right," Andy said. "From now on, I'll keep my thoughts to myself whenever Miguel Diaz is around. But I would like to know where we are headed."

"Only Miguel knows for sure," Julio replied, eyelids dropping like a veil. "Maybe we go to trade with more Comanche."

"I hope not. I intend to reach Santa Fe," Andy told his friend and protector, "and I'll only stay with you as long as we keep heading westward."

Julio nodded with understanding but would say no more.

They traveled slowly during the next several weeks, always moving west at the sluggish pace of the Mexican cattle, the ponderous *carretas*, and the bleating band of sheep and goats. Miguel Diaz was the only one of them who rode horseback and his mount was a handsome black stallion with a long flowing mane and tail. One of Diaz's lieutenants kept the animal groomed to a shine, and with its silver bit, braided bridle and reins, and a saddle with the biggest horn Andy had ever seen, Miguel Diaz cut a dashing figure.

On two more occasions, they met and traded with Comanches. Their sudden and always explosive appearance filled Andy with a mixture of sickness and rage, even though they were not the same ones who had robbed and murdered his friends. When the Indians entered the Mexicans' camp, Andy had to leave because he did not trust himself and feared that he might again try to kill them.

"Indians," Julio told him one warm evening when he stood alone, shaking with raw and powerful emotions, "are no better or worse than any other people."

"Yes, they are." Andy choked. "They're godless heathens! They like to kill and mutilate."

"And there are not whites who also like to kill? Or Mexicans?"

"I've never met any."

"Then you have been very fortunate. There are many and they are not difficult to find on both sides of the border. I have learned to trust only a few friends and to be wary of all others."

"Why did you save my life?"

"Why not? Maybe someday you will save mine? Who knows?"

"I would if I could," Andy said, unable to imagine such a thing happening. "Are you going back to Mexico?"

Julio smiled. "No," he said, "we *are* in Mexico, only now you call it *New* Mexico."

"We're in New Mexico!"

Julio shrugged to indicate that it did not matter much to him what a place was called. "Or maybe Colorado or Oklahoma. Who knows? Soon we come to the Cimarron River where it touches two, maybe even all three at once."

"Then Santa Fe can't be so very far away."

"Santa Fe is still many, many days' ride to the west. It is beyond those mountains which we call the Sangre de Cristo."

"Which means?"

"The blood of Christ."

"Would you like to come with me to Santa Fe?"

"No. I have been there before." Julio motioned to the sheep. "I take my sheep where the grass is best and where my children are safe."

"How many children do you have?" Andy asked.

Julio looked at him for a moment, then said, "I have work to do. You stay away from the Comanche and they will leave soon. Promise me this."

"I promise."

"Good."

The Comanche left the following day after feasting most of the night on goat. Andy did not ask what they had brought to trade, nor did he care. Two days later he saw a long, wavery ribbon of trees on the southwestern horizon and pointed. "Julio, is that the Cimarron River?"

"The Cimarron, yes!"

Andy had heard much about this river and knew that it was not large and, in fact, was nearly dry in some places late in the summer. By now, it ran with spring snowmelt. At the scent of the flowing water, the sheep began to bleat piteously and the cattle that pulled the Mexican carts picked up their pace. Four hours later they were standing in the sandy river bottom drinking the cool water and enjoying the shade of trees.

"Will we stay here long?" Andy asked his friend.

"Maybe a week," Julio replied.

"Then where will Diaz lead us?"

"Do not ask so many questions," Julio warned him.

Andy was feeling strong again and wondering if he dared to strike out on his own for Santa Fe. Surely it could not be that far. But they were still in hostile Indian country and the memory of his dead friends had left a deep fear that he would also be scalped and mutilated. Andy owed his survival to luck, not skill or daring. Had he not gone off to hunt and been led far from his camp by the sight of the buffalo, he would be as dead as poor Gizzard and Mr. Ford. So Andy stayed with Miguel Diaz and his mixed band of Mexicans and half-breed Indians, waiting to see what would happen next.

What happened was that they soon had more visitors, only this time it was not the Comanche but instead, a large band of heavily armed white men. At the sight of them, the Mexicans went into a panic, driving their sheep and carts into the trees that would offer some cover while Diaz shouted for every man to grab his weapons and prepare to fight for his life.

"Julio, who are they!" Andy cried, excited to see white men again. "And why are you so afraid!"

Julio gripped his rifle and said, "They are cowboys who hate both Mexicans and sheep. Stay down and get ready for a bad fight!"

Andy ducked behind the *carreta*'s solid wooden wheel

in time to see half the cowboys climb off their horses with their rifles and take cover in the trees along the opposite bank. The other half fanned out to cross the river both above and below the Mexicans and then encircled them in a deadly cross fire.

"Are you comancheros!" yelled a tall cowboy wearing a Stetson and cowhide vest with the hair on the outside.

The Mexicans dug in and prepared to defend themselves.

Andy was confused. "Julio, why don't we just tell them we're peaceable and put a stop to this craziness!"

But Julio wasn't really listening as he watched the fast-riding cowboys splash through the Cimarron River, both up and down from them and just out of rifle range. "First, they will start shooting our cattle that pull the *carretas*, and then they will shoot our dogs, sheep, and goats."

"But why?"

"Because they hate Mexicans . . . and sheep."

"That's it?" Andy exclaimed, hardly believing what was about to happen.

"That," Julio said, "and because, even more than Mexicans and sheep, they hate comancheros."

"Well then why doesn't Diaz tell them that we're not comancheros?"

"Because," Julio said simply, "we are."

Andy almost fell over backward. "*We're* comancheros?"

"Yes, because we trade with the Comanche. And for that, they will try to kill us."

The truth of Julio's words hit Andy hard. Of course they were the hated comancheros who traded with the raiding Comanche, Kiowa, Apache, and other warring Indian peoples. Kill off the comancheros and you ended the source of weapons and other precious supplies needed by the hostiles. Kill off the hated comancheros and you took away much of the incentive of the Indians to rob, murder, and steal from whites on the Santa Fe Trail and all along the frontier.

"Holy Jesus," Andy whispered, "and I'm one of them."

"Maybe we can survive until the darkness allows us to sneak away," Julio said, not sounding very hopeful as the cowboys started systematically to shoot Mexican cattle, sheep, dogs, and even Diaz's beloved black stallion.

When his stallion dropped, thrashing in death, Diaz went berserk. Firing both pistols, he charged into the river screaming curses at the cowboys, who coolly riddled him with bullets.

"We are doomed," Julio said, making the sign of the cross and bowing his head to pray.

Without any forethought, Andy grabbed a piece of white cloth from the Mexican's cart, tied it to a stick, and began to wave it back and forth while shouting, "Don't shoot! I'm an American! Don't shoot! We surrender!"

"Hold up!" the tall cowboy yelled. "Everybody hold your damn fire for a minute 'cause there's a *white* man in there amongst 'em!"

Andy stood and plowed forward, eyes on Miguel Diaz's body and the crimson stain added to the water. Diaz was lying facedown in the gravelly shallows and the current was slowly spinning him around in preparation for carrying his body back to Kansas.

"Who are you!" the leader of the cowboys shouted.

"My name is Andrew Parmentier! I'm from Indiana."

"What are you doin' with them comancheros, and you better not be one of 'em or you're a walking dead man."

Andy was so scared he could hardly spit out the words. "They're *not* comancheros. They're just poor shepherds trying to get back to Mexico."

The cowboy stood up in full view and Andy prayed

that his Mexican friends did not shoot the man and start an all-out war that they could not possibly win.

"Well, that dead Mex with the bandolier and two pistols sure wasn't no poor sheepherder!"

"He was a bandit, all right." Andy's mind was churning now. "These people hired him to protect themselves and their flock from predators."

"That still don't explain you bein' with 'em!"

"They saved my life!" Andy cried. "You see, I was with a supply train that got attacked and wiped out by Comanche. The only thing that saved me from being scalped was that I was off hunting when it happened. A few days later, I was lost and almost dead from thirst, and these good people found me and saved my life."

"What did they want in repayment?"

"Nothing," Andy said. "They're just poor but kind people trying to get their flock back to Mexico."

Andy felt a nervous tic at the corner of his lying mouth. Well, at least part of what he'd just said was true.

The leader of the cowboys frowned, scratched his massive jaw, and growled, "Where the hell is Indiana, anyway?"

"It's way up north between Illinois and Ohio."

"Tex, I heard of them places," another cowboy said, daring to poke his head up. "Maybe the kid is telling the truth and these greasers really *are* just a bunch of stupid sheepherders."

"Yeah, but I still hate sheepherders," Tex growled.

"I sure wish you'd let these poor people go on to Mexico," Andy hollered, standing in ice-cold water up to his knees.

"Kid, where are *you* going?"

"I was headed for Santa Fe."

"You'd never make it alone."

"Then maybe you could let me join you awhile."

The cowboys went into a conference that must have taken at least fifteen minutes while Andy stood shivering beside Miguel Diaz's body.

"Do you fellas mind if I remove and keep his six-guns?" Andy finally asked, for lack of anything other to do or say.

"Naw," Tex answered, "you can have 'em. But don't forget his gunbelt and holsters. And I want to try on that dead Mex's fancy boots. Mine are near worn-out and his look like they might fit me just fine."

"I'll take them off and bring them over," Andy said, whispering to Julio that he and his friends ought to leave pronto.

Andy felt bad about what had happened to Miguel Diaz. He felt even worse about the Mexican's fine stallion, but it had been a mean and sneaky animal that no one else but Miguel Diaz could have ridden for long without getting bucked off or raked off under a low tree limb or some such treacherous act. Andy's father had warned him about stallions and it turned out he'd been right. They were generally not to be trusted and always better to be castrated. But it was too late for that now. It was also too late for some of the sheepdogs for which Andy had taken a strong liking, but he wouldn't miss the sheep themselves. The only fortunate part was that no one but Diaz had been killed . . . yet.

Andy sure did admire the six-guns and their handsome tooled-leather holsters and gunbelts. He suspected that the dead Mexican's boots would have fit him just fine, but was plenty willing to hand them over to Tex in exchange for the favor of saving his life and that of his comanchero friends. And while it might be wrong to have lied and saved Julio and the others, they'd saved his life, so he had no choice but to save theirs, or so he felt in his heart.

Tex was a rugged-looking man in his early thirties, handsome and dark-eyed, with big hands, a lantern jaw, and a deep cleft in his chin. He hardly looked at Andy as he tore off his own run-down boots and replaced them with Diaz's fancy ones.

"They're pretty damned tight," he grunted, "but the best way to break in a new pair of boots is to soak 'em good anyway. All I got to do is wipe off the blood and wear 'em until they dry. That way they'll fit like a pair of woolen socks."

Tex stomped his feet deep into Diaz's boots and grinned with satisfaction. "Guess this was my lucky day and that Mexican's unlucky one, huh?

"You kick off them Mexican foot floppers and pull on my old boots. Ain't right that an American should wear a pair of damned old sandals."

"Yes, sir."

"Tex. My name is Tex Marcum. I'm the ramrod of the Monarch Ranch and don't you never forget it."

"Oh, I won't, Tex," Andy assured the big cowboy. "Now, I sure would be grateful if you let my friends and what is left of their sheep, dogs, and cattle go."

"I guess we might," Tex allowed, marching around in the wet boots, making squishy sounds. "Any more of them Mex have fine boots like these?"

"No," Andy said, removing his sandals and replacing them with Tex's old boots, which weren't nearly as comfortable, "but there's a good saddle on that black stallion you and your cowboys just shot."

"Ain't any self-respecting cowboy gonna sit in a *Mexican* saddle," Tex snapped. "They can keep it or leave it on the dead horse. Makes no matter to me."

"Boss?" another cowboy not much older than Andy dared to ask as he emerged from cover with a gun in his fist.

"What is it, Pete?"

"I'd sort of like to have that silver bit and braided reins I saw on the black stud we shot."

"We'll see," Tex answered. He appraised Andy for several moments then said, "Kid, can you stick a horse?"

"You mean ride one?"

"Of course that's what I mean. You slow in the head or somethin'?"

"No, sir! I mean, Tex. And yeah, I can ride."

"What'd you do in Indiana?" Tex asked suspiciously.

"I . . ." Andy was quite sure that Tex would look upon a corn-and-pig farmer with as much disdain as he looked upon a sheepherder, so he lied again, saying, "My father raised stock."

"Horses?"

"Some."

"Saddle . . . or plow?"

"Both."

"Hmmph," Tex grunted, really giving Andy the once-over. "Well, why didn't you speak right out before the shooting started if them Mexicans ain't really comancheros?"

"I never been in a gunfight before," Andy lied again. "I was scared you'd mistake me for one of them."

"Damn near did, being as how you were dressed like 'em, with sandals and that serape."

"When they found me, my clothes were in rags," Andy explained. "I was grateful for anything to keep warm at night."

"I guess you would be. Where'd you say you and your friends were attacked by Comanche?"

Andy described the place as best he could and that seemed to satisfy Tex, because he said, "I been there. You was a fool to take the Dry Route."

"I guess we were. But I'd never been out west before."

"I expect that you're useless as balls on a bird," Tex grumbled, "but maybe we can still make a cowboy out of you."

"What?"

"Thirty dollars a month and found," Tex announced. "Forty after you prove up, and that will take some doin'."

That sounded like a fortune to Andy, but stubbornness made him say, "I was going to prospect for gold in the Colorado Rockies."

"Then you was going to ruin," Tex said with contempt. "Cowboyin' is a far better way of life. Steady work year 'round on the Monarch Ranch. Two, sometimes even three meals a day and Sundays generally off unless it's roundup time. You won't do better than to come to work for us, kid."

"But I don't even have a horse or saddle!"

"The company will provide those and whatever else you need to cowboy. What do you say?"

"What choice do I have?"

"None, unless you want to join them sheepherding greasers and run all the way down to Mexico." Tex scratched his jaw and added, "The truth is, I'd be hard-pressed to believe any man that would choose them greasers over his own kind. In fact—"

"I'll take the job," Andy blurted, noticing a hardness edging back into Tex's close, deep-set eyes that might yet spell doom for Andy's friends.

Tex didn't grin, but somehow he looked pleased. "Kid, I figured you might. You can ride double on Pete's horse until we get back to headquarters. But first, you wade back across the river and tell them greasers they got fifteen minutes to clear out of my sight!"

"Yes, sir!"

"Boss or Tex is what you had better remember to call me from this day on. And get rid of that damned serape! Pete, give him your coat until we get back to headquarters and can find him some decent cowboy clothes."

Andy had grown to appreciate the serape. It was warm

at night, easy to work in, and comfortable for sleeping, and it was a gift from Julio, a man he'd come to like and admire. "Tex, do you mind if—"

"Shut up, greenhorn! Tex don't tolerate any backsliding or back talk, especially from a kid from Indiana who don't know how damn lucky he is to have a chance to cowboy for the biggest, finest cattle ranch in this whole damn Cimarron country! So git that trash outta my sight before I kill every last sheep and dog they own!"

Andy splashed back across the Cimarron River. When he reached Julio, he told his friend what he'd done and that he had to leave on the quick.

"You have saved our lives," Julio said, with a trace of bitterness because the lives of several good dogs, sheep, and Miguel Diaz had not been saved.

Julio and the rest of the comancheros cleared out fast. With only a few cattle left standing, the Mexicans hitched themselves up and dragged away their *carretas* to the hooraying and guffawing of the Monarch cowboys, who thought a man pulling a cart like a cow was about the funniest thing imaginable.

Andy waded back across the Cimarron and jammed his dripping boot into Pete's stirrup, then crawled up behind the young cowboy to ride double.

"You better hang on, greenhorn! If you take a tumble, we might decide to just leave you."

"Might be a blessing in disguise," Andy said, glancing back over his shoulder at the Mexicans, who were disappearing behind their flock over a hilltop.

Pete sank his spurs into the ribs of their mount so hard the animal leaped forward, almost flipping Andy over its rump. But he managed to hang on as they all went galloping back to wherever the hell the Monarch Ranch was located.

Chapter
Fifteen

Andy figured they'd never get to the Monarch Ranch headquarters, and if they did, by then he'd be plumb pounded to pieces. It was the first time he'd ever ridden double on the back of a galloping horse and damned if there ever would be a second time. The insides of his knees were already rubbed raw and ready to bleed and his tailbone felt as if it had been driven halfway up his spine. Andy had ridden his pa's plow horses and a few others, but he never could have imagined riding a cow horse, especially one that was racing over the roughest, most gawd-awful country imaginable.

"How you doin'?" Pete shouted as they trotted fast down the side of a ravine after the others in a cloud of dust so thick that Andy couldn't even see the bottom.

"How much farther!"

"Another six or seven miles. Gonna have to trade you off to someone else, 'cause this horse is startin' to fade."

Andy didn't care. In fact, he would have preferred to have gotten off the back of this animal and *walked* the six or seven miles, which would have been a whole lot easier on his body and mind.

Tex Marcum finally reined up on a high stretch of barren land and the rest of the Monarch cowboys did the same.

They were covered with dust and all the horses coated with sweat and well lathered.

"Kid, you climb down and ride behind Gideon on his big sorrel gelding."

Andy almost fell off the back of Pete's horse. When he landed, his legs buckled and he sat down hard on a small cactus.

"Ouch!" he cried, jumping up and grabbing the back of his britches and grimacing with pain.

All the cowboys burst out laughing, which made Andy furious. But there wasn't much he could do about it, so he said, "I guess none of you have probably ever had to ride double over this hellish country at a high gallop!"

His remark made them laugh even harder. All except Pete, who just smiled.

"What are you gonna do?" Tex asked. "I got a pair of pliers in my saddlebags. You drop your drawers and I'll pull out the cactus spikes."

"No thanks!" Andy was so mad he knew that if these cowboys kept hoorahing him, he was going to do something he'd regret. "Why don't you just point me in the right direction and I'll meet you at headquarters."

Tex quit smiling. "You'd *walk* seven miles?"

"Sure. How do you think I got here from Indiana?"

"I figured you rode something."

"I didn't. I was a bullwhacker and they walk."

Tex studied on that for a minute and then said to his men, "You boys go on ahead and I'll meet you back at headquarters."

Andy put his hands on his hips. "I don't need your help," he said, deciding he didn't want to become a cowboy. In the first place, this was a cruel bunch for shooting the black stud out from under Miguel Diaz and then shooting Diaz himself just because he was a Mexican. In the second place, they'd slaughtered the Mexicans' dogs and stock.

The more Andy thought about that, the angrier he became. In the third and last place, these cowboys rode like crazy men and had taken far too much pleasure in watching him suffer. Given all that, Andy decided that he could do without cowboying on the Monarch Ranch even though the high, steady wages were tempting.

"Tex, do you mind if I stay behind with you and the greenhorn?" Pete asked. He looked at Andy and chuckled. "I could hold him down while you use the pliers."

"You try that," Andy warned, "and I'll whip you good."

"Oh yeah!" Pete challenged.

"Yeah," Andy said, balling his fists.

Tex dismounted. He was as tall as Andy and twenty pounds heavier, but Andy wasn't afraid. He knew how to fight, and after all he'd been through since leaving Independence, he was bound to be tougher and faster.

"Simmer down, kid," Tex said, raising his hands, palms out. "I'm not looking for a fight, and if you've a mind to strike out on your own, that'd be okay with me. Cowboying is the best job in the world, but it takes a lot of work to learn the trade."

Andy cooled down some. "To tell you the truth, I don't even know much about horses. We had a couple of plow animals and my father was really just a corn farmer."

Tex visibly winced. "Kid," he finally said, rolling a long, twisted cigarette, I wouldn't spread that bit of your past around, was I you."

"You're not me and I'm not ashamed of being the son of a farmer. My father was a good man and he was making a go of things when he got a fool notion to fight in the War Between the States."

Tex lit his cigarette. "If your daddy fought for the South, you have my deepest sympathy and respect. But if he fought for the North, I don't want to ever hear about him again."

"Don't worry, you won't," Andy vowed, "because I'm striking out for Santa Fe. Just point me in that general direction."

"You'd need to go back to the Cimarron River and follow it west," Tex said. "That would take you a good part of the way, but you'd never make it on foot. The country is too rough and wild."

"I have guns now," Andy said, patting Diaz's fine pair of matched revolvers. "I could make it just fine."

Tex shook his head and sighed. "If you're not going to work for the Monarch like you agreed, I'll take back those handsome six-guns, the gunbelts and holsters, as well as my old working boots."

"What!"

"You heard me," Tex said, squinting around the smoke of his cigarette. "I couldn't abide the thought of a *quitter* wearing my boots, sorry as they are."

"I'm no quitter!"

"Yes, you are," Tex argued. "I offered you a job at thirty dollars a month and found. You accepted, but now you just quit. If that isn't being a quitter . . . well, I don't know what is."

"I don't like being laughed at and made fun of," Andy said, looking over at Pete to see if he was grinning. If he was, Andy was fixing to drag him off that horse and rub his face in the same cactus he'd just landed on.

Pete wasn't grinning. In fact, he sounded pretty serious when he said, "Cowboys laugh whenever they get the chance, Andy. We tease each other all the time. It's just the way we do things. You'll learn."

"Maybe I don't want to learn."

"Kid, that's entirely up to you," Tex said, "but you owe it to yourself to at least give cowboying a fair try. I don't offer a job to just anybody. Reason I offered you one is that you seem to have grit. I can also see that your life has been pretty tough taters and that you're used to scrapping. The Monarch Ranch can always use scrappers."

Andy wasn't angry anymore. Mostly he just hurt from the waist down, and so the idea of walking barefoot all the way back to the Cimarron River suffering cactus spikes was not to his liking. "Tex, do you really have pliers in your saddlebags?"

"I do and I sure ought to pull them cactus spikes out before they begin to fester."

"Oh, all right. But don't either one of you dare start laughing or I'll fight you both."

"If you did that," Tex said matter-of-factly, "you'd be in even worse shape than you are right now."

Knowing that there were times in every man's life when he had to swallow his pride and back down, Andy turned around and dropped his pants. His only way to redeem his dignity was not to howl, and as Tex began to yank out the cactus spikes, keeping silent took every last ounce of determination he could muster.

By the time Tex was finished, Andy's backside was far too sore to ride, so he walked. The surprising thing was that Tex and Pete walked, too. Walked their *horses*, that is, because Tex explained that a real cowboy always avoided walking like the plague.

"Andy, the Monarch Ranch," Tex explained, "is unlike anything you've ever heard about in the West. It's owned by a royal family named Chamberlain who can boast dukes, earls, barons, and all those fancy pedigrees. They built a big English Tudor stone house and a livery and carriage house for their blooded horses and coaches."

"A carriage house?"

"With ivy and a flower garden," Pete added, rolling his eyes around to show his disdain for it all.

"The thing is," Tex continued, "the Chamberlains or their friends rarely come to enjoy the ranch, so me and my daughter, Della, live in it while they're gone."

"What happens when they return?"

"We move back into the foreman's house, which is nicer than most anyplace you've ever seen, though it seems small by comparison. I get paid very well to ramrod the Monarch. The Chamberlains would like me to earn them at least a small profit, but in this dry and tough country, that's not really possible."

Andy frowned. "You mean that the Chamberlain family is so rich they can stand to *lose* money?"

"That's right."

"But that doesn't make sense!"

"There's a lot in life that doesn't make sense," Tex said. "Still, I've learned that something that doesn't make sense for someone might make sense to someone else."

"I still don't get it," Andy told him.

"I'm not sure that I do either," Tex admitted. "I was raised on a poor horse-and-cattle ranch just down south of Houston. Every day I was growing up was a struggle and a man either made a thing profit, or he picked up and moved on to find a place where he could make some money."

"That's the way I was raised, too," Pete said. "Only my pa raised mules in Missouri."

"Well," Tex said, trying hard to explain, "with really rich people, the game is altogether different. The Chamberlains view the Monarch Ranch as kind of a . . . a prize."

"A prize?" Andy asked.

"Yeah. A prize. Seems that the Europeans think that the American West is a very exciting place—which it is. But having a ranch in America sort of gives them even more to brag about to the other royalty."

"Seems pretty ridiculous to me."

"Well, it does to me, too, but the pay is better than I ever expected to make and I like this country. The Chamberlains come about once a year, if that. When they arrive, they bring their friends over to show off the cattle we're raising. For years they kept trying to get me to raise fox so they could hunt them on horseback, but that was where I drew the line and said no. So now they hunt coyotes or even rabbits and blue bugles and all sort of nonsense that I'll have nothing to do with."

Andy shook his head. "I can't imagine such craziness in this rough country with Indians running wild."

"We've pretty well cleared out the Indians," Tex said. "They know our range and they know we'll come after them if they cross the line. As for the coyote and rabbit hunting, I stay out of that part."

"Sounds like you have a good situation."

Tex glanced at Pete then back to Andy before he said, "We *all* do. But you have to understand that the people I work for look at people as belonging to . . . classes."

He'd just lost Andy. "What do you mean?"

"I mean that they think they are a whole lot better than we are."

"Like you think of yourself as being a lot better than Mexicans or Indians?"

Tex didn't appreciate Andy's example but finally nodded in grudging agreement.

"We get big year-end bonuses," Pete interrupted. "If we increase the size of the ranch, the English give us extra money at Christmas."

"Pete's right," Tex said. "Part of my job is to keep increasing the land holdings. That's why I was so rough on those Mexicans. They were trespassing on our new range."

Andy shook his head in amazement. "Clear back there to the Cimarron River?"

"Yep," Tex said. "Andy, you ever hear of Richard King?"

"No."

"He was born in New York of poor Irish immigrants. King ran away when he was thirteen and became a Gulf Coast and Mississippi River captain. In a few years he founded a steamship company and his ships still manage to smuggle cotton into the Confederacy through Mexico. Richard King is already a hero in Texas and some years ago he bought over fifteen thousand acres of the old Santa Gertrudis Spanish land grant."

Andy wondered what any of this had to do with the Monarch Ranch or the English royalty who owned it.

"The short of it is that Richard King has been gobbling up Texas like a turkey vulture standing on a dead deer. No one knows for sure how much land he now claims title to, but it is nearing a million acres."

Andy almost fell over. "A *million*?"

"Yep. And the Chamberlain family hate the Irish even worse than I hate comancheros. They have vowed the Monarch Ranch will become the largest spread on the American frontier and cannot abide the idea of it being smaller than the King Ranch, owned by the son of poor immigrant Irish."

"In school I learned about the great potato famine and the way the English mistreated and starved the Irish."

"Don't ever let on that you know that or have any sympathy for Irish," Pete warned. "The Chamberlains consider all Irish scum and trash."

"So that's it?" Andy asked, hardly able to believe what he'd just learned. "You work for these rich Englishmen who are willing to lose money because they have made it a point of pride to become bigger than Irishman Richard King's ranch?"

"That's it," Tex replied. "So we keep adding to our

range every year, even though we already have more land than we'll probably ever need for cattle, and I'll be damned if I'll see it ruined by sheep."

"But how do you keep getting bigger?"

"The Chamberlains have the money to buy lawyers and politicians in all the right places. They insist upon getting *legal* title to all this land, which until recently belonged to Mexico."

Andy was utterly fascinated. "So how big is the Monarch right now?"

"We're half a million deeded acres—but that's only a guess, because the Chamberlains never give me exact figures. They've made it real clear that my job is to raise cattle and horses and to keep squatters off any land in this part of the Cimarron River country until it is legally deeded to the Monarch."

Andy saw the way of things now. Saw how Tex, for all his toughness, was really just a pawn in the game that the English were playing.

"I'm not sure that I want to be a part of this," he said.

"Give it a try," Tex urged. "You'll make far better money than you could anywhere else and learn to cowboy. After a year you can change your mind and prospect and go broke, if you want."

"The food is the best and you can see we all ride good horses," Pete said. "Best damn job I ever hope to find."

"All right," Andy said, "if your cowboys don't prod me into a fight, I'll stick awhile."

"Fight or don't fight," Tex said. "But I got a feeling you can hold your own in a scrap with the best of them."

"We'll see," Andy told these men. "Like you said, life has been tough for as long as I can remember."

"If you'd have taken off walking back to the Cimarron River unarmed and in your bare feet," Pete said, "you'd have found out how bad things can really get."

"After the Comanche killed, scalped, and shot my friends to death, they got about as tough as they'll ever get," Andy told them as he walked along beside their horses.

"Another five miles and we're there," Tex said, pitching his canteen down to Andy. "I'd better go get the men back to work. See you at sundown!"

Pete stayed with Andy all the way in to the ranch. At the first look of it, the young cowboy saw the surprise on Andy's face and said, "We told you it was like a small English castle."

"Amazing," Andy said, starting across a mile of open rangeland toward the huge stone monolith and shaking his head.

"You'll like working for the Monarch Ranch," Pete promised. "You don't know how many good cowboys have tried to work for us but have been turned down by Tex."

"Then why did he hire me?"

"That's the thing I can't understand," Pete said. "But then, Tex just makes up his own mind about a man as quick as you can snap your fingers. He either likes or hates 'em and there isn't much ground in between. He took a liking to you the minute you jumped up and ran into the Cimarron River. I think he figured you had sand."

"What does that mean?"

"It means you have grit," Pete explained. "Just stay on the right side of Tex and do what you are told, and you'll find you never had such a good life. Tex is as fine a cowboy and ramrod as ever there was and he knows cattle and horses. You can learn plenty from Tex Marcum. But don't you dare get to sparkin' his daughter, Della."

"She pretty?"

Pete's face went soft and he nodded. "She's pretty all right. But big trouble. Just give her a wide berth and you'll do fine. She likes to flirt and tease the new cowboys until they go half-crazy. Those that can resist stick with the outfit; those that don't are bound for a whipping."

"Thanks for the warning." Andy looked up at the young cowboy. "Why are you doing it?"

"Can you keep a secret?" Pete asked.

"Sure."

"Swear on your father's grave?"

"Yeah!"

"Well," Pete said, "my father was a farmer, too. He had a few mules, but mostly he raised corn like your father. And by the time I was ten, I knew that foul-smelling end of a Missouri mule better than I knew the look of my own hand."

Andy had to grin. It was good to know that there was another farm boy in this outfit, and maybe a bunch more, if they were brave enough to admit it.

"You'll do fine!" Pete hollered over his shoulder as he put spurs to the sweaty ribs of his horse and galloped on to the Monarch Ranch headquarters.

Chapter
Sixteen

Andy stopped dead in his tracks the moment he saw the Monarch Ranch headquarters. Nestled in the center of a large, grassy valley fed by a sparkling stream, the main house was a sprawling two-story stone mansion prettier than any house Andy had ever seen, with vines growing up the walls and a handsome front porch shaded by immense trees. It was better than a picture and Andy stood admiring the place for several minutes before he noted what he was sure was Tex's house. It was tiny in comparison to the mansion, but still finer than any house in Brighton. Like the main house, this one was made of rock and had a porch. The other structures were all painted white and consisted of a bunkhouse, the cookshack, tack room, and blacksmith shop as well as a carriage house and an enormous barn, the only building painted a coppery red.

Nothing but money here, Andy said to himself as he headed down into the valley. The Chamberlains must be as rich as the king and queen of England.

Andy cut down to the stream and washed himself as best he could. He combed his long, shaggy hair with his fingers and then followed the cold, rippling stream into the ranch yard. Tex had his cowboys working again; some were in the shops while others were out in the paddocks repairing fences and exercising some of the finest-looking horses Andy had ever laid eyes upon. As he entered the ranch yard, a pair of brown-and-white-spotted hounds bolted out from under the porch to bark at him, tails wagging like crazy.

"Andy!"

He turned to see Pete emerge from a building then motion him to come on over. Andy bent for a moment and let the hounds get a good whiff before he continued across the yard.

"This is the bunkhouse," Pete said with obvious pride. "Come on in and I'll show you where to bed down."

The bunkhouse was pretty darn nice and neater than Andy would have supposed, which he guessed was because Tex wouldn't stand for sloppiness. It was made of split logs like a cabin, but the inside walls and ceiling were plastered white. There were big railroad spikes in the center posts where men hung their coats and things and a long row of real beds instead of the crude bunks he'd expected. Between each set of beds were two sets of cabinets, and each of them had little doors with brass knobs. The place was so neat it made a fella almost expect there to be lace curtains on the windows.

"Pretty nice, huh?" Pete said, indicating to Andy which bed he'd been assigned.

"Better'n I ever had at home."

"Me, too," Pete said, looking around proudly. "Tex was an officer in the war with Mexico. He insists that this place is kept clean, swept and dusted every Sunday morning before the men can take their leisure. He inspects it, and if it ain't clean, we don't get the day off until he's satisfied."

Andy shook his head. "It sure isn't what I expected."

"Nothin' on the Monarch Ranch is like anything you'd expect," Pete replied. "The thing of it is, the English often don't bother to let Tex know when they're arriving. And when they do, they march around with their big noses up in the air and everything had better be in order or Tex catches hell. And if *Tex* catches hell, you better believe life is going to be even worse for us cowboys."

"I'll keep my stuff in the cabinet and everything neat and clean," Andy promised. "My ma raised me right."

"Good to hear that, because you sure look rough now. In addition to the new clothes you'll be receiving—and they'll come out of your first month's wages—you need a haircut and a shave."

"Why?"

Pete shrugged. "I reckon Tex don't think it makes much sense for the place to be all slicked up for royalty and the ranch hands to look poorly."

"I see."

"He allows a man to wear a mustache or beard, but you had best keep it short and trimmed."

"How am I going to do that?"

Pete grinned. "It just so happens that I am one of the best barbers in the neighborhood and I'll do your hair and give you a shave for six bits. It's Saturday night and Tex likes to have the new man for dinner at the main house."

"I'd sure rather eat with you and the others."

"You'll do what you're told, Andy," Pete warned.

"Well, dammit, I'm broke, so I can't pay for a shave and haircut right now. I would like a bath, though."

"You'll have both and we'll settle up on payday," Pete said, opening the cabinet above Andy's bed and dragging out a comb, razor, scissors, and shaving cup. "We'll sit on the back steps and I'll be finished in no time. Then you need to take a bath and try on your new duds."

"Jeez," Andy complained, "what sort of cowboy am I supposed to be?"

"Oh, don't worry," Pete assured him, "as low man on the payroll, you'll get more than your share of rough, dirty work. But for this one night, you get cleaned up and go to the big house to dine like a gentlemen. Enjoy it, Andy! It's the last time you'll ever set foot in either one of the stone houses."

An hour later, with a pretty good back-step haircut, shave, and smelling of strong soap from his bath, Andy tried on his new clothes. They were too short at the ankles and wrists and baggy at the waist, but they were new and felt good.

"There's a mirror over there on the side of the out-house," Pete said. "Take a gander at yourself."

Andy was shocked by his appearance. He looked respectable and almost human again, although leaner in the face than he'd been back on the farm. "Pete, am I going to get a cowboy hat?"

"Yep, but not today. Cowboys aren't allowed to wear hats inside the mansion."

"Why not?"

"That's the rules."

By now the sun was dipping into the western horizon and the day's work was done. Several of the other cowboys stuck their heads out the back door of the bunkhouse and grinned or even whistled at Andy, which made him turn red with embarrassment.

"Pay 'em no mind," Pete said. "Any one of them would give a week's pay to have supper in the mansion."

"Is Della a good cook?"

"Naw! She don't cook. They got an old lady that cooks and keeps the place up inside. Her name is Nettie and she's a real corker, but you hardly ever see her beyond the garden. Nettie is also supposed to teach Della how to cook, sew, and all that, but I don't think she learns much."

"Then what does Della do?"

"She goes off to a boarding school in the fall and is gone until spring. She's here for the summers and likes to ride horses and go hunting. Or sometimes she'll hang around the barn or the shops and visit. Tex don't like that much, though. He's real touchy about her and he'll whip a cowboy near to death if he gets fresh."

"What is Della going to do with herself?"

"You mean when she's grown up?"

"That's right."

"How should I know? I expect her to marry someone important. Maybe even one of the Chamberlains, although she's as much out of her class with them as we are with her."

Andy shook his head. "I never imagined I'd be working for a place like this and getting all spiffed up for a dinner party my first day on the job."

"Don't let it go to your head," Pete warned. "After this evening you'll go from prince to toad. Tomorrow morning, you can bet that Tex will have you digging postholes or some other miserable job. And that might be all you'll do for a month or two before he'll even allow you near a horse or a cow."

No matter, Andy thought. For thirty dollars a month, I can stick awhile and save my money, then light out for Santa Fe. He heard the clang of an iron triangle and heard the cowboys go out for supper.

"It's time to eat," Pete said, "and I'll be going to get my share."

"What am I supposed to do?"

"Walk right up to the big house and knock on the door. You'll be invited inside. But remember to mind your best manners. Don't scratch in the wrong places or slop your food nor belch nor pass a foul wind."

"Of course not!" Andy snapped. "I was raised proper!"

Five minutes later he was invited into the mansion, and glory be, but it was something to behold! Marble floors, beautiful, ornately carved furniture, a grandfather clock with a gold pendulum bigger than a dinner plate, and some paintings that Andy would have liked the time to study and admire.

"I'm Nettie, but you'll call me Miss Wilson," said the short, sixtyish, but still attractive woman as she smoothed her apron and peered through spectacles at Andy to make sure he passed muster.

"Yes, ma'am."

"Are your hands washed?"

"Yes, ma'am!"

"Then come into the dining room and meet your hosts. Dinner is about to be served. And for heaven's sake, don't *stare* at Miss Della!"

"Of course not, Miss Wilson. Why . . ."

But the woman was already marching into the dining room, where the biggest table Andy had ever seen stood empty except at one end, where Tex and Della awaited.

"Andrew Parmentier," Tex said without rising from his seat. "This is my daughter, Miss Della Louise Marcum."

Dear Lord but she was pretty! A heart-shaped face, big green eyes, and lips as red and puckered as springtime roses. Andy had no idea how old Della was, but she was old enough to turn the head of any man. She smiled and eyed him so boldly that Andy momentarily forgot to breathe and nearly fainted.

"Mr. Parmentier," Della said, extending her hand, "my father told me that you come to us under rather remarkable circumstances."

"I was almost scalped by Comanche," Andy managed to say. He gulped and added, "But I got lucky and was saved by some Mexican shepherds."

"How fascinating."

Since she thought it was fascinating, Andy was prepared to elaborate, but Tex said, "Be seated, Andy, and don't you be telling Della about what happened between us and the Mex out there by the Cimarron River. No need for a young lady to hear that sort of thing."

"No, sir."

"Nettie, bring on the food!"

The rest of that evening was a blur for Andy. Dazed, trying hard not to embarrass himself or his mother, who had taught him the rudiments of good manners, he concentrated so hard on behaving properly that he forgot everything that was said, although he did recall that they had some mighty tasty things for supper and apple pie for dessert.

"Andy," Tex said, lighting a cigarette and rising from his chair, "it's been real enjoyable having your company."

"Yes," Della was saying, "it has been. Perhaps we can do this again after you—"

"Now, Della, you know the rules. Once to dinner for every man, twice for none."

Tex came around and almost shoved Andy toward the front door, saying, "You'll be digging fence posts for the first month or two. Tough work. Evenings, you can learn a few things just by hanging around the cowboys."

"When can I ride a cow horse?"

"Soon as the fence repairing is finished. If you last through that, you'll get your chance. In the meantime ask Pete to show you how to toss a rope. Practice on a fence post or a bucket. But mostly, you'll want to watch and listen and that's about all you'll have the strength to do in the evenings."

Andy tried to conceal his disappointment. Tex had hired him to learn cowboying, but he was going to be a fence fixer and that was hard and boring work. "Yes, sir."

For the next three weeks Andy worked pretty much out in the paddocks from sunup until sundown, digging up and replacing rotted fence posts. Sometimes they lifted up easy, but most times he had to pound, pry, and bust his gut to get the old posts out and the new ones in. The earth was hard and rocky. There were whole days when the best that Andy could do was to replace four or five and then collapse on his bed after supper and fall asleep while the other cowboys talked about women, weather, cattle, and horses.

"Some cowboying," he muttered to himself as he attacked the heavy posts and the unyielding ground each morning.

He worked awful hard. So hard that one evening Pete said, "Everyone is saying you can do the work of nearly two men. Maybe you ought to ease up, Andy."

"The harder I work the sooner the fence repairs will be done and I can start cowboying."

"Well," Pete said, "you're putting some of the other men to shame that have already worked on that posthole digging and fixin'."

Andy was pleased. "That just goes to prove that *farm* boys really know how to work. Were the other hands city boys?"

"Some of 'em."

After supper, one of the most recent posthole diggers and employees, a big, loud fellow named Luke Page, picked a fight with Andy.

"You're just a gawdamn show-off is what you are!" he snarled. "Are you trying to make me look bad?"

Andy knew what was coming. He'd been warned by Pete about Luke and knew he was about to face his second test at the Monarch Ranch.

"Luke is strong as a mule and can kick like one. Even worse, he has a rock jaw," Pete had warned. "Andy, if he gets you down, you're in big trouble, but Luke knows better than to break you up so you can't work. If he does that, Tex will skin him alive."

"Tex won't have to interfere," Andy had answered with more confidence than he felt right now.

"I don't like the looks of you," Luke was saying as he

poked Andy in the chest with his thick forefinger hard enough to rock him back on his boot heels. "You're way too pretty. You need some scars and a broke nose. Yeah, kid, that's what you need. And you'll never make a cowboy, 'cause you're a stinking Mexican sheep lover!"

Andy had learned early on that the only way to silence a bully was to hit him first and where it hurt the most. And so, without warning, he ripped a short uppercut to Luke's crotch that raised the Monarch cowboy to his tiptoes. Then he threw a vicious left cross that connected just below Luke's ear. The bully's eyes rolled up in his head and Andy chopped him on the other side of the head as he was falling. Luke hit the floor so hard his head rattled the windows.

The whole thing hadn't taken more than two, maybe three seconds and now the cowboys were staring open-mouthed at Andy, who had his blood up and was ready for more.

"Anyone else have something to say about me and sheep?" he challenged.

One after the next they shook their heads and turned back to their bunks until only Pete remained. "Damn, Andy!" he whispered, eyes frogging back and forth between his tall young friend and Luke Page, still quivering on the wooden floor. "You didn't learn to fight like *that* on no corn farm!"

Andy took Pete's arm and led him out the back door and they moseyed out to the main corral. "My father was a bare-knuckles fighter in his youth. He came from Boston and his father was known to be the toughest man in the Irish section of town. So I inherited some natural talent and good teaching. Mostly, though, the winner is almost always the man who hits first and hardest."

"Luke probably won't be able to walk for a couple of days," Pete fretted aloud. "You might have fixed him permanent with that first punch."

Andy shrugged. "That would be a lasting favor to the painted women. Besides, a mean bully like him doesn't deserve to ever father a child."

Two days later Luke was able to go back to work . . . replacing rotted fence posts. For his part, Andy was promoted to grooming horses and learning how to repair tack. He was also given a grass rope and lessons from the best roper on the payroll, Hank Montgomery. Hank spent a good deal of time teaching Andy how to throw an overhead toss, which, when executed correctly, passed over other horses to catch the particular animal that a cowboy chose to ride that morning. The *mangana* was an underhanded throw that was even more difficult and used to catch the forefeet of a stubborn, running horse and flip it hard.

"You can't ride one until you learn to rope your own every morning," Hank told him. "Now watch me most of all and don't take any advice from Pete, 'cause he's the worst roper in the whole outfit."

It was almost five weeks to the day that Andy finally snagged his morning horse, but it was due more to luck than skill and he accidentally dropped his loop over the worst bucker in the corral, a big buckskin that the cowboys called Spud.

"What am I supposed to do now?" Andy asked, crushed by this stroke of ill fortune.

"You can either let go of your rope and look like a scared greenhorn, or reel Spud in to saddle and ride."

"To hell with Spud," Andy swore. "I've seen him unload good cowboys nearly every morning. And besides, everyone on the payroll already knows I'm a greenhorn."

"Yeah, but if you toss that rope away, you and Luke are going to get real well-acquainted digging post holes."

Andy got the message. "All right," he grated. "Spud, why don't you show me a little mercy and I'll figure out some way to repay you."

But Spud was not merciful, and although he allowed himself to be saddled and bridled, the moment that Andy climbed on board, the powerful buckskin started bucking so hard that Andy did a double somersault over his head and almost broke his back on the top fence rail.

"He'll probably wear down in an hour or two," Hank said hopefully.

"An *hour or two*," Andy moaned, pressing both hands against the small of his back and noticing that Tex and Della were coming across the ranch yard to join an already growing crowd of grinning spectators.

"Look good for the young lady," Hank said under his breath in a mocking tone, "not to mention your boss."

For the next couple of hours Andy looked anything but good. Spud pitched him every and any way he pleased, but Andy got mad and kept coming back for more. Bloodied and battered, he had to be helped up into the saddle by Hank *and* Pete and finally by Hank, Pete, and a couple of other cowboys that were trying to give him advice on how to ride the buckskin bucker to a standstill.

In the end, Andy *did* ride Spud, but he recalled no more of it than he had of that special dinner in the Chamberlain mansion. He thought he saw Tex grin, and had Della really shouted a gusty and unladylike "Yahoo cowboy"?

Andy didn't know, but the other cowboys said she did, so he guessed that she might have gotten carried away in all the excitement.

The next morning was torture to get out of bed, but Andy did it and danged if he didn't lasso Pokey Joe, one of the outfit's gentlest geldings. When a half-bent-over and pale Andy saddled and rode Pokey Joe, there were grins aplenty from the cowboys and Della.

"When can I take him out on the range?" Andy asked through clenched teeth, because he was so stove up and achy.

"Go for a long ride today," Hank told him. "Ride on

past Luke Page and give him a snort, then head upstream a few miles."

"To do what?"

"Oh, I don't know that it matters. Just look things over. I'll tell the boss you are checking on cattle."

"Why?"

"Andy, if I were you, I'd ride awhile then tie Pokey Joe to a tree and lay in that cold stream for an hour or two before I took a snooze in the sun."

"But, Hank, won't I get caught?"

"Naw! Anyone who looks as sorry as you look deserves the afternoon off."

Andy didn't argue. He even prodded Pokey Joe into an easy gallop, although it nearly killed him. His big reward was seeing Luke's sweating, sorry face as he sailed by the latest posthole and forced a big, triumphant grin. Luke bawled out something that Andy really didn't want to hear.

After they were out of sight of the ranch, Andy reined Pokey Joe into a slow walk and headed for the stream and the shade of big old cottonwood trees. He'd forgotten to bring hobbles, but the grass was good and Andy figured Pokey Joe wasn't any more interested in going to work than he was.

All in all, it was going to be one mighty fine day. Andy did partially undress and soak in the cold stream and then he took a long snooze in the sun. He might have slept the whole day through except that Della awakened him by using a blade of grass to tickle the bottoms of his bare feet.

He awoke with a start to her giggling. "What are *you* doing out here?"

"I ride this way at least a couple of times a week. What are you doing *sleeping* on the job?"

Andy started to say that it was Hank's idea but caught himself in time and replied, "I got tired and rested my eyes for a few minutes."

"Why, Andy, you most certainly did not! You went swimming and then you took a long nap."

"So what?"

Della glared at him. "I'm not sure that you're anything near as nice as I thought."

"I'm probably not," Andy told her. "And anyway, I was warned loud and clear that your father won't tolerate you being around the cowboys."

"Yes," she said mischievously, "but Spud proved that you're *not* a cowboy."

He wouldn't give her the satisfaction of his anger. "That's true."

Della looked disappointed and changed the subject. "I heard that you whipped Luke Page pretty bad one evening in the bunkhouse."

Andy didn't say anything.

"Luke is mean. He's beaten up several of the hands. I don't know why my father even keeps him on the payroll."

"Maybe now that he's had a taste of his own medicine he's a changed man."

"I hope so. But my father says that you like Mexicans."

"That's right. And I especially appreciate them when they save my life."

"I don't like them at all."

"Why?" he asked.

"They're dirty and lazy." Her voice went flat and sharp. "They lie, cheat, and steal."

"No more or less than anyone else." Suddenly Andy wasn't enjoying their conversation anymore. He reached for his shirt and put it on in a hurry, then started to button it up the front. He was so sore that he could not help wincing with pain.

"Here," she said, "let me help you."

"I can do it."

"Yes, but I can do it better."

Up close Della was even prettier than she was at a distance. She smelled real nice, too. Like lilacs. Andy could hardly get away from her fast enough.

"I'll ride back with you," Della decided.

"I'd rather you didn't."

"Why, because of my father?"

"That's right."

"He really likes you, Andy. First for whipping the bunkhouse bully, then for sticking it out to the end with Spud. He says you got the makings of a good cowboy and that is about the highest compliment he'll ever give to a man."

"I'm grateful to hear that," Andy said, meaning it. "Your father is to be respected and admired."

"I think so," Della replied. "But then the English arrive and he starts toadying up to them, saying 'yes, sir' this and 'yes, sir' that."

Andy had to struggle into his saddle. "Della, have you ever wondered why your father puts up with the Chamberlains and their snobbish friends?"

She frowned. "Because he gets paid an awful lot of money."

Andy shook his head. "The money is nice, but I'll bet he's putting up with them on account of you."

"Me?" Della's green eyes widened with genuine surprise.

"That's right. He's willing to do it so that he can afford to send you to that boarding school."

"Who told you about that?"

"Pete. But it sure isn't any secret."

"No," she had to admit, "it isn't. And it isn't my idea to attend a boarding school. It's father's."

"Well," Andy said, "Tex wants the best for you."

"He wants me to marry a Chamberlain, but I'm not good enough for them. Their young men would like to take me up in the hayloft and mess around, but . . . I won't."

Andy felt his cheeks warm with embarrassment. He guessed they had each said more than they should have, so he reined Pokey Joe around and started back to headquarters.

"Andy Parmentier," Della said, riding up to his side and studying him thoughtfully, "you are different."

If she knew how many men I've killed, she'd understand why, he thought.

"Della, don't go analyzing me. And I'd prefer you keep your distance."

His words stung and Andy saw the color rise in her cheeks. Della had a quirt tied around her waist and she tried to lash Andy across the side of his face, but he grabbed it and almost tore her out of the saddle.

"Dammit, Andrew Parmentier!" she cried. "You're . . . you're awful and I hate you!"

"Better *you* hate me than your father!" he yelled as she galloped away.

Andy watched Della disappear over a hill, wondering if he'd done the right thing. He wasn't sure why, but he had the feeling that girl could be almost as tough, ruthless, and unforgiving as her Mexican-hating father.

Chapter

Seventeen

A ndy stood poised in the center of the circular pole corral with a lariat twirling overhead as a big roan gelding charged around and around him. The dust was choking but Andy hardly noticed as he concentrated on the bronc, which was smart enough to know it was being singled out for another hard bucking session. Suddenly the rope in Andy's fist snaked out in a perfect figure eight, with each loop catching a foreleg. Andy leaned back and braced himself as the powerful gelding hit the end of his lariat and somersaulted, crashing hard. The animal was dazed, and with the wind knocked out of its lungs, Andy had it bridled before its head cleared.

"Lester," he shouted through the boiling dust, "bring that saddle and cinch it down hard and fast!"

The greenhorn sprinted forward and had his saddle on the gelding's back and cinched in seconds. Andy looked at the excited kid and said, "Mount up and ride like I showed you yesterday!"

The kid didn't lack for courage. He was tall and gangly

but game and he hopped into the saddle, planted his boots in the stirrups, and yelled, "Yahoo!"

Andy released the roan's ear. The wild horse shook its head to clear the cobwebs and commenced bucking. It was a pile driver and landed stiff-legged, causing Lester's head to snap back and forth like a bullwhip. Six jumps later the roan hurled Lester to the earth, knocking him out cold.

"Ah hell," Andy swore, striding across the corral, grabbing the unconscious kid, and dragging him to safety. He turned and ran after the still-plunging, bucking roan, then vaulted into the saddle, burying his spurs into the gelding's ribs. Andy tore off his Stetson and began dusting the animal's foam-flecked haunches with his hat and rode the horse to a standstill. Head down, quivering and cowed, the bronc wanted no more punishment. Andy replaced his hat on his head and trotted the whipped horse over to the gate shouting, "Pete, let me out!"

Pete jumped for the gate and swung it open.

"Yahhhh!" Andy shouted, spurring the bronc into a hard run. They shot across the ranch yard and the fields. Andy sent the roan flying across the stream and up the valley as if its tail were on fire. He made the horse gallop until it was covered with sweat and puffing like a steam engine.

"All right," he said, finally slowing the exhausted animal to a staggering walk. "I'll ease up on you for now, but if you broke Lester's neck, I'll run you into the ground tomorrow."

Andy forced the roan to trot on back to the Monarch Ranch, where he saw Tex and his cowboys still huddled around Lester. Andy spurred the roan over to them and said, "How is he?"

"He'll live," Tex answered. "I'm not too sure you should have allowed him on such a big, rank horse."

"How else will the kid learn?"

Tex frowned. "I just don't see any point in getting a new hand all busted up. That's all I'm saying, Andy."

"Eight years ago you sure enjoyed Spud pounding me into the ground."

Tex had to smile at the memory. "You were game."

"And so is this kid. Lester just needs to land on his south side instead of his north."

"Andy, get down and come join me at the house. The rest of you cowboys get back to work."

"What about Lester?" Hank asked.

"Carry him over to the bunkhouse and he can sleep awhile. Andy, what do you think about Pete riding that bronc around for another hour or so?"

Andy winked at his old friend, one of the few left from his greenhorn days on the Monarch. "Sure. I think Pete can handle the roan now that I've taken off his rough edges."

Pete grinned and pretended to yawn, saying, "Thanks, Andy, I could use a long afternoon nap in the saddle."

Andy followed Tex up to the foreman's porch, where they eased into cane rocking chairs. It was a fine spring afternoon and the valley was greening fast. There wasn't a cloud in the sky and the air was filled with butterflies that reminded Andy of his best childhood days.

Tex said, "Watching that tall greenhorn get bucked off did remind me of the day you bucked Spud out and then rode Pokey Joe up the valley. I remember you yelling something out to Luke Page, who I'd put on the posthole-digging job."

"Luke was sure mad that day."

"Yeah, but he was afraid of you," Tex said, "and you gave him a long overdue lesson in humility that evening in the bunkhouse when you busted his face and his pride."

"I heard that Luke was knifed to death just a month ago in an Abilene saloon," Andy said quietly.

"That doesn't surprise me," Tex replied. "We all knew that someone would kill him sooner or later. Once a bully always a bully. You never had to whip another man on my payroll and you just sort of took control of our bunkhouse."

"Naw," Andy said, "I just kind of let it be known that I wouldn't stand for any more bullying of greenhorns."

"You made my job easier and have for quite some time."

Andy blushed at the unexpected compliment from a man he'd come to think of almost like a father.

"I've got some more Hereford bulls coming in from England," Tex said, rolling a cigarette and studying his handiwork for a moment before striking a match and enjoying his smoke. "I'm going to meet them at the railhead next month. We need to keep upgrading the quality of Monarch cattle."

"We've already introduced eight Hereford bulls and gotten some handsome crossbred offspring."

"That's what I mean," Tex said. "That Hereford blood is going to make Monarch beef superior to anything on the market. Right now the Longhorn is still king, but that will change. It might take a decade or two, but the time will come when cattle buyers will be demanding a better grade of beef. When that times does arrive, we'll have it for them . . . and get a premium price."

"What about the Angus or some of those other English beef breeds we're starting to hear about?" Andy asked.

"I've talked to the Chamberlains and they've asked me to come to England and shop around for more blooded bulls of exceptional quality. They don't know a cow from a crawdad and I sure haven't been all that impressed with the ones they've sent so far, even though they must have cost a small fortune."

"I think one of the Englishmen told me the Herefords they sent over here averaged about two thousand dollars apiece," Andy said. "Add on the shipping charges and the price probably doubles."

"No doubt," Tex agreed. "Those bulls are worth a fortune and I can't tell you how it worries me that they're going to get shot, or sick or stolen. The Chamberlains want to see each one of them every time they arrive."

"I sure don't think they are that all-fired special."

"Me neither," Tex admitted. "For one thing, they're just real small. We may have calving problems with the next generation or two of crossbreeds. But that aside, I'm going to try and find the best cattle that I can in England and the rest of Europe. I might buy some Angus or shorthorn bulls, although I'm worried about them being able to forage well enough in this tough, dry country."

"That could be a problem," Andy agreed. "But England! I'll bet you are looking forward to that trip."

"I am," Tex admitted. "I've wanted to see England and Europe after all these years of catering to the English and hearing their brag. I'm hoping I'll be disappointed and continue to believe that this Cimarron country is the best ranch land in the world."

"I expect that to be the case," Andy said, still not sure where this conversation was leading. "Will you see Della and her family up in Kansas City?"

"Yes. I've got another grandchild I haven't yet seen."

Tex turned and looked straight into Andy's eyes. "Do you know what they named him?"

"Haven't a clue."

"Andrew."

Andy's jaw dropped.

"Della named that boy after *you*."

Andy popped out of his rocking chair wagging his head. "Oh no! Not me, Tex."

"Sit down and don't argue."

Andy took a deep breath and forced himself back into

the rocking chair. On the one hand he felt flattered, but, on the other hand, threatened, and he was confused about Tex's true feelings.

"Take it easy, Andy. I know that Della was smitten with you for a long time before she finally got married. And I know you never took advantage of her innocence. That's another reason you became my favorite hand. That and the fact that you've become the best cowboy on my payroll."

Andy was getting uncomfortable. It just was not Tex's style to give a man so many compliments. He forced a laugh. "Tex, if you keep talking like this, I'm going to get so swelled-headed I'll have to buy a new hat."

"Even though you're already getting top cowboy wages, I'm going to give you a twenty-dollar-a-month raise and the title of assistant foreman."

"Now wait a minute," Andy protested. "There's Pete and a couple of the others who hired on with Monarch long before I did. Putting me over them isn't going to sit too well with that bunch."

"That's the price you have to pay for a title," Tex said without a hint of sympathy.

"Why are you doing this?"

"Because Pete and those other cowboys that were here before you just don't have the leadership it takes to get the tough ranching jobs done and keeping out the squatters who'd like to settle on this range. If they were given the job, I'd fire them within a month. But I'll never have to fire you."

"I hope not."

"I won't," Tex declared. "You're loyal, tough, and responsible. You'd make a good rancher."

"You mean starting my own outfit?"

"That's right. And, as I explained to the Chamberlains, if I don't give you some authority and a title, you'll be leaving the Monarch to do that soon, and we don't need your kind of competition."

Andy was surprised by this insight because he actually had been toying with the idea of starting his own outfit. He'd saved a good deal of money over the years and he could make a go of it with all the knowledge and skills he'd learned cowboying under Tex Marcum. When you learned from the best you became the best, or so Andy hoped.

"I hit it right, didn't I?" Tex said.

"I had been thinking about some ranch land I could get cheap in southern Colorado."

"Don't think about it any longer."

"Tex, I'll stick with the Monarch for at least a couple more years."

"You could retire off this ranch. The Chamberlains know who you are and they know your abilities. I didn't have to talk very hard to get you a promotion."

"Thanks," Andy said, meaning it.

Tex was quiet for several moments, then said, "Now and then even I think about doing something completely different. I'm nearly forty."

"That's not old."

"It is in this business. But the opportunity to finally visit Europe has given me new life. I need you here to handle things in my absence. I want to cross the ocean and not be worrying that the ranch is going to hell."

"I'll see that it doesn't," Andy promised.

"I know that," Tex said. "Do you want me to make the announcement to the crew, or would you prefer to make it yourself?"

"I'd better do it," Andy said, pushing out of his rocker.

"By the way," Tex said, "there'll be some workmen arriving next week."

"What kind?"

"Carpenters. I convinced the Chamberlains that their assistant foreman needed his own furnished house."

"Aw, now wait a minute, Tex! I enjoy living in the bunkhouse."

"Sorry," Tex told him. "But I'm sure I don't have to explain that you can't live with the men that are taking your orders. It just doesn't work. You'll have to distance yourself from Pete and the others. I know you don't want to, but that's an important part of the new job."

Suddenly, becoming assistant foreman for the Monarch Ranch seemed a whole lot less appealing to Andy. But he'd made an agreement and he'd keep it, at least for a couple more years. Tex needed him.

"Two years," Andy promised. "I'll give it that long. But after that, I'll probably be striking off on my own."

"Fair enough," Tex said. "I can't blame you. If the Englishmen's money wasn't so good, I'd do it myself. Might get out of ranching and become a cattle buyer. They make pretty good money and I could work out of Kansas City and see Della and my grand-kids more often."

"How many acres does the Monarch own?"

"Nearly eight hundred thousand . . . and counting. We just have to keep scaring and driving off the gawdamn squatters."

"But we don't have a legal right to do that," Andy said quietly. "That is all open range."

"Not for long," Tex said. "The Monarch Ranch lawyers are getting title to it as fast as the English money rolls in. We're buying it for practically nothing, but someday it'll be worth a hell of a lot of money. I've often thought the Chamberlains might lose a fortune over the years in cattle and ranch improvements, but they'll earn it all back and then some on land appreciation."

"I see. Will they *ever* have enough land on the Cimarron?"

"Nope."

"That's what I thought," Andy said, mind leaping ahead to the difficult task he had this evening of telling the other cowboys that he was now assistant foreman and that they'd be taking his orders when Tex went cattle shopping in Europe.

Pete and the others had accepted Andy's promotion without rancor or envy. For a month afterward, however, they'd hazed him unmercifully, until his own house was finished and he'd moved in permanent. Fall roundup went exceptionally well and the Monarch cattle had never looked better. Tex had made two short trail drives to eastern Kansas to deliver cattle at the riotous cow-town railheads, and Andy figured that it wouldn't be long before the Chamberlain family finally started making an honest profit.

And why shouldn't they? The cattle trade was booming and the new crossbreeds were beginning to generate a lot of interest all the way back to the Chicago stockyards. Not that the Monarch was the only big outfit experimenting with European breeds, but the increasing numbers of their crossbred cattle were as good as any being shipped to market.

The Civil War had finally ground to a bloody victory for the North, President Lincoln had been assassinated, and Andy had begun to write a letter home every Christmas and receive one each February in return.

The news gave him a lot of comfort. It reinforced his conviction that he had done the right thing in killing that bastard Eldridge Loomis. His mother had never remarried but sounded happy and content with town life. Unfortunately, little brother Gilbert had turned into the hellion that Andy had always expected and had nearly burned down the schoolhouse last winter while playing with matches. His sister, Wilma, was already attracting boys, so Andy guessed she wasn't too homely anymore.

Andy missed Brighton Township and often wondered if Ginny had ended up marrying Emory Bayer. Emory really hadn't been such a bad fellow and his family did have lots of money, so Ginny would probably never have to worry about finances. Andy knew that if they'd married, he'd have made Ginny's life miserable by dragging her into the Western frontier. Back then, he'd been far too footloose and restless. Sort of like poor Gizzard, God rest his whiskey-sotted soul.

Two days later the weather turned sour. A norther came in and the temperature plunged. "It's going to be a long, cold winter," Hank predicted that night as the cowboys ate their supper.

"Hope that new shipment of English can stand the snow and cold," Pete added grimly. "They got lucky last winter. But this one is acting like it could be a lot worse."

"Amen," Hank and Lester said together.

But the storm didn't pack much of a wallop and the weather cleared in a few days, to everyone's relief—although the air was cold. Andy was happy enough in his own house and was starting to adapt to the privacy. Back in Brighton he'd never even had his own bedroom and now he had three whole rooms all to himself.

"Andy?"

He opened the door to see Tex shivering in the darkness. "Come on inside and warm up."

Tex stomped over to Andy's new potbelly stove and began to rub his hands together briskly. "I've got a problem that needs fixing."

"What's that?"

"We've got squatters burrowing in up near the head-waters of the Cimarron."

Andy took a deep breath because he knew what was coming next. Despite how much he admired and liked Tex, this was an area where they would never reach agreement and one that had caused friction right from the start.

"How many?"

"Maybe a family, but probably just one man. I dunno," Tex answered. "But this fella is pretty cagey, because he built a dugout into the side of a hill. He found a seep down in the draw with enough water so that he doesn't have to go over to the river very often. There's no corrals or anything. Just a damn dirty dug that's almost impossible to find."

"Who spotted him?"

Tex drew the makings for a cigarette out of his shirt pocket. "A drifter that passed through while you were out working cattle this morning. He was looking for a job, but I couldn't help him."

"What did he say?"

"He was hungry, so we fed him and then sent him packing. I didn't like his rough looks."

Tex carefully rolled his cigarette, avoiding Andy's eyes. "The drifter told me that he was coming over from Raton and just happened to see a thin trail of chimney smoke. Thinking maybe he could get something to eat, he went to investigate but was turned back by a warning shot from inside the dugout. He never saw who fired. He was angry and wanted us to get even for him. I promised we would."

Andy digested this information, then asked, "Where, exactly, is this dugout?"

"Right near the headwaters of the Cimarron."

"That's a long, long ways from here, Tex."

"We want the whole damn river!" Tex grated. "And those are my orders from the Chamberlains."

Andy reached for the pot of coffee he had made that morning. "Want some?"

"No. I want you to take four or five of the boys and ride over there and run that gawdamn squatter off."

"Sounds like he's dug in pretty good and means business."

"And we don't?"

Tex lit his cigarette from the stove and studied Andy closely. "I've got to go to Cimarron City on business in the morning. When I return tomorrow evening, I expect you to tell me that you ran whoever was in that lean-to off our range."

Andy wanted to tell Tex that it *wasn't* their range. In fact, it was *miles* from their deeded land. However, he held his tongue, knowing that there wasn't anything he could say to make Tex listen to reason.

"Go pack your guns and rifles," Tex ordered. "One way or the other, move that squatter."

"I don't want to shoot him."

"Then scare him!" Tex shouted. "Put the fear of God in him so he tells others that the Monarch Ranch won't abide anyone on the Cimarron!"

"Yes, sir." Andy was furious and it must have shown, because Tex grabbed his arm in a viselike grip. "Andy, when I promoted you, I did it believing you'd always carry out my orders without question. Was I wrong?"

"No, sir. They'll be gone tomorrow," Andy promised, adding wood to his stove.

"I know they will," Tex said as he headed back to his own house.

That night, Andy sat up late warming himself by the stove. He had a bottle of rye whiskey and he drank more of it than he should have, thinking about how much he hated running off poor nesters and squatters from a land that barely offered them a chance to eke out a livelihood. Even more, he detested the Englishmen and their high-and-mighty ways. How dare they lay claim to American lands so very far removed from their birthrights.

Year after year and with mounting anger, Andy had

heard them talk about squatters in the same tone of derision and contempt that Tex and some of the other cowboys used. Hell, his own father had homesteaded that Indiana farm and struggled hard trying to make a living.

"The rich get richer and the poor get poorer," he said to himself as he drank his whiskey.

Finally, Andy went to bed and slept in past daybreak, which made Tex angry again and brought him back into Andy's house. "It's a long ride, kid. I suggest you skip breakfast, saddle your horse, and get going!"

"Yes, sir," Andy replied, deciding that he might even quit the Monarch when he returned. That way Tex and the Englishmen could do their own damn dirty work.

Chapter
Eighteen

It was late in the afternoon and the weather was turning raw again with the threat of snow. Andy was freezing and anxious to turn back to headquarters when they finally spotted the dugout hidden down in a lonesome draw about a half mile north of the Cimarron River.

"What do you think?" Pete asked as they studied it from a distance and tried to keep warm.

"I think whoever was here has gone."

"We probably ought to make sure," a cowboy named Ernie suggested as he wiped his runny nose on the back of his coat sleeve. "Tex is going to want us to be sure."

"He's right," Pete agreed.

Andy could feel them waiting for his orders to ride on down and investigate. What was he going to do now?

"Listen, boys," he hedged, "if there's someone hiding in there with a rifle, he could shoot us all out of the saddle. There's not even a rock to hide behind in that draw. We'd be riding into a death trap."

"So what do we do?"

"I'll go on in alone," Andy told them. "Keep me covered."

"Are you sure?" Pete asked.

"Yeah," Andy replied, not sure at all.

He checked Miguel Diaz's matched pistols, hoping like hell he didn't have to use them in the next few minutes.

"I'll go in with you," Pete offered.

"Thanks for the offer, but this kind of thing is why I get paid extra."

"We'll cover you real good," Ernie promised, dismounting to yank his rifle out of its scabbard.

Andy was mounted on his favorite horse, a sorrel with four white stockings. He'd hunted antelope off the gelding before and knew that it would not raise a ruckus if he suddenly had to go for his guns and the bullets started to fly.

"You be real careful!" Pete shouted into the swirling wind and first flakes of snow.

"Don't worry, I will!"

Andy was sweating underneath his heavy sheepskin-lined coat and it wasn't because he was too warm. The length of the draw gave him the opportunity to study the dugout, but there was no sign of life and he began to convince himself that the place was abandoned. Most likely, whoever had been there had been scared off by the drifter. At least that was Andy's fervent hope. If he was wrong and there was an outlaw hiding inside, he was probably a dead man.

"Hello in there!" Andy called, reining the sorrel in about forty feet from the dugout and squinting to peer into the gloomy interior.

No answer. No sound. No movement.

Drawing his gun, Andy dismounted and stood behind his sorrel for a moment. If someone plugged his favorite cow horse, there'd be hell to pay. But the only movement Andy saw was that of a ragged tarp that flapped in front of the dugout's entrance. It had been pegged over the entrance by a pair of crude stakes.

"Anyone inside?" he called over the wind. "I got friends up on the hill, so you better come out unarmed!"

Nothing.

Taking a deep breath, Andy cautiously moved forward, staying close behind the sorrel until he was near enough to rush the dugout.

Was that flickering candlelight back inside?

Andy couldn't tell for certain, so he unholstered both pistols, ducked under the gelding's neck, and plunged headlong into the dugout.

There was a lighted candle inside and beside it lay a Mexican with a crucifix clutched in one fist and a pistol in the other. The Mexican blew out the candle and fired.

Andy threw himself to the floor, rolled, and returned fire until he heard a soft moan. Heart hammering against his ribs, he held his breath and waited for the Mexican to stop breathing. Instead, the man began to recite the Rosary.

So what was he to do now? Wait for the Mexican to finish his dying prayer?

"Señor," Andy hissed, "I work for the Monarch Ranch and you are trespassing." Realizing how foolish that sounded, he added, "For what it's worth, I am sorry I plugged you, but you gave me no choice."

"Señor Parmentier?"

Andy's heart leaped into his throat and he choked, "Julio?"

"*Sí!*"

Andy crawled forward, raging at the cruelty of fate that forced him to shoot the very man who'd once saved his life. He leaned so close he could feel Julio's shallow breath on his cold cheek.

"What are you doing here?" Andy asked, scarcely able to recognize his old savior and friend. Poor Julio seemed to have aged thirty years. His hair was silver and he was so gaunt that his flesh hung in folds upon his face. Worst of all were his eyes, which were dull and nearly lifeless.

"That is a long and a sad story, *amigo*."

"Then it will keep," Andy said. "Are you here alone?"

"No, my daughter, Magdalena, is with our burros. She has gone to bring back firewood from the river but will return soon."

"Dammit, I need a match!"

Julio pressed a match into his palm and Andy's hand shook badly when he relit the candle and studied his friend. Julio's breathing was labored and his face was damp with cold sweat. Andy was no doctor, but he figured Julio might be dying.

"*Amigo*, where were you wounded?"

"In the side and now also in the leg." Julio forced a smile and joked, "It is good that you are a bad shot, eh?"

Andy raised Julio's blanket and saw the dirty, blood-soaked bandage strapped to the Mexican's side and knew the wound was serious. "I'm sorry, Julio."

"No matter."

"It does matter." Andy leaned close and quickly inspected the fresh bullet wound. "I'm afraid this looks bad."

Julio shrugged as if it did not matter anymore. "My life has no more meaning except for Magdalena," he whispered. "We had to leave our peaceful farming village in Mexico."

"It is none of my business."

"Please," Julio begged, "it is best that you know."

"You should save your strength," Andy told the man, "whatever—"

Julio's voice grew fierce with pride. "Magdalena's husband was the *alcade* of our village!"

"What is that?"

"The most important official," Julio explained.

"You mean, the mayor?"

"*Sí!* And he had much land and cattle. To us, he was very rich and powerful."

Andy had a bad feeling about where this story was

headed, but because it seemed so important to his suffering friend, he let it play out.

"Her husband's name was Ignacio Zavala and he could have married any young woman in all of Mexico—but he chose my beautiful Magdalena. You see, Ignacio was in love and did not listen to his friends and family, who told him not to marry the daughter of one so poor."

"What went wrong?" Andy asked, wanting to get to the end of this tragedy so that Julio could rest.

"They had a son that was christened Pablo. He is handsome and strong! A good boy! But Ignacio and his family did not want Pablo to live among the poor people of her mother."

Julio took a deep, ragged breath and seemed to gather the last of his strength and then continued, his voice now stricken with sadness. "When Pablo was five, the Zavala family took him far away—to Mexico City, where they said that he would be better raised and educated."

"What about his mother?"

"Magdalena begged on her knees for them to leave Pablo with her in our village, but they would not listen. Not even Ignacio, who beat her when he became drunk. I tried to talk to him once, but . . . One night I heard her screaming and knew that she and Ignacio were having a terrible fight. I got up and went to help, but . . . by then it was too late. Ignacio had beaten my daughter very badly this time and she lost her second child. Ignacio did not care. He was so jealous he accused my Magdalena of sleeping with another man who had fathered this dead child!"

Julio's eyes filled with tears. "I could not bear this!"

"So you killed Ignacio," Andy said, desperate to bring this tale to its tragic conclusion and somehow get rid of the Monarch cowboys waiting for him on a nearby hilltop.

"Yes, but in the fight I suffered this wound in my side. After that, we escaped across the border."

"Don't be ashamed or feel guilty about killing Ignacio Zavala," Andy heard himself say. "The bastard deserved to die and you had no choice but to help your daughter."

"But—"

Andy placed his fingers over Julio's feverish lips, thinking of how similar were his own past circumstances and the death of Eldridge Loomis. "You did the right thing, Ignacio."

"No!"

"Yes," Andy insisted.

"God will be my judge and that will be very soon."

"You're going to make it," Andy promised. "Your daughter and I will keep you alive."

Andy watched tears fill the eyes of his suffering friend, but then he heard a faint shout and remembered his waiting cowboys.

"Julio," he whispered, grabbing a piece of the man's serape and fashioning a crude bandage for the leg wound. "When Magdalena returns, she must get you away from here *muy pronto*!"

"But to where?"

"Go to . . . Santa Fe. That town is full of good Mexican people who will help you. I'll be along as soon as I can and give you and your daughter money so you don't have to worry about that anymore."

"You are a good friend!" Julio said, coughing quietly.

Andy didn't like the sound he heard, didn't like it at all. Julio's lungs sounded as if they were filled with phlegm or blood. If he'd been lung-shot, the man was as good as dead.

"I have to go," Andy said, knowing his cowboys might arrive at any second. "Have Magdalena take you into Santa Fe and find a doctor."

"*Sí, médico.*"

"You must not wait!" Andy said with urgency.

"I know Santa Fe well," Julio whispered.

"Good! I will meet you there as soon as I can. I swear it!"

Julio reached out and grabbed Andy's hand. "*Amigo*, leave my poor fate to God. But if I die, try to help Magdalena!"

"I will," Andy promised, hearing the hoofbeats of his cowboys as they charged down the ravine to his rescue.

Andy didn't know what he could do to keep the cowboys from finding Julio, but he was so desperate that he had an idea that might just work.

Jumping up and running outside, he threw up his hands and shouted, "Cholera! Cholera!"

The cowboys slid their horses to a standstill and gaped at Andy. Pete said, "Andy, we heard gunfire. What—"

"I finished the Mexican squatter off," Andy panted, throwing his eyes around like he was half-wild with fear. "But he was already dying of cholera."

"Cholera?" Hank gulped, backing his horse away from the dugout. "And you went *inside*!"

"How was I to know he was sick!" Andy shouted as the others also began to back their horses away from him and the dugout.

"Andy, what are we going to do now!" Pete cried.

"What do you mean?"

"Well, you can't come back to the Monarch and maybe . . . well, dammit, I'm sorry, but you know what I mean!"

Andy marched over to his sorrel gelding and climbed into the saddle. "I ain't stayin' to die like that!"

And right then, before the cowboys had any idea of how to react, Andy spurred the sorrel gelding in among them and they scattered like leaves. Andy watched them flog their horses up the ravine and he smiled despite everything that had gone wrong.

He had a little more time now. Pete and the rest would

reach headquarters long after dark and Tex would be told immediately. After that, Andy didn't have any idea what would happen. He tied his horse and hurried back inside.

Julio was awake and whispered, "Why, *amigo*?"

"It'll give me a little time to think this out," Andy said. "And also to help you get ready to leave."

"Magdalena has heard me speak of you many times," Julio said as Andy began to wash and replace his friend's bandages. "But I thought you had gone to California."

"I'd meant to, but I became a cowboy instead."

"A cowboy?"

"Yes," Andy said. "I work for the same bunch that ambushed us and shot Miguel Diaz off his horse eight years ago."

Andy half expected a scolding or reprimand but didn't get it. "Look," he said, "I needed work and the idea of becoming a cowboy for one of the biggest ranches in the Southwest was too good to turn down. I work for Tex Marcum."

"So, you also have met a devil, eh?" Julio said, closing his eyes. "I know of that man and the Monarch Ranch. They have beaten and killed my people. Driven them off their lands and slaughtered our sheep, dogs, and cattle."

"Not when I was around."

"Maybe you close your eyes to what you do not wish to see."

Andy wanted to change the subject. "I can't stay but a few minutes longer," he said. "Where is your daughter and those burros we can hitch to the cart to carry you to Santa Fe?"

"They will come."

Andy curbed his impatience. "I can't afford to wait. I'll go hunt them up and get the cart hitched. Then I have to go back to headquarters and see if I can smooth things over with Tex."

"As you wish."

Andy *didn't* wish. Not for any of this trouble. And if Tex ever found out what he'd done to deceive the cowboys in order to give Julio a chance to escape . . . well, there would be hell to pay.

"You said that she went to the river?"

"*Sí.* There is spring close by, but it is not very good water."

"I'll go find her," Andy said. "Will you be all right?"

"It is not my life that is important," Julio replied. "Andy, you must promise me that nothing more bad will happen to Magdalena."

"I'll do my level best for her, *amigo*. That's the best that I can promise."

Julio nodded and Andy hurried outside. The wind was picking up and the snowflakes were thicker. It was going to be a bad night and he had a long cold ride ahead of him back to headquarters.

He climbed into the saddle, then headed directly for the Cimarron, but had not gone a half mile before he saw a girl hurrying along, head down, leading two stubborn burros who did not want to hurry.

Andy spurred his horse forward and shouted so as not to surprise and frighten Magdalena. But that backfired, because when she saw him, she reached into her serape, drew out a gun, and fired.

"Hold it!" he shouted into the wind. "I'm a friend. *Amigo!*"

In reply, the girl fired again and Andy swore he could hear the whine of the bullet.

"Magdalena, I'm Andy Parmentier. *Amigo!*"

It was a miracle that his words reached her, but they must have, because she lowered the pistol and waited. But he noticed that the weapon was cradled across her left forearm.

Andy dismounted and raised his hands as he walked forward. "Magdalena, do you speak English?"

She nodded and he expelled a sigh of relief. She was quite attractive. Tall for a Mexican girl and slender. He could not see well enough to judge her age, but he suspected Magdalena was in her late teens. Shouting to be heard over the wind, he told her what had happened, except for how he'd shot Julio in the leg.

"We have to get him to a doctor in Santa Fe!"

"No!" she shouted. "Not in this storm. He is weak and would die on the way."

"But you don't understand. The cowboys might come back tomorrow."

She pushed past him, jerking savagely on the ropes leading the burros. Andy had no choice but to follow her back to the dugout, cussing under his frosty breath.

When Magdalena saw that her father had been wounded again, she let out a howl of fury and probably would have killed Andy on the spot had she suspected he was the culprit and not one of the other cowboys. Luckily, Julio did not reveal the truth to her either.

"He cannot be moved in this storm," Magdalena said, lighting several more candles and throwing a heavy woven robe over her father. "Andy, you must go back to your people and tell them that we will stay here until my father is strong enough to make the journey."

"Tex Marcum won't cut him any slack," Andy warned. "He'd ride a hundred miles in a day to drive out squatters."

"You go now and tell this Tex I will shoot him dead if he tries to hurt my father or our burros." To emphasize her point, Magdalena patted her gun.

Andy knew better than to argue with an armed woman. "With luck, I'll be able to convince Tex that there's no danger to anyone. I don't know what he'll do with me given I told the boys that Julio has cholera."

"The sickness?" she asked.

"Yes."

"Why did you say this?"

"If I had not, they would have wanted to come inside and see what they could steal. If that had happened, they would have seen that your father was not dead and that I'd lied."

"What would you have done then?" she asked bluntly.

"I don't know."

"You don't know?"

"Your father saved my life on the Santa Fe Trail. I wouldn't have allowed them to kill him."

"But if he had not, you would?"

Andy was getting frustrated and upset and so he grabbed the girl by the arm and dragged her outside where they could speak in private. "Señorita, I've got a long, cold ride back to ranch headquarters tonight. I told your father that he must see a doctor. He looks very bad."

"He is better than before. Getting stronger."

"Then he really must have been in terrible shape," Andy said as he pulled his hat down low and headed for his horse.

She followed him, and when he was mounted and began to turn away, she reached out and grabbed the gelding's bit and held it tightly. "Will you help my father if they come back?"

"Don't be here, Magdalena! I owe your father my life, but I'm not ready to kill my friends."

"I see."

"No," he told her, "you don't see at all. But that doesn't make any difference. I'll do what I can, you do what you can. Fair enough?"

She nodded and said something, but the wind snatched her words away.

Andy wheeled his horse around and put the spurs to it, knowing that he had to run while there was still a little daylight left and the footing was not yet too slippery. He didn't know what would happen when he reached headquarters, but it couldn't be anything good.

Tex threw Andy's door open and stood just outside on the porch. "The boys say that you went into a Mexican dugout and shot a man dying of cholera. Is that right!"

Andy was feeding the fire. It was well past midnight and he was frozen half to death and shaking violently. He kept feeding the cast-iron stove, not even turning around.

"I asked you a question!"

Andy shut the metal doorway on the stove and turned around to face his boss and his mentor. "That's right. He would have died of the cholera."

"And you went *in* there!" Tex was yelling, face white with rage.

"How else would I have found out he was dead?"

"You're quarantined."

"I'd expected that."

"Two weeks," Tex said. "And not one day less. We'll put your food on the porch. Relieve yourself behind the wall. Don't get near anyone. Is that understood?"

"Yes."

"Did you stay to burn the dugout?"

"No. It was snowing and I couldn't get a fire started."

"Then I will," Tex told him. "As soon as the storm breaks, I'll ride out there personally and burn that dugout to ashes."

Andy didn't say a word.

"I'm sure not happy about this," Tex said, the tension finally going out of his broad shoulders. "But then, I guess it's not your fault."

"I damn sure don't think so," Andy said. "I went in alone trying to save my men from being shot. And now . . . now this. Don't seem fair or right to me."

Tex's voice softened. "Yeah, I guess it ain't. You got any liquor?"

"No."

"I'll send over a few bottles, if you want."

"I could use some right now to warm my insides."

"I'll get a bottle," Tex said, then added: "Just one?"

"For now."

"No," Tex said, "I meant one dead *Mexican* in the dugout?"

"Oh. Yeah. That's right."

"That's funny," Tex said. "They're as groupy as sheep or cattle. Where you see one, you'll most always see at least a couple more. Might be there were more and they're spreading the cholera around. If so, I damn sure hope it stays among the Mexicans. With luck, maybe they'll even infect all them greasers in Santa Fe."

"I wouldn't wish that on my worst enemy."

"Mexicans *are* my worst enemies. Mexicans and comancheros. I'd as soon kill them as I would a pesky horsefly."

"They're all human beings, Tex. The Bible says that all people are God's children, made in His image."

"How can that be, or is God like a chameleon that changes colors?"

Andy was so astonished by this blasphemy that he simply gaped at his boss. Seeing this, Tex barked a loud laugh that chilled Andy right down to the bone and then he stomped away, still laughing as if he'd said something terribly funny or clever.

As soon as Tex was gone, Andy took the cork out of the bottle and drank deep. Next, he pulled his chair up beside the potbelly stove and fed it, staring into the fire. He wondered how long the storm would last and if Magdalena was going to be gone when Tex and his men arrived to reduce their dugout to cinders.

Probably not. She had been right; exposure to this weather would kill Julio, although Andy figured he'd probably die anyway. And if he did, what would Magdalena do with her father's body? Bury it there? Not likely. Mexicans were pretty religious people and he suspected she might seek the services of a priest. Andy shook his head, feeling desolate. What if Magdalena did try to bury Julio and was caught by Tex? Andy hadn't seen any digging tools, but there must have been at least a pick or shovel about for them to have made the dugout.

The thing that was making Andy drink more than he should was the image of that beautiful young señorita trying to bury poor Julio in the hard, freezing ground. She'd be dumb with grief, of course, and not even see Tex and the cowboys when they stormed down that draw shouting and twisted up with hate and whatever other feelings they held toward all Mexicans. And what would they do when they saw that the only thing they were facing was a young woman trying to bury her beloved father? Would they take pity on Magdalena, maybe help her bury Julio, and then hitch up her burros to the *carreta*? Andy didn't think so.

Even if they didn't harm Magdalena, they would be callous. And if she should be angry and grief-crazed enough to try to shoot them, they'd kill her in a heartbeat. She'd be dead, and he'd given Julio his solemn promise to help and protect Magdalena. Given his word to a dying man. To a friend.

"I got to go back and help her," Andy said aloud, taking a last pull on the bottle and corking it before he went to change into his very warmest outfit. "No matter if Julio dies or not . . . or Magdalena gets away or not, Tex is going to study that dugout and tracks and realize I lied. I'm finished on the Monarch."

Having decided this, Andy went into action. He pried up one of his floor planks and extracted a heavy metal box containing more than four thousand dollars—all the money he'd saved for the past eight years. He wrapped the money in an oilskin and crammed it into an extra pair of saddlebags along with ammunition, a couple pounds of cold beef and cheese, and every letter he'd received from his mother.

He had a gold watch that he'd bought in a weak moment and a two-shot derringer of good quality. Extra matches, extra gloves, and his best pair of spurs were also added to the mix.

"That's it," he said aloud, barely able to buckle the saddlebags. "Anything else I need I can buy in Santa Fe—if I get lucky enough to reach it alive."

And so in the deepest, coldest hour before dawn, Andy went back to the corral and saddled his second-favorite horse, a Roman-nosed blue roan he had named Blueberry. The horse was an often ornery but iron-tough four-year-old gelding that Andy had broken himself. Blueberry could be a bucker on a cold morning like this, especially when the sun wasn't even up. He might even bite a cowboy who jerked his cinch up too quick and too tight and pinched his skin. And Blueberry had been known to cow-kick a fella in bad weather after having an ice-cold bit forced between his teeth. Despite all that, Blueberry was a demon for work. The roan could run all day long and still have something left at sundown. He was also surefooted, intelligent, and as fine a cow pony as there was on the Monarch. Every man on the ranch payroll coveted Blueberry and would have given up most anything to have him for their own. But now he was Andy's to keep.

Warming the bit in his gloved hands, Andy got the

horse ready to ride. Blueberry's ears were laid back tight the whole time he was being bitted and saddled, but he didn't kick or bite.

"Our life is changing," Andy told the horse as he opened the barn door and took a quick pull on the whiskey before shoving the bottle deep into his coat pocket and climbing into the saddle, "and I'm afraid not for the better. Blueberry, like it or not, we're finished here with the good life working for Monarch. From now on, we are on our own."

In response, Blueberry snorted and tried to run to get his blood warm, but Andy held him in check until they were well out beyond the ranch yard and even the paddocks where the pretty English horses played in good weather. Then he gave Blueberry his head and let the tough young gelding run west toward a tiny dugout on the Cimarron.

Chapter
Nineteen

The storm blew over about two hours after daybreak and the sun appeared through cracks in the billowy clouds. Best of all, the bitterly cold wind had died, leaving a foot of glistening, crusty snow. It was beautiful, but Andy was too cold and worried about his Mexican friends to notice. He pushed Blueberry hard and the gelding eagerly responded. Andy knew that Tex and the other cowboys would leave almost as soon as it was discovered that he and Blueberry were missing. By now, Tex would have figured things out and he'd also be pushing for the Cimarron dugout just as hard as Andy.

Either way, Andy was pretty sure that he was in for a fight that he could not win. But there was no way that he could abandon Magdalena or Julio, whose *carreta* would be overtaken long before they could reach Santa Fe.

Andy took a deep breath, exhaling a cloud of billowing frost. He was very cold and wanted to warm his insides with whiskey, but knew he needed a clear head for whatever trouble he'd face this day. So he kept his hat brim pulled down low, squinted into the brilliant whiteness, and let Blueberry do the tough sledding until they finally reached the dugout.

"Hello!" he shouted, pushing fast down the draw and noting that the *carreta* was still unhitched. "Magdalena!"

She came outside with a rifle clenched in her hands and he dismounted.

"How is your father?"

Magdalena lowered the rifle. "Much stronger."

Andy had been thinking that if Julio was dead, they could cave the dugout in over him, ride Blueberry double, and maybe even make it all the way to Santa Fe. Once there, he had no doubt that they could find people who would protect Magdalena. As for himself, he'd just keep running so that Tex and the cowboys could never overtake him.

"We've got to run," Andy told her. "The Monarch people are probably no more than two hours behind me."

"It is still too cold for my father to travel."

"Magdalena, you don't understand. To stay here is to die. We can wrap your father up in blankets and put him in the *carreta* and he'll be fine."

"If the cowboys are that close, they will catch us anyway. Why not fight and die here?"

"Because the closer we get to Santa Fe, the more I like our chances. Tex will be miles away from any possible land he can claim for the Monarch and killing us could get him in big trouble."

"My father has told me what happened long ago at the Cimarron when they shot Señor Diaz. Miguel was my uncle. Did you ever think that he might have a wife and children?"

"I'm sorry, but that was *eight years ago*! We haven't time to think about that now. We have to run!"

Magdalena stared right into his soul and asked, "If we run and then are caught, will your heart remain strong?"

"What do you mean?" he asked, knowing.

"I mean will you leave us behind and try to save your own life?"

"Never!"

"You swear this on the sacred blood of Jesus?"

"Yes, and also on the Holy Bible. I won't do that, Magdalena. Trust me."

"You are a cowboy."

"But also a man."

"And also a . . . a gringo."

Andy could see the doubts rising up from the very deepest part of Magdalena and he didn't know what he could say that would satisfy them, but he had to try. "If I ran and left you and Julio to the Monarch Ranch cowboys, I wouldn't be able to live with myself. I don't want to die, but a bullet would be a mercy compared to knowing I was a craven coward. That I'd abandoned and betrayed the man who saved my life when I was still just a foolish farm boy."

"All right, then," she said. "We go now."

While Magdalena got the burros hitched, Andy went inside the dugout and knelt beside his old friend. "We're leaving, *amigo*. We're going to Santa Fe."

"It is too late."

"Nope," Andy said, scooping the man up in his arms, appalled by how much weight he'd lost. "Magdalena was right, your color is better."

"But the burros are very slow."

"We're in no big hurry."

"Then why are we rushing when it is still freezing cold?"

"Don't ask so many questions," Andy said, carrying Julio out into the glistening world and placing him in the rickety, wooden-wheeled cart. The burros were hitched and ready to go.

"I will be right back," Magdalena said, dashing back into the dugout.

Andy turned the burros away and started leading them toward Santa Fe. The wooden wheels began to screech, but Andy had no time to grease them. Every moment counted, despite an overwhelming sense of futility he could not shake.

"There," Magdalena said, catching up and taking the lead rope from his hands. "It is done. There will be nothing for them to find or steal."

Andy turned and saw smoke seeping under the tarp that shielded the entrance. Magdalena had torched the dugout, but he doubted that would affect their chances. Tex would still follow their tracks westward and overtake them. What would happen then? Andy shook his head and climbed into the saddle.

"Magdalena," he said, kicking a stirrup free, "climb up behind me and let's hope that Blueberry isn't going to buck too hard."

"I can walk. I have *always* walked."

"Mount up," he said sternly. "But first, hand me that lead rope."

"Why?"

"Once you're on board and we've got this gelding settled, we're going to drag them damn burros into a trot or else yank their stupid heads off."

"They will dig in their heels and refuse."

Andy took the lead rope and wrapped it around his saddle horn, saying, "Yeah, well, they can try, but you have never seen Blueberry drag a big longhorn steer out of the brush. He has no mercy."

"He is like the cowboys," she said, climbing up and throwing a leg over the back of the roan's rump.

Blueberry snorted and tried to force his head down between his hooves so that he could throw them both. But Andy anticipated the move and reared back, fighting to keep the horse's head up so that he couldn't buck. What happened next was sort of a compromise and Magdalena wrapped her arms around him tight. Blueberry couldn't buck, but he sure could crow-hop, and so, with the burros skidding along behind and braying like babies, they hurried west.

Andy let Blueberry trot even though the contrary son of a gun would have liked to gallop. After several minutes of being strangled alive, the burros stopped fighting and began to trot fast and the squealing axles really began to whine.

"See!" Andy yelled.

"But my poor father will be shaken to death!"

"No, he won't," Andy said, thinking maybe he would but seeing no help for it.

Andy focused on the land ahead, which he knew very well because every year he'd taken the time to ride to Old Santa Fe and have a week on the town. He'd traded there, drunk too much bad liquor there, and even—God forgive him—occasionally given in to the weakness of flesh there. And given how many men he'd killed, Andy supposed that he was not only bound for Santa Fe but also for hell this day. He just hoped that Magdalena and her father could be saved. And with that in mind, he decided that when Tex and the cowboys overtook them, he would give Magdalena his horse and go back to face them on foot. Maybe, if he killed Tex . . .

"That's crazy," he muttered.

"What?"

"Never mind. Cowboys talk to each other a lot and also to their horses."

"Mexicans talk to their animals, too," she said, hugging him tight.

Andy liked the smell and feel of her pressing against his back and almost wished his coat hadn't been so thick.

"It's a beautiful day, isn't it!" he shouted so that she could hear him over the screaming *carreta*.

"You are loco!"

Andy laughed, and with Blueberry pacing the unhappy burros, they trotted on toward the large and friendly Mexican *barrio* of Santa Fe.

The burros were almost played out and even Blueberry was starting to flag a little when Andy chanced to look back over his shoulder and saw the glimmer of steel in sunlight. Maybe it was the sun glinting off a buckle, polished bit, or even a spur. Andy wasn't sure, nor did it matter, because he knew it meant that Tex and the cowboys were closing fast.

"We're going to make a stand and I have to choose a good place to fight!" he shouted back to Magdalena.

"How about up on that little mountain?"

It was the cone of a long-extinct volcano. Not tall, maybe only fifteen hundred feet, and Andy knew that it had a crater inside where outlaws sometimes took refuge. They were crossing through a lava field that was making things even more difficult, especially for the *carreta*.

"Up ahead are some big lava boulders!" Andy shouted. "We'll pull in behind one of them and make our stand. Can you use your rifle?"

"Of course!"

When they reached the large lava boulders, some of which were larger than a wagon, Andy took shelter and grabbed his own rifle, yelling, "Magdalena, stay with your father and the animals! I'll try to reason with Tex."

Then he was climbing up into the volcanic rocks and taking a good firing position. When Tex and his cowboys appeared, they would be riding straight into his line of fire, and given the difficulty of traversing this lava field, Andy knew that he was in an excellent defensive position.

He laid his pistols out and stretched out on the rock to wait, rifle in hand. When Tex and the rest appeared, Andy raised up, took aim, and fired a warning shot. The shot wasn't meant to hurt anyone, but, unfortunately, it ricocheted off the lava and nicked one of the cow ponies, which caused near pandemonium among the rest. Tex and the others yanked their pistols out and tried to return fire, but their horses were so crazed that they weren't any real threat. So Andy held his fire, waiting to see what would happen next.

The cowboys retreated back up the trail, probably to take cover among the boulders. Everything was going fine until Magdalena appeared.

"Dammit, Magdalena, I told you to stay with your father!"

"He is dead," she whispered, wiping tears from her eyes. "The rough road caused his wounds to reopen and he lost too much blood."

Andy bowed his head. "I'm sorry. Julio was a very good man. You were right. We should have made our stand at the dugout."

"No," she answered. "If we had done that, we would all be dead by now. Maybe now we can still escape to Santa Fe."

"Not unless they decide to give up on us," Andy said, fighting waves of bitterness. Tex hadn't killed Julio, not directly, but Andy felt he was partly responsible.

"What are we going to do?" Magdalena asked.

"That depends on Tex."

"Maybe he will let us bury my father."

"I doubt it."

Magdalena began to cry. Andy pulled her close and stroked her long black hair. "Look," he said, "why don't you just go down and ride for Santa Fe?"

Her head snapped up and her eyes were defiant. "Never!"

"The truth is," Andy argued, "it's me that they really want. I've betrayed Tex and he isn't the forgiving kind."

"Then we should kill him first," Magdalena decided, rubbing her eyes dry with the back of her hand.

Andy was struck by Magdalena's character and passion. Here was a young woman who apparently had been badly mistreated by her cruel husband, the mayor of her poor village, then hounded by his relatives all the way up to New Mexico. Her father had been gravely wounded, but she'd somehow managed to get him to safety. After that, Magdalena had excavated a dugout and taken care of Julio, probably hunting small game while he mended. She had chased off an intruder and now witnessed the death of her father. Despite all that, Magdalena remained unbroken and unafraid.

Andy was trying to put his admiration into words when Tex appeared from behind a big rock waving a white bandanna. He shouted, "Andy, we need to talk!"

"What about?"

"You lied and betrayed me. I have to do something about that."

Andy raised up a little but not too much, because there were a few cowboys down there that could, if Tex had ordered them to, shoot him through the head, given a clear shot.

"You don't have to do anything, Tex. Just get on your horse and take the boys back to headquarters. It's over between us."

"No, it isn't."

"Why!"

"You *know* why, Andy. I taught you everything about cowboying. I took you in when you were wearing rags and living among a band of cattle-rustling greasers! I treated you like a son, and in return, you betrayed me."

"Where is Phil? He's your best marksman."

"He's with the others," Tex replied. "This is between you and me."

"Have them come out in plain view," Andy shouted. "Then we'll talk."

Tex wasn't happy, but he complied. One by one, the cowboys appeared, each leading his horse. When Andy was sure that no one was missing, he stood up, whispering, "Magdalena, before you run for it, take a dead aim on Tex. If they try to kill me, shoot him. With Tex gone, maybe the others will quit this fight."

Tex was walking up the boulder-strewn trail toward Andy after handing his reins to Pete. Andy wondered what was going through his friend's mind but then decided he really didn't want to know. Pete had been a good friend and they'd shared a lot together these past eight years, but Pete would shoot his own brother rather than oppose Tex Marcum.

"This is between us," Tex shouted.

"What do you want from me!"

"An apology, for starters."

"I'm sorry, Tex. But the Mexican in the dugout once saved my life. Now he's dead."

"What about the other one?"

That told Andy that Tex knew about Magdalena, although he doubted the man knew she was a woman.

"He's got a bead on you, Tex. And I think you've come far enough."

But Tex kept advancing. Andy took a deep breath, knowing that he ought to kill the man, but that would be murder. "That's far enough!"

"I'm coming for you," Tex vowed. "So you'll either have to shoot me down in cold blood or fight me man-to-man. I've told the others to back off and leave us settle this between ourselves without interference. May the best man win. That's how it has to be."

Now Andy understood. Tex had been shamed and betrayed and his pride demanded a fight to the death.

"Don't go out to face him," Magdalena pleaded. "It is a trick!"

"No, it isn't," Andy replied. "Tex is filled with hatred and too much pride, but he is also a man of his word."

"He is not to be trusted!"

Andy placed his hands on her shoulders. "Magdalena, I promised your father that I'd take care of you and I'll be all right."

"Unless he kills you."

Andy felt a shiver of fear as he steeled himself to fight Tex, but he tried to make light of it by joking, "Thanks for your vote of confidence."

"Be careful," she warned.

"If he wins," Andy said, "the cowboys will try to rope and shame you—but probably nothing worse. It would be best for you to ride hard for Santa Fe now. With a head start on Blueberry, they'll never overtake you."

"You really want me to do this?"

"Yes."

"Very well, then," she said, giving him a quick kiss on the cheek and hurrying off.

When she was gone, Andy went to face Tex. As far as he was concerned, there could be no good outcome to this fight. He didn't want to kill or even hurt Tex, no matter what had come between them. But he damn sure wasn't gong to let Tex kill or beat him, either. He'd done nothing wrong except try to help an old Mexican friend who didn't deserve to be harassed, humiliated, or driven from free land.

"Tex," he began when they came face-to-face, "we don't need to do this. I'm sorry I lied to you but—"

"Shut up, Andy. I never listen to a man that has lied to me once."

Andy stiffened. "A lie isn't a big enough reason to kill."

"It is in your case," Tex said, hand shadowing the gun on his hip. "Make your play."

"Now wait a minute," Andy said, moving in closer.

Tex went for his gun and Andy was caught with his arms held outward almost in a pleading gesture. In the split second before he would have been shot, he threw himself forward, slashing his right hand down against the barrel of Tex's revolver. The gun exploded and Andy felt the muzzle blast burn his hand as Tex howled in pain. Andy's left hand caught his foreman with a short but powerful blow to the jaw that dropped Tex and sent his gun flying.

"Damn you!" Tex shouted, gaping at his bullet-shattered knee.

Andy scooped up the man's gun, and when Tex whipped a knife from his boot top and tried to use it, Andy pistol-whipped him across the forehead, opening up a deep gash that blinded the Monarch foreman with blood.

Tex tried to get up and find his gun, but Andy hurled it into the rocks. He half expected Pete and the other cowboys to kill him, but they did not. However, their grim expressions made it clear that they would the next time their paths crossed.

Andy didn't wait around to bandage Tex's ruined knee or to wipe clear the blood flowing into his eyes. Instead, he turned and sprinted back up into the rocks and almost collided with Magdalena, who had been hiding with her rifle.

"Thought I told you to run!"

"I would never leave my father—and I won't leave you, either," she said, chin raised and black eyes flashing. "We bury him in Santa Fe and then we go away together."

"Why?" he asked as they hurried down to the burros, the *carreta*, and Blueberry. "Why together?"

"Because I have no one left to love and protect, and nowhere else to go now," Magdalena told him as if it should have been obvious.

Andy could hear Tex cursing and raving like a wild animal back in the rocks. He was sure that the Monarch

Ranch foreman would recover, but Tex's knee was ruined and he'd limp for the rest of his days. Andy also realized that what had just happened between them would never be forgiven or forgotten. They were sworn enemies now, and the next time they met, one or the other was going to die—no matter how many years passed.

_____ Chapter _____
Twenty

Founded on the banks of the Santa Fe River in 1610 and meaning "Holy Faith" in Spanish, Santa Fe was the oldest seat of government in the United States of America. Andy knew that the safest place to obtain a Christian burial for Julio was at the old Barrio de Analco resting on the east bank of the river. It was from this humble yet enduring collection of rambling shacks and crumbling adobes that the oppressed Pueblo Indians had once revolted to drive out the Spaniards, slaughtering many and causing the rest to abandon the city for years. Other uprisings had occurred over the following centuries but Santa Fe had endured, even flourished.

Julio's funeral ceremony was simple and too brief, but not without a splendid casket and flowers that Andy paid for out of his ranch savings. When the funeral mass ended, Andy slipped the old Mexican priest ten dollars and was rewarded with a toothless smile but also a troubling reminder of things old and past.

"It is my understanding, Señor Parmentier," he said with a heavy Spanish accent, "that blood was shed in Mexico and that there is a question of mortal sin."

Andy beat down his first taste of anger. Wanting to avoid any confrontation over religious matters he did not pretend to understand, he replied, "Julio saved the life of his daughter, *padre*. Before he died, I agreed to protect her from danger."

The priest nodded with understanding. "I have heard that the señora is married to a very rich and powerful man in Mexico. If this is true, then she must return to him."

"That is not possible," Andy declared with an edge to his voice. "Magdalena would be punished, imprisoned, or, at the very least, disgraced by her husband's family."

"We believe that it is better for one to lose their earthly life than their immortal soul. And while I appreciate what you have done to help this beautiful young woman, you cannot..."

Magdelena had been kneeling beside the fresh grave of her father but now joined them. She overheard the *padre* as she approached and Andy saw her face turn even paler.

"Father, forgive me, but you speak without compassion or understanding!"

"Did you marry according to the holy sacraments of our church, or not, my child?"

"I did but—"

"No, no," the old *padre* said, wagging his finger and smiling tolerantly, "it is not up to you to decide that you can be excused from your holy vows. That is for God and Mother Church to decide."

"My husband," Magdalena choked, "beat me so badly that my child was crushed in my womb!"

"Then perhaps there can be an annulment, but, of course, that would be very difficult given the circumstances and Señor Zavala's esteemed position. However..."

Magdalena placed a forefinger to her lips, a sign that silenced the *padre* and then she whispered *adios* and hurried away. She was so upset and running so hard that Andy had to chase her all the way to the old plaza. When he finally caught her, she folded into his arms and wept with such desperate sadness that he could find no words of comfort. Mexicans, Indians, and whites all stared in passing, but Andy did not care, for only now did he fully realize that this girl had lost not only her father, but her deep Catholic faith.

That afternoon they bought a basket of warm tortillas, corn, and beans from a street vendor and sat in the plaza under the tall trees and ate, watching the ebb and flow of Santa Fe until after dark.

"I need to find you a place to stay," Andy said, breaking a long but easy silence. "Do you have friends here that you could live with in safety?"

"I want to stay with you," she told him as a pair of wandering musicians began to strum their guitars.

"Are you sure?"

"Very sure, and for as long as you want."

Andy thought of the many places where he had stayed while alone in this colorful old city and knew that none of them was proper for Magdalena. He also was sure that he could not take her to respectable lodgings because they were not married. Caught in this dilemma, he was not sure what to do, until Magdalena opened a small leather pouch and extracted two worn silver rings.

"What are those?" he asked.

"They symbolize the sacred marriage of my parents," Magdalena replied as she slipped the smaller of the pair onto her wedding-ring finger.

Andy's mouth went dry and his pulse pounded in his ears when she looked at him in a way that no woman had ever looked at him before, not even the coquettish Ginny of his long-lost Brighton Township days. And he trembled as he placed the other silver band on his own wedding-ring finger.

Magdalena kissed him tenderly and then he kissed her not so tenderly and the first thing they knew they were at-

tracting attention again and the guitar players emerged from
the darkness and began to serenade. Passersby paused to
smile and someone tossed a red rose to Andy, who placed it
in Magdalena's lap.

"Man and wife?" He gulped.

"Husband and wife forever," she replied.

Andy found respectable lodgings in the *barrio*. They
were simple but clean, and the husband and wife who hosted
them for the next few weeks were gracious. As far as Andy
was concerned, he had found true happiness, a state of bliss
beyond any he could have imagined, until late one morning
when they had a visitor from the local constable's office.

"Mr. Parmentier?" the nervous young marshal in-
quired as he stood outside their room with his hand near his
pistol.

Andy heard Magdalena's sharp intake of breath behind him and then the quick whisper of her feet on the
adobe floor. When she pressed up against his back, he felt
her hand slip his derringer into his pocket.

"Why do you ask?"

"My name is Edward Bates," he said, glancing down
as if to make sure that his badge was still pinned to his vest,
"and I'm afraid that you must come with me."

Andy had the feeling that this young Santa Fe official
was even more worried than he himself was. They were
about the same age, but Andy towered over Edward.

"May I ask why I am being summoned?"

"Official business. Very important."

"Am I being arrested?"

"Only," Edward managed to reply, "if you refuse my
request."

Andy returned his derringer to Magdalena, saying, "I
had better not be found with this in my pocket. I'll return
soon."

"I am going with you!"

Andy turned back to Edward. "My wife says she wants to come with us."

"She said that she *is* coming," Edward corrected. "That is okay with me."

In a few minutes they were escorted past their kind and now almost tearful old landlords to the marshal's office by the plaza, where they were formally introduced to Edward's superior, a man in his fifties who Andy thought was of mixed blood because of his dark complexion.

"First of all, my name is Marshal Lorenzo Cordova, but it is okay to address me as Marshal. Please sit down."

"No, thank you," Andy replied, "and if this concerns the death of Alcalde Ignacio Zavala—"

"It does not, though I am aware of that," Cordova said, studying them both intently. "It is about *you*, Mr. Parmentier."

Andy heaved a deep sigh of relief and squeezed his wife's hand. "What is wrong? Has the foreman of the Monarch Ranch accused me of shooting him in the knee? Well, I didn't do it. We were fighting and he shot himself by accident."

"You have witnesses to back this up?"

"I saw everything," Magdalena said. "And I will swear to it under oath!"

"Good!" Cordova displayed perfect white teeth under a perfect pencil-thin mustache. "That is good news, but I am afraid that there is another . . . more serious charge against you, Mr. Parmentier. I am afraid this second charge cannot be easily overlooked or dismissed."

"What is it?"

"Horse thievery. You have been charged with stealing a horse from the Monarch Ranch."

"Blueberry!"

Lorenzo shrugged. "Edward has located this animal

in a livery only a little ways from where we found you. Isn't that true, Edward?"

"Yes!"

"And," Lorenzo added "didn't the owner of this livery say that the horse belonged to this Mr. Parmentier?"

"That he did."

"And that the saddle and also the bridle and blanket were in his possession?"

"Yes, sir."

"Listen," Andy said, getting more upset by the moment, "I roped and broke that big roan gelding when he was still a two-year-old outlaw. I was the only man who could have broken and trained him to be a good cow pony. No one else—with the exception of my wife—has *ever* been on his back."

"My deputy tells me the roan is a very fine horse," Cordova said, "and no doubt worth a good deal of money."

"He is," Andy agreed, "but—"

"I am afraid," Lorenzo interrupted, "that the punishment for horse stealing is death by hanging."

"No!" Magdalena cried.

"Yes," the marshal of Santa Fe agreed, turning his palms upward, "but what can I do? The roan wears a Monarch brand. Clearly, the animal belongs to the Monarch Ranch."

"Marshal Cordova," Andy said, desperate to be understood, "I worked for the Monarch Ranch for more than eight years. I started punching postholes in the ground, and when I left, I was assistant foreman."

"Congratulations, but—"

"Please," Andy said, "hear me out. I have earned Blueberry a hundred times over from the Monarch. But that aside, I think you should know the true reason behind this charge of being a horse thief. Was it filed by Tex Marcum?"

"Yes, that is the name on the warrant for your arrest and request for extradition to Oklahoma Territory."

"He was my foreman and friend," Andy explained. "And I would still be working for him had he not been intent on killing my wife's already badly wounded father."

Lorenzo glanced at Magdalena with upraised eyebrows. "This is true?"

"It is," she answered. "We were living in a dugout not far from the Cimarron River. It wasn't anywhere close to the Monarch Ranch, but still those people intended to kill my father, who could not defend himself."

"Why would they want to kill a helpless old man?"

"Let me explain," Andy said, trying to calm himself but not quite being able to purge the feeling of a noose tightening around his throat. "Marshal Cordova, Tex Marcum hates Mexican people. He will kill them on sight because he believes that they are all thieves, shiftless cowards, and backstabbers."

"You have seen him kill a Mexican in cold blood?"

"I have!" Andy exclaimed. "Eight years ago Tex Marcum and his men gunned down my wife's uncle in the middle of the Cimarron River without provocation, reason, or regret."

"And why didn't you inform the officials?"

"There were no officials then," Andy said, "and besides, I was just a runaway farm boy and no one would have believed me. I'd have been either horsewhipped or shot by Tex Marcum, so I kept quiet."

Lorenzo took a deep breath, then turned and marched over to his desk. He took up a pen and paper, paused a moment, then returned to hand them to Andy, saying, "You will sit down and write out everything you have told me."

"About the horse, too?"

"Yes, *especially* about the horse. Never mind about the saddle and bridle. If it belongs to the Monarch Ranch, I am sure you would be willing to buy both the horse and the saddle for . . . say, one hundred dollars?''

"Make it two hundred," Andy said, "so they can't say they were cheated on that, too."

"Then write everything in your own words. You, too, señora."

"Thank you, Marshal."

"I will ask you to swear your words are true before a magistrate, then I will have one of my men copy these documents and send the copy—with our signatures—to a town called Cimarron City in the Oklahoma Territory, where the arrest and extradition papers originated."

"What then?" Andy asked.

"I will send off our documents and your two hundred dollars to Tex Marcum and consider this matter officially closed. It was clearly a . . . a misunderstanding."

"What if they don't accept my money or the documents?" Andy asked, knowing full well that what Tex really wanted was his hide nailed to the barn door.

"They have no choice," Marshal Cordova replied. "I have made my decision. And I will inform Tex Marcum that, should I find and arrest him, he will be tried for the murder of your wife's uncle."

"Thank you!" Magdalena cried, hugging the marshal, who looked embarrassed.

"It is only justice that is being served. But I have one very important question yet to ask."

"Anything," Andy told him.

"Was this shooting *in* New Mexico Territory?"

"I can't be certain," Andy replied. "It might have been in the Oklahoma Territory, but I think it was here in New Mexico."

"Good," Lorenzo said, looking pleased. "If Marcum and the Oklahoma authorities are uncooperative, you must show me this place on the Cimarron where her uncle was shot to death. I am confident that it was, in fact, in New Mexico."

"Yes," Andy said, barely suppressing a grin. "The more that I think about it, I'm almost certain the attack and killing was on this side of the border."

"Can we go now?" Magdalena asked.

"I'm afraid there is one other small matter."

Andy blinked. "And that would be?"

"About the same time that you say the señora's uncle was shot on the Cimarron, there was another matter brought to my attention by a man named Walter Bean. Have you ever heard of this man?"

"No," Andy said, "never."

"Well," Cordova continued, "Walt Bean was a bounty hunter, and at the time he was very interested in locating two young men who had apparently stolen a great deal of money from a Missouri riverboat captain. I can't remember the captain's name."

"What has that to do with my husband?" Magdalena asked.

"Well," Cordova said, "I'm not sure. I had some notes, but I threw them out after Bean was gunned down up in Taos about two years ago. As for the captain who was robbed, Bean told me that he died of consumption. But I suspect that the money in question was a sizable amount."

He waited for Andy to say something, and when he did not, Cordova added, "Do you happen to have any recollection of a riverboat captain and a kid named . . . let's see, I think his name was Gizzard. Or perhaps Lizard. I'm not certain, but it was an unusual name. I never was good at remembering them."

"I sure don't have much money," Andy said, sidestepping the question. "Wish I did, though."

"Then you are without funds?"

"Oh no," Andy said. "I've saved quite a small nest egg

from my cowboying days on the Monarch. That's why I'm able to pay double what Blueberry is worth just to settle the matter in a friendly way."

"Let's be honest," Cordova said. "I know of Tex Marcum and his reputation as a Mexican hater. I had a . . . dispute with him a long time ago when he beat up a few of the locals. I warned him never to come back to Santa Fe. What I am getting at, Mr. Parmentier, is that I believe you, but we both know Tex Marcum isn't the kind of man who forgives or forgets."

"You're right."

"My advice would be to leave Santa Fe and just disappear."

"To where?"

"It doesn't matter and it might not even be necessary. But Marcum would not be above hiring a bounty hunter like Walt Bean to settle a score. Do you follow me?"

"I do."

"I was certain you would," Cordova said. "And one last piece of advice—never go back into the Oklahoma Territory. If you do that, you might wind up being the featured guest at a necktie party."

Andy stood up and extended his hand. "Thank you for believing me, Marshal. And for the advice."

"Then I won't be seeing you anymore?"

"No," Andy said, looking at Magdalena. "I think we will be going prospecting in Colorado."

Cordova smiled and stroked his thin mustache. "Excellent idea! But don't lose all your money."

"We're going to strike it rich," Andy predicted. "I've dreamed of doing that since I was just a boy."

Lorenzo Cordova extended his hand to Magdalena. "Good luck, Mrs. Parmentier."

Her eyes glistened and she nodded, too overcome with gratitude to say anything more.

But when they were outside, she took Andy's arm and said, "Colorado?"

"Yes. If you are up for some adventure in the high mountains. But it won't be easy."

"I do not know what 'easy' would feel like, my husband."

Andy lifted his chin. With a little luck, his good horse, and new wife, he wasn't worried at all. In fact, he *already* was a rich man.

Chapter
Twenty-one

Dear Mother:

*It is almost Christmas and I wanted you to know
that I have had some awful good things happen
to me this year, although at first I thought them
terrible. To begin with, I got fired from my job
on the Monarch Ranch. Actually, I decided to
quit for reasons too complicated to explain
right now.*

*I told you all about my friend Tex Marcum in
earlier letters, but I want to take back everything
good I said about him, other than his abilities
with horses and cattle. He has accused me of
stealing my own horse, Blueberry. Anyway, if I
ever return to the New Mexico Territory, I might
be hung, so I won't go back.*

*The other piece of big news is that I married a
Mexican girl named Magdalena, who is brave
and beautiful. I know that you don't know any
Mexicans, but they are good folks. If ever I get
the chance, I will bring her to visit you. Someday
when there is time, I will also send a photograph.
We were married by a justice of the peace just*

before we left Santa Fe for the Colorado Territory, where we are now living in a cabin and working some very promising Rocky Mountain diggings. We have a good claim and money in the bank, but everything is real expensive here, so I need to find gold as soon as the snow clears. It is too cold right now to pan gold in the stream, so I am doing some hard-rock mining. Magdalena cooks pies and does some mending to help with the money.

Do you remember how I always used to believe I could find gold? Well, most of the ore around here is silver, but I'm sure there is also gold. There are a lot of other men up here, some even working the icy streams and hoping not to get pneumonia. If I strike it rich, I'll send you some money. You can send me your news at the address on the envelope.

Your loving son,
Andy

The snow was gently falling when Andy trudged down to the trading post, saloon, and general store that served the small but energetic mining community of Ouray, lying high up on the eastern slope of the Uncompahgre Range. The nearby San Juan Mountains were covered with even deeper snow and the entire valley, located at a height of well over seven thousand feet, glittered as if it was warmed by a blanket of diamonds. Andy thought this had to be one of the most beautiful alpine valleys in the world—but also the coldest.

"Say, Andy!" the general-store owner, Mike Dalton, called out. "You're just the man I've been waiting to see!"

"Uh, oh," said a miner, examining a meager selection

of tinned goods halfway down the aisle, "watch out, Andy, that sounds like trouble."

"What do you need?" Andy asked.

Mindful of eavesdroppers and knowing that everything that was said in his store quickly became common knowledge, Mike led Andy through the back door and into a nearly empty storeroom that seemed even colder than outdoors. "Andy, just take a look at this place."

"Why? It's freezing in here!"

"Yeah, but it's also very empty. I've got a big problem and maybe you're the solution."

"Keep talking."

"All right. As you can see, my shelves up in front are nearly empty and I've got hardly any stock in this storeroom."

"Then you'd best get some goods in here or you're going to have some mighty unhappy customers."

"I'd like to, but I loaned my supplier money to replenish and then he ran off with all my cash."

"You shouldn't have trusted him, Mike."

"I know, but I was desperate. For collateral, I kept one of his freight wagons and a team of good oxen, but I guess he decided he would rather have my cash."

"I guess," Andy said, not sure where this conversation was headed.

"Andy, I remember someone mentioning that you were a bullwhacker."

"Now wait a minute."

Mike held up his hands. "Just hear me out. If you'd be willing to go down to Santa Fe for supplies, I'd *give* you the wagon and team of oxen."

"I'm not interested in driving oxen on icy, snow-covered mountain roads."

"Sure, it's risky, but the wagon and oxen are worth a lot of money."

"The answer is still no thanks."

Mike took a deep breath. "Then let's form a partnership. For far less than it's worth, you can buy half my saloon and this store."

"You must really be desperate, Mike. You've a good business here. Nothing to compete with it in Ouray."

"Oh, it's good all right and it will get a lot better. I figure to triple my business next year."

"Are you serious?"

"Dead serious. Don't tell a living soul up here, but I'm almost out of whiskey. When that goes, the people of Ouray might riot and hang me. Without whiskey and supplies, I'll go under by next spring. That's why I've got nothing to lose by selling you half of everything at far less than market value."

"I don't think so, Mike. I've got a good claim and I'd best keep working it."

"Listen, I'm forty-three years old and I've been in this business for the last fifteen years. I've seen boom and bust in the goldfields, but I've never been in a position to really cash in on one until now. When this mining district booms next spring, we'll make a killing."

"You think so?"

"Yes! And I promise that you'll earn far more money in partnership with me than you could ever hope to make prospecting. Magdalena could also help us out and be your eyes and ears when you're making supply runs."

"I don't know," Andy hedged, not wanting to let on how excited he was about these possibilities. "Magdalena and I like to work together."

"You'd only be gone maybe ten days a month to Santa Fe or Denver and back. The rest of the time you could still work your claim and play prospector. Hell, Andy, you'd have it both ways!"

"Mike, you're a very persuasive man."

The largest business owner in Ouray quivered with excitement. "Andy, I *smell* money here. This is definitely the opportunity of a lifetime. And since you have some money to help me out with the first run, and the know-how to handle mules and oxen, we're a perfect match for a winning partnership."

"Magdalena wouldn't agree to being left behind even for ten days a month."

"Then she can haul freight with you and help me out when you're working your claim—that is, unless you expect her to sort gravel or swing a pick all day."

"She does it," Andy said, "but I'd rather have Magdalena working in the store, where it's easier. I'll talk to her, and if she's agreeable, we'll write up a contract agreement."

Mike clapped him on the shoulder. "I've been watching you and I know we'll get along and make a fortune, if this camp really takes off as I expect."

"Sounds good. I really am enjoying being a miner and I always dreamed that I'd strike it rich."

"Yeah," Mike said cryptically, "and so did every other poor devil who ever dug a tunnel or mine shaft or froze his feet in a cold mountain stream with a big pan in his shivering paws. But they're all dreams. What I'm talking about is a surefire thing and I speak from long, hard experience. This mining camp *is* going to produce and it'll make us rich."

"Maybe."

"No maybe about it," Mike assured him. "And if it's mining you crave, well, when we are rolling good, then hire us bullwhackers and mule skinners and oversee that part of the operation. If things go as expected, we can expand into other nearby mining districts and—"

"Whoa there, Mike! I haven't even decided to do this yet!"

"Why would you turn me down?" Mike asked. "Take it from me that the ones who get rich mining are almost always the suppliers. It's a rare man who strikes pay dirt and manages to stay that way for long. I've only seen it happen a couple of times, but I've watched hundreds—no, *thousands*—of gold-fevered men go broke, get hurt, get killed, or ruin their health trying to hit pay dirt. Buy into my operation. Keep me in business this winter and you'll thank me all the way to the bank next summer!"

"I'll talk to Magdalena," Andy promised, "but right now I'm freezing. You got *any* whiskey left to warm my innards?"

"You bet! And don't say anything about this to anyone else. If you don't accept, I want to be able to pick my own partner and not have half of Ouray pestering me for the same deal I've just offered you."

Andy purchased a bottle and a few supplies, then hurried to his cabin. It wasn't much, but he'd bought it along with his good mining claims from a man who'd injured his back and, with winter coming on, needed to leave the high mountains badly enough to sell cheap.

That night he and Magdalena sat around their stove talking about Mike Dalton's proposition.

"Do you trust this man?" Magdalena asked with her usual directness.

"Yes," Andy said. "I do. And Mike really needs me or I'd never have such an offer. Without our financial help and me freighting, he is going under and everyone in this camp will suffer the consequences. So what do you think about me freighting?"

"It will be difficult for us this winter."

"That's true. We'd have to fit special shoes on the oxen to give them better footing. However, there is a blacksmith in town."

"I think we should take the risk," Magdalena told

him. "I think Mr. Dalton is a good businessman and also honest."

"So do I," Andy agreed. "I keep wanting to prospect, but other opportunities keep getting in my way. Yet I can't help but feel that Mike is right that Ouray is going to be a boomtown."

"But what if it isn't?"

"Then at least we'll have a freight wagon and the oxen to dismantle and haul our saloon and store on to another mining town."

"I would enjoy working in the store and meeting ladies."

"Some won't be ladies."

"I know," Magdalena said, "but they still deserve respect and need to have a few nice things."

"All right, then," Andy said, pouring two glasses of whiskey and raising one in a toast. "Let's accept!"

And that was how it began. That winter was hard freighting, but their mining community did boom in the spring, bringing them more business than they'd dreamed possible. By August, Andy had six teamsters working every day of the week, traveling to Denver, Raton, and Santa Fe. Even better, on a crisp October afternoon when the aspen were dazzling splashes of red, orange, and yellow against the spectacular mountainsides, Andy discovered a thin but unbroken vein of gold in his latest mine shaft. The vein was hidden by sparkling quartz rock and he might have missed finding it except he accidentally struck an overhang of quartz, and there it was, gleaming dully as it twisted into the mountainside.

Andy was staggered as he scooped an egg-sized nugget off the floor of the shaft and whispered, "I think I've just struck it rich!"

Moments later he was flying down the rough mountainside like a farm boy racing through a tall cornfield. Andy didn't stop until he burst into their general store. "Magdalena, we did it!" he shouted. "We *really* did it!"

He slapped the nugget down on the counter, scooped up his wife, and swung her around and around, shouting, "We're rich!"

Their celebration was wild but brief, and ended when one of the customers that Magdalena had been serving said with real bitterness, "You folks were *already* rich, but don't let the poor ones spoil your fun."

Andy set his wife down and his joy died. This was Mrs. Emily Alexander, the wife of a drunken prospector who had deserted her and their four children several months earlier. "I'm sorry, ma'am," he said, feeling ashamed of himself.

The woman scrubbed her tears away and said, "You don't have anything to be sorry about, Mr. Parmentier. I had no right to spoil your party. Congratulations and . . . good day."

Mrs. Alexander collected her coin purse and started to leave without making a purchase, but Magdalena caught her sleeve, saying, "Andy?"

"Go ahead," he answered, knowing exactly what she had in mind.

"Mrs. Alexander," Magdalena began, "gold is a gift of God. Take this nugget with our blessings."

The poor woman was nearly dumbstruck and she finally stammered, "Why, the nugget is huge and worth a *lot* of money!"

"Then all the more reason you should have it," Andy told her, feeling much better now.

"God bless you both!" Emily Alexander cried, hugging them and then hurrying outside to call for her ragged brood.

Several months later Andy learned that the woman had gone to Denver and married a Baptist preacher. He and

Magdalena hoped that she had picked a good husband and not one just after her money.

Andy traded their company's oxen for more surefooted mules, and even though their gold production wasn't what they'd hoped, between the mine and their partnership with Mike Dalton, they made a considerable fortune during the next few years and often went to Santa Fe to combine business and pleasure.

One day they happened to see Marshal Cordova, and after some small talk, the marshal said, "I've heard about your good fortune both in merchandising and prospecting. Some men have all the luck."

Andy grinned. "My best luck was in finding Magdalena. In fact, when I did that, my luck suddenly went from bad to very good."

"I'm happy for you both," the lawman said, "and I'm also happy to tell you that I have heard nothing more about that warrant for your arrest on the ridiculous Oklahoma horse-stealing charge."

"I didn't expect that you ever would," Andy replied. "Is the Monarch Ranch still riding roughshod over innocent people?"

Cordova's perfect smile faded. "Yes, and if Marcum or his cowboys ever visit Santa Fe or I hear word that they've even crossed *my* border, I'll have them arrested. They've killed several Mexicans and one Indian that I know of for trying to settle open land. Someone needs to stop them once and for all, but my hands are tied because they keep to the Oklahoma Territory and employ the sharpest lawyers money can buy."

"It's not right." Andy complained.

"I know. If I had your money and enjoyed raising cattle, sheep, or horses, I'd buy up Cimarron River ranch land on *this* side of the border and give Tex and his English noblemen a taste of their own bad medicine."

"It's a thought."

"It ought to be more than just a thought," Cordova said. "The fact is, that bunch respect nothing but force . . . and power. Also, I understand that they have stocked their range with some *very* expensive English bulls. A lot of people in New Mexico wonder how they'd taste at a fiesta."

"Marshal, you aren't suggesting . . ."

"Nice meeting you both," Cordova said, tipping his hat to Magdalena before walking away with a smug grin.

Andy was confused. "Did I hear him right? Was the marshal really suggesting we rustle and roast a few prized Monarch Ranch bulls!"

"Maybe more than a few, but that could get you killed."

"Yes," Andy said, taking her arm and continuing down the boardwalk, "it could. I could be shot, like Tex and his men are still shooting lawful settlers."

They didn't talk about it anymore. But by the time they returned to Ouray, the suggestion was consuming Andy. So much so that he was no longer interested in freighting or even of striking another rich vein of gold. No, what he was thinking about was cowboying. Of founding a cattle empire on some very fine grassland along the Cimarron River.

Two days later he finished his investigations and had found out that a big ranch was for sale and it was located exactly where he wanted along the river at a price he could easily afford.

"Why are they selling almost sixty thousand acres of prime grazing land so cheap?" Magdalena wanted to know.

"They're afraid of the Monarch and especially of Tex," Andy said. "I had to dig a little, but that's the reason they want out."

"Then we should be even more afraid."

"I'm not," Andy told her. "This time I won't be just some poor farm boy that can be abused and bullied. This time I'll be a force to be reckoned with if they come across the border and try to raise hell in New Mexico."

"Andy, do you have to do this?"

"I think I do," he answered. "Will you stand by me on this one?"

"Of course," Magdalena replied.

Andy kissed his wife and held her close, thinking about cattle and ranching. "I wonder," he mused aloud, "if me and Blueberry can still make a pretty fair roping team."

"I have no idea."

"We probably can," Andy said, "especially since those expensive purebred bulls are so slow."

"Andy!"

Chapter
Twenty-two

A ndy soon discovered that he and Blueberry were still a very good roping team. Why, they could lasso and drag a bawling purebred Monarch bull all the way from Oklahoma to New Mexico without any big strain. For appearances as much as anything else, Andy bought some of his own cattle, mostly young cows and heifers. He also saw to it that they were bred by either a Monarch Ranch Hereford, Angus, or shorthorn bull. Andy sort of liked to spread the genes around and see what turned up interesting.

He was examining one such calf that needed some special attention when a rider appeared on the eastern horizon. Andy checked his sidearm and wondered if this was a hired gunman sent by Tex to kill him.

"Mr. Parmentier?"

"That's me," Andy said, noting a Monarch brand on the cowboy's sweaty dun, but also how young the rider was and how nervous.

The cowboy cleared his throat. "I've been sent over from headquarters to warn you to stay off Monarch property."

Andy had to admire the kid's brass, if not his intelligence. "I'll do that," he said in the friendliest tone he could muster, "but you tell Tex and the others to do the same."

"Yes, sir." The cowboy started to wheel his horse around and gallop away.

"Whoa up there!" Andy called. "What's your name?"

"Billy Boyce."

"Are you any good at cowboying?"

"Actually, no," Billy admitted, looking down at his saddle horn as if it were suddenly the most interesting thing in the world.

"Why not?"

"My father was a Nebraska corn farmer. He did well at it and I'm not ashamed that I spent so much time following the ugly end of a pair of mules. But I always dreamed of being a cowboy, so I left Nebraska, followed the old Santa Fe Trail, and wound up on the Monarch."

Andy couldn't help but appreciate that answer. "Kid, you'd do a lot better working for my new outfit. I just bought this spread last week, and as you can see by the looks of the house, corrals, and buildings, it needs considerable work. But the grass is good and I've already got some cattle on my range. This ranch is going to be pretty special someday and you could play an important part."

"Why would you hire a greenhorn like me?"

"I appreciate your honesty and I know that farm boys are used to hard work."

Billy blushed. He was slightly bucktoothed but otherwise a fine-looking young fella, with sandy-colored hair and bright blue eyes. "Thank you for the offer of employment, Mr. Parmentier, but I have a job."

"I'm offering you a better one. I'll pay you forty dollars a month to start."

"Sir, the Monarch started me at forty-five."

"That's good," Andy replied, "but when Tex orders you to bully or gun down innocent people, is it worth the extra five dollars a month?"

The cowboy took a deep breath. "Mr. Parmentier, I've

heard a lot of stories about you. Heard you got rich up in
Colorado after working for the Monarch. They say that
you turned on Mr. Marcum after he made you assistant
foreman."

"That's what you heard?"

"Uh-huh. You're definitely the man that shot him in
the knee, so's he can't ride without pain nor walk without it
either."

"Tex would have killed me if I hadn't shot him first.
Even then it could have gone either way, because we were
both struggling over his six-gun. And once he was down, I
could have killed him but didn't."

"Tex sure isn't grateful," Billy said. "He can't even
speak your name without turning red in the face and cuss-
in' a blue streak. I come from a family of God-fearin'
Methodists and I must confess that kind of salty talk of-
fends me."

"A foul mouth is the least of Tex's many faults."

"That may or may not be true, sir, but I ride for the
Monarch."

"I respect that," Andy replied. "Take a message back
to Tex warning him that if he ever crosses into New Mexico
onto my land, he's a dead man."

"I'll do that."

"And then ask around until you learn what *really* happened that day we fought beside the Cimarron River. When
you learn the truth, maybe you'll change your mind about
coming to work for me. I could use a strong young fella like
you around here helping me repair corrals and fix up the
buildings."

"That's not cowboying."

"You'd get to do some of that, too. And besides, if
you're not a good hand yet, I don't expect you cowboy
much for Tex, either."

"No, sir, I don't. Mostly, I dig postholes."

Andy almost laughed out loud. "You'd do a fair share of that here, too. But I'd work alongside. One more thing. Tell Tex and his British bosses that they were right all along—pure English beef tastes better. At least, that was the popular opinion at our last big Santa Fe fiesta."

Billy's eyes popped and his jaw fell. It was all that Andy could do not to laugh out loud. And before the kid could recover, he added, "Inform Tex I'd like to invite him over here for dinner next Sunday. Just so there's no mistake, we can meet at noon where he was going to kill my wife and her wounded father in a dugout."

"Mr. Parmentier, I don't think—"

"Tell him I'm coming alone and he ought to do the same—if he has the guts."

"Yes, sir!"

The cowboy galloped away and Magdalena came out of their house, still holding a rifle. "I heard that, Andy, but why?"

"Because I know that sooner or later Tex will send a sharpshooter out to ambush me. One minute I'll be sitting on Blueberry, the next I'll have a hole the size of a melon in my chest. Trust me, this is my best and only chance of staying alive."

"If anyone should hate or feel the need to kill that man, it is I," Magdalena said with passion. "Tex killed my uncle, and if he hadn't been coming to run us off, my father would not have bled to death trying to reach Santa Fe in that wooden cart!"

"Magdalena," Andy said quietly, "do you realize that your father and uncle were comancheros?"

"They were just poor people trying to make a living. If my uncle and father had not given the Comanche what they needed in trade, I believe they would have killed even more."

Magdalena was upset and went back into the house,

leaving Andy standing in their ranch yard to watch Billy
Boyce become a small black dot on the eastern horizon.
Andy had no regrets about issuing his challenge, and he
knew that life was just like a big eternal circle; the seasons
went around and around and so, too, did the good or the evil
of every man.

Andy had risen long before dawn this Sunday. He'd
dressed, shaved, and because his stomach was too upset for
food, he'd strapped on his gun, grabbed his rifle, and gone
to saddle Blueberry. He considered waking Magdalena to
say good-bye, but they'd said that already and it had been
difficult. Better, Andy decided, to just ride the boundaries
of his new cattle ranch and then drift over toward the
Cimarron River and the old dugout. Over the years it had
crumbled until there were just a few timbers extending out
of the hillside, leaving hardly enough room inside for a fox
or a raccoon to take shelter.

The day was perfect, with nary a cloud in the sky.
Andy spent all morning checking on his cattle and thinking
that if he survived this showdown, they would make the
foundation of a pretty decent herd. Sure, they were just
longhorns, but far better than the wild cattle a man could
still chase out of the brush down in Texas. When crossbred
with the English bulls that Andy was so fond of "borrow-
ing," his stock would soon become much improved.

Andy roped cattle twice that morning just to get the
kinks out of Blueberry and put his mind on things other
than Tex. They'd never roped better and Andy took that as a
good omen.

Tex would come alone, Andy was sure of that much.
Billy Boyce had carried a public challenge to the old cattle-
man, making it impossible for him to back down or bring
reinforcements. Andy had been waiting a good long while
to confront a Monarch Ranch cowboy for just that reason.

"It's just a matter now of who shoots first and straightest," he told the roan as he coiled his lariat and studied the Cimarron River snaking off to the east. It was, he thought, a handsome but not a mighty river, and he had a sudden urge to follow it just to see where it might flow.

Andy crossed the river and gave Blueberry free rein. The roan broke into a hard gallop that lasted until they could see the long draw and the remains of the old dugout where he'd first met Magdalena.

Andy's thoughts were cut short by the appearance of a buggy. It was a handsome rig pulled by two black horses so well curried that their coats glistened. Having no other purpose or plan, Andy rode down into the long draw and reined Blueberry up near the dugout. He checked his six-gun, which was a newer model Colt with metallic cartridges rather than the old black powder pistols that he'd inherited from Miguel Diaz.

"One gun. One bullet. One man rides away," he said to himself, one eye on the pistol and the other on the approaching buggy.

Tex looked old and unwell. His cheeks were hollow and all that Andy recognized were his broad shoulders, hooked nose, and burning black eyes. Tex was dressed in a red flannel shirt and a black hat. No coat but a lap blanket spread across his lame knee and the walnut grip of a six-gun sticking out from his waistband, butt first.

"Same old cross draw," Andy said to himself as the buggy drew to within fifty yards before stopping.

"Parmentier, you've been stealing my prized bulls!"

"That's because their meat is so tender and all my Santa Fe friends have gotten spoiled."

"You're a horse thief, a cattle rustler, and a no-good Mexican-lovin' son of a bitch!"

"I'm also the man that whipped and shot you!"

Tex's face turned bone white. His matched horses

began to paw nervously and Tex let them march forward to meet Blueberry.

At twenty-five yards, Tex pulled the team in again and said, "I'm going to kill you now, Andy. I've been wanting to do it a long, long time."

"Make your play!"

"I already have," Tex shouted, whipping a sawed-off double-barrel shotgun out from under his lap blanket.

Too late Andy saw his fatal mistake. He threw himself sideways, jerking hard on his reins. Blueberry reared and caught the full force of both shotgun barrels. Andy struck the ground, rolled, and tried to drag out his gun, but was pinned under the wildly thrashing roan.

"You lose, farm boy!" Tex shouted, quickly reloading two shells into the shotgun.

There was no time for Andy to say his prayers. No time to think of Magdalena. Only time to take a quick glance up at the old man's mocking face and see a pair of shotgun barrels that looked as big as cannons.

A rifle shot boomed and Tex stiffened, then lifted up in his seat. A second shot sent the foreman of the Monarch Ranch crashing over backward as his team bolted in panic and the runaway buggy went flying up the draw past Andy and the crumbling dugout, where Magdalena emerged with a rifle smoking in her capable hands.

"Shoot Blueberry," Andy managed to gasp. "He don't deserve this!"

Magdalena shot the cow pony and somehow found the strength to lift the dead animal's weight enough to free Andy's leg. She helped him to his feet, and together, they hobbled over to collapse before the dugout.

"I'll be right back," she said, vanishing inside to reappear a moment later with medicine, bandages, and a bottle of whiskey.

"I thought you'd burned and destroyed that dugout," Andy said.

"I reopened it as a shrine to my father. I never told you, but sometimes, when his memory was with me strong, I would come here to pray for him and feel better."

Andy reached for his wife, his woman. "You make *me* feel better," he said. "You always have and you always will."

She kissed him, then examined his leg and said, "It isn't even broken. God must have heard my prayers for you last night."

"It might not be broken, but it sure feels like it. Make a big fire and let's drink some whiskey and watch the stars come out. I'll be ready to go home in a while."

She gave Andy whiskey and he drank deep and watched her head for the Cimarron River to collect firewood just as she must have done many times for poor Julio.

The leg throbbed and he felt terrible about losing Blueberry, but at least Tex had shot or run off his last nester. Andy figured that matched pair of blacks would take him home to the Monarch.

He leaned back against the hillside, thinking of his life since Indiana and all the men he'd known that had lived and died. He'd made mistakes, but everything had turned out all right. The only real regret he had now was that he and Magdalena could not have children. Well, Andy thought, taking another pull on the whiskey and feeling the pain in his leg diminish, there were orphanages in both Denver and Santa Fe. Maybe they could adopt a couple kids to help them turn this ranch into the pride of northeastern New Mexico.

Andy Parmentier figured everything would turn out just right. All he had to do was keep setting his sights high and follow the Cimarron River home.

About the Author

GARY McCARTHY grew up in California and spent his boyhood around horses and horsemen. A prolific novelist of the American West, Mr. McCarthy has written several historical novels in the Rivers West series including *The Gila River*, winner of the prestigious Spur Award, and *The Humboldt River*. He makes his home in Arizona.

The exciting frontier series continues!

 **RIVERS WEST**

Native Americans, hunters and trappers, pioneer families—all who braved the emerging American frontier drew their very lives and fortunes from the great rivers. From the earliest days of the settlement movement to the dawn of the twentieth century, here in all their awesome splendor are the RIVERS WEST.

___56800-0	THE RED RIVER	FREDERIC BEAN
___56798-5	THE CIMARRON RIVER	GARY MCCARTHY
___56799-3	THE SOUTH PLATTE	JORY SHERMAN

each available for $5.50/$7.50 Canada